THE CASE

OF THE

HERMIT'S

GUEST BEDROOM

RRGall

THE DUMFRIES DETECTIVE TRILOGY

PART 1

THE CASE OF THE PIG IN THE EVENING SUIT

PART 2

THE CASE OF COLOURFUL CLOTHES AND KILTS

PART 3

THE CASE OF THE HERMIT'S GUEST BEDROOM

TO YVONNE

My thanks to Ambrose and Carol

Cover: detail from a painting of Dumfries by Irene Gall

www.artist-irene-gall.co.uk

One

The tramp was beckoning me over. He stood on the far pavement. The road was shiny with rain. It reflected the yellow of the streetlights. There were no cars, the town was deserted: it was two in the morning on a wet Dumfries night.

I thought about ignoring him. I was tired. I wanted my bed. But he was showing me something in his hand, teasing me across. He held it high, in the flat of his palm. I chose to approach, crossing the road to his corner on Queensberry Street. Habit made me look both ways – I knew the street was empty.

The tramp's long, dirty, unfastened, brown coat weighed over his rounded shoulders, its two side pockets bulging like boils: the huge hood of the jerkin worn underneath enclosed his head. His trousers hung at different heights.

It was difficult to make out what he held: it was small and flat and tempting. He shuffled a few steps back, allowing space on the patch of pavement in front of him. There was a smell of blocked drains over here.

He cradled the object in his shaking, outstretched, upturned hand like an enticing gift. It was a little brown envelope of sorts. Slowly, he unpeeled each lightly stuck flap, using the thumb and forefinger of his thinly gloved hand, his hood springing a glance in my direction after each movement.

In the darkness I sensed his eyes staring at me, sizing me up. The tip of his nose was exposed: it was bent, broken, discoloured, and the flesh on his chin, behind the dirt of his unruly beard, appeared swollen.

The first flap, the second, then the third, and the fourth leaf. What was this – a demonstration of anti-origami? Unthinkingly, I edged in closer. The full force of the tramp's stench grabbed and overwhelmed me, stopping me in my tracks. I braced against it and tried to cover up by forming a smile: to show him nothing was wrong.

He shambled forward: I forced myself to hold ground. Matted hair escaped from under his hood and fell as rats' tails as he leaned forward, holding the envelope at eye-level, showing me the mound of exposed speckled powder.

It wasn't a lot to see – certainly not worth the trip over. This man was a player short of a full team, a match without a ball, the Gretna of the Scottish Division One. He needed help: I thought of options.

As I opened my mouth to speak he sucked in an almighty breath and blew. The powder, unleashed, blasted into my face like a sandstorm. I was slow to react.

My eyes stung with a million hot, sharp tacks. Gasping, tottering, I staggered backwards onto the road, my right foot slipping from the kerb. I stumbled. I was reeling, rubbing, gulping in air, groaning. And the pain, filling my head, was excruciating: scorching needles driving up through my nostrils, straight into my brain. The back of my throat roared in flames, as the envelope floated to the ground.

He seized me under the arm. It steadied me. He pulled me sharply up and towards him: the unwanted, brisk movement ricocheted through my head like a bullet screaming for a way out. I registered his putrid breath, the stink of his decomposing rags, and the filth clinging to his hair and smeared over his coat. It made me gag.

I lost control of my legs. My weight was too much for him: he couldn't hold me up and both my knees collapsed and clacked on the harsh street like coconut shells.

I remained kneeling in front of him, eyes streaming, crying like a baby, as the rain flowed over my face. The plastic bag, containing my make-shift ice-pick, rubber gloves and saw, fell from my grip and kept me company on the wet ground.

He yanked my hair and hauled on an ear, raising me up like a submarine from the depths. He barked out a laugh as the punch smacked into my left temple, as I heard the crunch of his knuckles against my fragile skull. It felled me. He grasped an ear again and pulled. My eyes struggled to focus as he gripped my shoulders, tugged me up, and hugged me against his rancid body.

And, with a jerk, we lurched forward. I bowked again. It splattered over my blurred shoes and his old boots as we walked. We didn't stop.

With grim determination, I put one foot in front of the other, again and again. In my garbled mind I thought he was taking me home and to safety. When he spoke, it was not as gruff as expected: it was a kind, comforting voice, as though he was talking to a frightened child. 'You'll soon get some rest. You'll get a lie-down. It's not far now...'

I didn't catch the rest: pressure was building up in my head, screaming through my ears.

*

We stumbled over cinders, stones. I caught my foot. He lost his grip. I fell. There was a smarting in the palm of my right hand: I'd landed on a piece of glass. I gave a yell. The sound from my mouth shocked me – as though it was the first noise I'd uttered in years. I should have been shouting for help. I should have been yelling at the top of my voice to be saved. I wasn't going home: somewhere in my brain I'd always known that.

He clapped a stinking hand over my mouth, destroying the beginnings of my scream. I was on all-fours. Instinctively, I grabbed the piece of glass and rose to my feet, flailing at him – my arms as wild and useless as ribbons in the wind. He thumped a fist into my gut. It burst the air inside and I slumped. He yanked at me and we clambered on, along the side of the train track.

*

The tramp allowed me to rest. I was leaning on him. We

were under a bridge. It was dark but it was shelter from the rain. He punched me in the stomach again. It wasn't as hard, I shouldn't have crumbled – but I was flat-dead exhausted and I fell to the ground, looking out through dizzying eyes.

He grabbed my head, using my ears as handles, and slammed it backwards, smacking it against a wooden sleeper. He crouched over, laid me out down the middle of the train track, as carefully as a father tucking in his son. I allowed him – there was no thought of resistance, no fight, no strength. My brain was numb, filled with mush. He removed my shoes and socks and splayed me out: star-shaped.

The cold steel of the rails played across the backs of my bare wrists. I was spread and positioned, my hands at head-height on either side.

'In the old films the woman is tied across the tracks, head on one rail, feet on the other. I prefer it this way: spread like a goalie waiting to save a penalty. I'll tell you why in a minute – once I get you fixed into place.'

I saw him pull something from his pocket and felt a rope tightening around my right wrist. He opened out my hand. 'You're bleeding.' He must have touched the blood of the wound. He tutted. 'That's probably a nasty gash: can't make it out too well. Normally I would suggest you get that seen to, in case it leads to an infection – but, as the hand won't be attached to your arm for much longer, I doubt if we need worry.'

He spat into the wound: the warm, cloying liquid slid slowly across my palm. He raised himself awkwardly to his feet, shuffled across, and started to tie more rope round my other wrist. A drop of water from the bridge overhead plopped onto my face. It sparked life into me. I shouted. Immediately, he slapped my face and clamped his grubby hand over my mouth once more. It smelled of the sewer. He fumbled in a pocket; seconds later he'd slabbed long strips of tape across my mouth, again and again. The sound was cut: my lips parted in mid-scream.

My left arm swung, still free. It missed his head and hit off his shoulder. I kicked my legs, knees pummelling into his back. He landed on top of me, thumping down onto my chest, pinning my arms. I kept beating at him with my knees but he managed to tie my hand and I was held in place. I fought on, kicking. He shifted his weight onto my legs and fastened my left foot to the rail. He fought with my other leg: hauling it wider towards the other side, pulling on me like a wishbone.

'It's no use – you're not tall enough. You won't stretch,' he said. There was disappointment. 'I'll have to tie it in with the other one, on the same side.'

He crossed my legs at the ankles, I squirmed, but he managed to attach my bare right foot to the metal: both heels dangling over the edge. He stood up and his hood made a nodding motion as he surveyed his handiwork.

Fear rose. I couldn't move. I lay in the middle of the track; I would be able to see the train coming towards me.

He knelt at my head and spoke softly, 'If you want my advice you should keep as steady as possible, keep your head down, and stay as low as you can. That way you might live. When the 2.25 am coal train comes through you will lose your hands and feet, but it should be a clean cut and you might possibly come out of it alive – if that's what you want. There should be enough clearance for your body and head not to snag. You're nice and slight: it would be different if you had a big belly. You should be thankful for that. It's all up to you now.

Keep low, that's my advice, because they won't see you – not here in the murk. And it's on a bend... But to be alive, that's something, at least – wouldn't you think? You have to try and stay positive: you never know what might happen. If the coal train doesn't run tonight, you'll be safe. At least for a while. Keep that in mind. The next train will get you, I daresay. But, for all I know, there could be a train strike – it's been known.

You can always hope for that.'

He bent closer, the shadow of his face stared into my terrified eyes. Then he checked each fastening in turn, opening out my hands, rubbing his fingers gently over my skin.

'No-one will find you here. The station is half a mile further up. Even if you could pull the gag off, there's no-one to hear you, not under here, not at this time of night. Your best bet is to pray for a train strike: stranger things have happened, you know.'

I heard the crunch of his feet as he walked away. I was left with the coldness of the rails and the quiet of the night sounding over the repetitive drips of rain falling from the bridge, landing on my head like water torture.

Panic hit me like a locomotive. I lost control. I broke into a shaking, heart-pounding frenzy. I was screaming inside, yelling at myself to move, move! My eyes were wide in fright as my arms and legs thrashed. Pulling, tugging, twisting my body and hands, arching my back for purchase. If I kept on I could tear away the bindings. The ropes were dirty and old: they would break and I would wriggle free.

My breathing was fast and I couldn't suck in enough air through my nose. Sweat built and coated my skin, my muscles drained of energy, and then my limbs became heavy. I had to stop. It was too exhausting. I urged myself to halt. There was a slight give in the ropes, a little bit of movement, but not enough.

I told myself to be calm – to work things through. How much strength would it take? How long would I need? How long before the train arrived?

The Tramp hadn't found the piece of glass. I'd picked it up. It was small: a broken top of a beer bottle. It wasn't much. When he'd inspected my cut palm, it was in my other hand. But he would have found it there too, so I had slipped it into my mouth – it felt the obvious thing to do. I thought it would be useful, a weapon: something that shouldn't be given up. Now it was trapped in my mouth, behind the tape across my face, lolling against my tongue – and useless.

I should have dropped it at the side of the track: he wouldn't have seen it in the darkness. I might have been able to pick it up and use it. Now, it was heavy in my mouth – it might even choke me. But what would that matter now?

I couldn't give up. There was still the chance my wrists could squeeze through the binding: even if it meant scraping away all the skin. I rotated them, round and back, round and back – the sweat helping, oiling. The rope burnt the flesh. I think I could smell it. If there's blood it might make it easier – grease the rope in blood, grease the rope, twist and back, twist and back.

I turned my head to one side; it rested on the dank sleeper. I stared through the gloom, watching my hand birl in its shackle. Nothing was happening, the skin was bunching up too much, stopping it slipping through – and the flesh stung.

Wait. Think.

The voice at my ear gave me a start. It shocked me. I heard a man talking. Close. I thought of my guardian angel – she was a man.

'I'll loosen your hands,' he said.

I made a grunt in reply. I'd never talked to an angel – only listened.

'I don't think it's all that fair,' he said.

The rope, attached to the rails, came away. My right hand was free, my arm was released. I felt a lightness along its length – as though gravity had ceased to exist. My hand floated towards my face as I sought to pull away the gag – to free my mouth and offer my deepest thanks.

Whatever you want in future – whatever you need from me – I will give it to you.

The punch to my stomach was deep: the fist almost

bouncing off the backbone and out. It forced the air from my lungs, bulging my nostrils as it sped out.

My right hand was yanked away sharply. I had no control over it. Held by the rope round the wrist, it was a puppet hand, going only where its master wanted.

'I'm letting your hands escape,' said the voice.

The sting from my skin made me groan.

'I don't want to be too hard on you. I see you've made quite a mess already: you've broken through into the gore. Sorry about that. You've been putting up a fight, eh? Couldn't you let it lie – let yourself lie? You should have done as I said: take your punishment and move on. Your wrists will need to be seen to later. Remember that: in case infection sets in.'

I followed the line of the rope through the dark of the night. I curved my head back and saw it end up in the hands of The Tramp. The depths of his hood bore down on me. I hadn't heard him return.

'I didn't think it was fair,' he repeated. 'Too big a price to pay. I had to come back. Hope you don't mind. This way, you'll lose your feet but your hands will stay intact, hopefully – if you keep them tucked in and still.'

He re-tied one end of the rope to my wrist and the other end round the rails. He did the same to my left hand. They were tethered to the track but with enough slack to fall inside – out of the way of the wheels.

He crunched my fingers into fists and wound masses of tape round so they looked like black stumps at the end of my arms. 'So you don't try to pick away at the knots,' he explained.

For a second time, I heard him walk away.

Thursday 24th August 2006

Chiara handed me the bottle of champagne and watched me scan its label. 'Don't worry,' she said, her words bouncing within her laugh, 'it was on special offer. Not expensive – nothing like the last one. You'll be able to drink this one without thinking of the price. But it should be a good enough quality – drinkable, at least.'

'That's all I'm hoping for.'

Last week, the wine had worked out at whopping £4 a mouthful – and I don't have a big mouth. Needless to say I hadn't enjoyed the taste: it was as sour as a jilted lover. I twisted out the cork, with a large pop, and glugged some foaming liquid into two crystal glasses, handing one over. She made another toast to our long weekend together and I made one to the mighty Queen of the South, the greatest team in South-West Scotland, if not the whole world, giving my hopes for the new season.

Chiara plonked herself on my lap; although she could have chosen one of the other two armchairs in her sitting room. Her free hand clasped the back of my neck and her bare legs stretched over the arms of this large easy-chair. I shuffled into a more comfortable position, allowing the seat to share some of her weight – but I knew better than to say she was heavy. And I also knew you'd always be asked to carry away a plate, a cup, or something, whenever leaving a room: I'd learned one or two facts about women in the last few weeks.

I took a sip of the champagne. It was nice right enough, with flavours of lemon and biscuit. I snuggled in close, my lips running up and down behind her warm ear. She smelled of the bubble bath she'd recently vacated and her skin still held its heat. The white, fluffy bath-robe, knotted unconvincingly at the middle, was soft to be touch. Her auburn hair was up as usual, she had no make on, and she was beautiful.

I ran a hand up and down the silky skin of her leg as we sipped away. We sat quietly, calmly, and once again I wondered what she was thinking.

The TV, in the corner of the immaculate sitting room, flickered away, its sound low. Our eyes rested on it from time to time, as the pulse of her body drummed through me. It didn't take long for the bottle to finish and for the first, luscious response from the champagne to spread through my brain.

Suddenly, she jumped to her feet, halting the lazy, circulating flow of well-being. I saw the gleam in her eye and knew it was the start of something.

She turned the TV off and, without any difficulty, slid the settee back against one wall, exposing a large area of solid, polished oak flooring. 'Take off your clothes,' she ordered, as she twiddled the wooden slatted window-blinds shut. The early evening light disappeared.

'Everything?'

'Everything.'

I stood in the middle of the floor and did as I was told, throwing my things into a heap by the TV. The lamplight, emerging from the corner of the room, emitted a soft glow, dim enough to comfort any body issues. Chiara watched for a while then crossed to the door and flicked on the main overhead light. It dazzled the white-walled room. In the spotlight I fought the urge to cross my hands in front, managing to keep one steadfastly by my side, whilst bending a knee to a dashing angle, placing the other hand nonchalantly on a hip.

She waited, one finger lingering on the light switch, the other tapping away at her lips. Then, apparently satisfied, she moved across the room, picked up a remote, and switched on the CD player. The display panel lit up and flashed, awaiting the next command.

'I think you might like this music,' she whispered.

'I never listen to any.'

She nodded. 'I know. It's a pity. Maybe we can change that. This tune will remind you of tonight. Whenever you hear it, your mind will return here. Have you experienced that before?'

I thought for a moment then offered, 'They played Flower of Scotland on the bagpipes at Hampden before an international match. It makes the back of my neck tingle – if that's what you mean.'

She gave a 'mm' sound and left the room, returning a few seconds later pushing a large cardboard box across the floor. 'I would like you to open this, take it out, blow it up, and then get inside it. You've got five minutes to do that.' She checked the clock on the mantelpiece.

'What if I can't get it up in time – will you help?'

'You'll manage on your own.'

I studied the picture on the lid. 'Do you have a foot pump? It'll make it easier.'

'You have to use your mouth – that's part of the rules.'

I knelt down and went about my task, Chiara calling out the minutes as they passed. The floor was hard on my knees: she wouldn't allow me a cushion.

When I'd finished, I was giddy from the heady cocktail of champagne and oxygen depletion. I rose shakily to my feet. She held my arm to steady me. The room smelled of rubber. I didn't like it. I sniffed my hands and held them out to her in protest.

She lifted my glass and put its last drops to my lips. I drank. Some of the bubbly fizzed down my chin. She mopped up the mess with her tongue.

'You're still not inside. There's thirty seconds left. The rubber'll be cold at first but I'll soon sort that out.'

'Inside – are you sure?'

She nodded and I didn't argue. The room was spinning. She left me alone.

There was a ping from the microwave and she returned

carrying a large glass bowl with a ladle. A sweet, heady fragrance grabbed the air in the room and overpowered it like dozens of smashed perfume bottles.

'I've made a mixture of frankincense and rose oil – and it's warm. Body warm,' she said softly. 'Good for your well-being.' She dimmed the lights, pressed play, and the music started.

'Sounds like sonar,' I said.

'Ssh. Close your eyes. Relax. Let it all flow over you. Breath easily, steadily.'

I barely felt the oil on my skin as she ladled it over. I lay calmly in the inflatable paddling pool, listening to the music, feeling the rhythm of her hands sweeping across me. She caressed my skin, from the soles of my feet, fingers locking into toes, to the temples of my head – her palms gliding, sliding and slipping in time to the music. I spread my arms and legs wide like a star and experienced the luscious flow over my senses: my brain melting with the pleasure.

'That's you,' she sighed.

It was quiet. I opened my eyes. I was shiny: head-to-toe in oil. She was dabbing her hands on a towel.

'So soon?'

'It's been twenty-five minutes,' she replied softly.

I tried to sit up and slipped. She handed me a single 2-ply paper hankie. 'This is all you have to wipe yourself, wherever that might be – so use it wisely. If any oil touches my skin, even one little drop, you lose and you have to stop what you are doing immediately. Are the rules clear?'

I took the tissue from her, delicately holding it between thumb and forefinger. Her hand pulled on the tie of her bathrobe and she let it slide to the floor.

*

As we lay in bed in the dark of midnight, side by side, flat on our backs, holding hands in the space between us, she said,

'It was going to be a surprise but you might as well know now: I'm going to sell this house. I'll organise it tomorrow. With the profit I've decided to buy two in Scotland. Gradually, I will move closer to Dumfries. Eventually, I'll have all my properties in the North – that way I won't need to travel as much. It'll make things easier.'

'You're willing to do all that for... me?'

'Yes.'

I sat up sharply. 'You shouldn't do that, Chiara. What if things don't go well between us? What if something happens?'

She switched on the lamp – it was hard on the eyes. She hugged me. 'I don't think you need worry. We'll be fine. And it's a financial decision I'm making as well: it's not just based on you. Don't worry.'

Friday 25th August

I woke prematurely – it nearly always happens when I'm beside her – and slithered from bed, my skin as soft as Gretna's defence, and wandered into Buckingham, searching for a newspaper shop.

It was my first visit to one of Chiara's houses – other than the one she had owned in Dumfries, the place where we'd had our very first, exciting night together back in March of this year. And this was also a nice enough house: modern, neat and tastefully decorated. It even had a double garage, allowing revered cars almost as much room as its human occupants. Nevertheless, she wouldn't be attached to it. It was how she made a living: buying early and selling on.

The sun was up as I strolled from the red-bricked housing development, turning towards the town centre. The road was busy, even at this early hour, with piles of belching lorries and fat cars elbowing their way in the direction of London and Birmingham. The fume-filled walk along the pavement was not a pleasant one.

We had spent the last few weeks working on my home – this was our break away from it. My apartment was nearly complete now, but the main part of the house lay untouched: a far bigger job for another time. Cash had flowed from my wallet like a burst beer tap and I had spent more money in the last month than the whole of my forty-three years put together. Nevertheless, it was money well spent: my flat had been sculpted, or, at the very least, painted, into another form, a long overdue and necessary rupture from the past and my parents' tastes. It placed the house firmly as our new home. It belonged to both of us now. The change had been freeing, exhilarating.

It didn't take too long to locate a newsagent and I found a more pleasant route back – along a path through some woods, skirting round the edge of the town. I had everything, I should be completely happy but there was a tiny knot of annoyance in one corner of my mind. It niggled like a failed two-foot putt and was unlikely to go away soon: I was going to miss my Friday session with the boys tonight. It was stupid, I knew that, but it kept at me. It was our ritual, starting from the first moments we were aged to drink – and I was breaking it.

When Chiara had suggested this short spell away, it hadn't occurred to me that this would matter so much. Missing my Thursday golf, yesterday, had been no great hardship – but this? I couldn't shake off.

As I emerged from the trees, turning onto London Road, my phone buzzed. It was a text from Jill Gittes: she wanted my help again. I'd given her my number in the steamy heat of last month when I'd found her husband's murderer, but, unfortunately, you can never ask for a number back. Actually, I'd forgotten she had it in her possession – getting careless. At least, the prospect of a new job tempered the irritation of the intrusion. It was the right time to start my work again – helping people. I didn't want to become as idle as a Dumfries litter bin.

Perhaps last month's success with her case would spur more folk to come forward. However, it might be necessary to reassure people that I am still willing to take on the slightest of problems as well – other than finding missing pets, of course – providing the reason behind the task is sound.

I returned a text saying I wasn't in town at the moment but would be back tomorrow night and she could get me then, if it was urgent. I replaced my phone, deciding there would have to be another change to my number: I allow my four closest pals and Chiara have it and that's all. Anyone else can get me through my local, The Bruce.

When I returned, Chiara was in her dressing gown again, making a pot of tea. I sat down at the kitchen table and watched. I'd never had a girlfriend before, never had the desire – any fleeting relationships lasting as long as warm toast – but I

19

knew I should keep my frustration at missing the pub tonight to myself. So I flicked through the newspaper like a man swatting flies.

'You were up early again,' she said.

I nodded.

'Was it the same dream – the one you told me about?'

'Yes, it's always that one.' I wasn't in the mood to talk about it.

'Anything different happen this time? Did you manage to get any further along?'

'Not really,' I answered, absently.

'Tell me.' She moved closer.

I looked up from my reading and saw interest in her face. I shrugged. 'There's not much to tell. I'm standing in a corridor, near some stairs. I'm nervous, my heart is beating hard – but I don't know why. I can feel the carpet under my bare feet. I keep thinking I'm in my own house, upstairs – but I don't recognise it at all.

This time I started to walk towards the door at the far end, and each step brings more and more fear until it is almost unbearable. There was a flash – and then I was fully alert, awake.' I shrugged again.

'And you've never reached that door?'

'A couple of times. Once I had my hand on the handle, ready to turn it, before I startled awake in a sweat.'

'When was that?'

'Back in March – when someone was trying to kill me.' I turned my attention back to the paper.

'Do you think you'll ever get through that door? Maybe that's what needs to happen – then the dream might not return.'

'Let's not talk about it now...'

The flash of the report on page seven stopped me dead in my tracks. Shocked me. In this paper, in the national news, was the photo of a man, a close-up – perhaps taken from his passport – and I recognised him. What on earth was going on? How could this be happening?

The headline read:

MYSTERY SURROUNDING ELDERLY MAN FOUND DEAD IN HIS EVENING SUIT ON A DUMFRIES PAVEMENT

Instantly, the picture of the pig I'd seen on the internet broke into my mind. *It* had been dressed up in an evening suit, dragged from a sewer, and left sprawled out on a pavement in Sydney, Australia. I'd found the photo whilst searching for leads on the Kingholm Pig case – and now the picture of a man I knew from my home town was here, right in front of me. He had ended up the same way. How could that be?

The report said it had happened on Wednesday night around ten o'clock, close to the town centre, in a side-street off English Street.

Chiara must have noticed something in my face. 'What is it? What are you staring at?' I turned the paper round to show her. 'I've spoken to this man,' I said, frantically tapping away at his photo. 'Not so long ago. I know him – not very well, mind you – but I know him… knew him. I didn't know his name was Lewis Chamberlain, but I was speaking to him up at the old ruined hotel only last month, when it was being demolished. Remember I told you about the place where Onion Sanny used to keep his caravan?'

Chiara nodded, vaguely. 'Onion Sanny? Is that the hermit man?'

'I suppose he could be called that: he keeps himself to himself right enough. Although, I've done a couple of jobs for him this year, so I'm not sure what that says. And there's a chance that this Lewis Chamberlain was a friend of Sanny's as well. I can't say for definite but I'm fairly sure I saw him walking towards Sanny's new home just after we'd helped with the flitting. Are hermits allowed to have friends?'

Chiara chose not to reply.

I went on, 'Mr Chamberlain used to own that hotel – the one they pulled down. That would have been years and years ago, of course: I've only ever known it as a ruin. He said it was a grand place in its heyday – and sounded very proud of it. I'm guessing this was back in the late fifties, early sixties – when he had it.' I shook my head in dismay, 'It was strange – our first meeting. Did I tell you?'

She shook her head.

'It was late one night and he was inside that old hotel, in a derelict room, with one of those old wind-up gramophones playing. He was on his own, arms outstretched, holding an imaginary partner, a gas lantern blazing away in one corner. He didn't give his name then, but he said it was the room where he'd first met his wife, and when he danced there, he felt she was alive again, and with him. That's why he did it. Naturally, I left him alone and I've always thought of him as the Waltzing Man. He was very smart in his evening suit.'

I added, 'It says here he was eighty-six. He was fit for his age, that's for sure. It's very sad.'

She said, 'It says he was strangled by a rabbit snare.'

I nodded, despondently. 'I know. Terrible. Another death in Dumfries. What's going on with the place these days? It used to be one of the quietest towns in the whole of Scotland.'

'A snare sounds nasty: I wouldn't fancy it. What are you going to do?'

I scrunched up my shoulders. 'What can I do? I'm here – for a start.' The words came out harsher than I'd meant.

'We'll be back tomorrow night.' If she'd picked up on any resentment, she didn't show it.

'But I didn't really know him,' I muttered.

'Don't you want to help out? That's what you do, isn't it?

22

It's your town, after all. Where you've lived all your life.' She set a cup of tea in front of me. As usual, it wasn't strong enough – she bought champagne costing as much as a night in a decent hotel but couldn't stretch to an extra tea-bag in the pot.

'Maybe I *can* do something,' I said. 'I could have a word with Asa – and Chisel as well.' I added, mostly to myself, 'I wonder why they didn't let me know about this?'

Before Chiara could speak, I gave the answer, 'Probably to keep me out of harm's way. It's been known to happen.'

'Is that what you want – to stay away from it?'

I swithered. 'I'm not sure. There might be nothing for me: I'm not going to poke my nose in if no-one wants me to. I would need to find out more. The boys'll be in the pub tonight – they never miss a Friday night.'

'Or any other night, for that matter.'

'That's a wee bit harsh, Chiara.'

She sat down and watched me as I re-read the article. I tried to avoid the intensity of her stare. Eventually, she said, 'You miss your friends.'

I knew it wasn't a question. I lifted my head and gazed back at her. It was a few moments before I spoke. 'I'm sorry – but I do. It's stupid – we've only been away for a couple of days. I'll get over it.'

She gave a smile. 'It's all right, Jin, it's only natural. Do you want to head up today? It's early yet: there's still plenty of time.'

'What about the business you've to do?'

'I don't need you to come along – I wasn't expecting you to either. I'll see to everything myself, and drive up tomorrow. You take the train back: I'll drop you off.'

'Then you'll be alone – that's not very fair.'

'I have friends as well, you know.'

'And they're all men,' I grumbled back.

'I thought you didn't mind.'

'I don't like you being on your own – that's all I said. I worry about your safety. It's better if there's someone around, but...'

She waited for me to continue – I didn't. So she said, 'You want me to stop seeing these other men?'

'I do, Chiara.'

*

The train journey home was easy enough. I arrived in Dumfries at a quarter to two in the afternoon – Chiara dropping me off at the station in Birmingham for ten o'clock. We had agreed on a compromise: she would stay one night with her father, who lived somewhere in the area, and she would drive up to Scotland the next day.

The back door of my house was reluctant to open, glued by its recent coat of white paint, and I had to put a shoulder to it to release it and all the pent up decorating odours. The made-to-measure kitchen had been installed last week but there were still some finishing touches needed to set it off.

Although every wall in my apartment was plain white now, each room had its own distinctive style through the use of bright curtains, new furniture and paintings. I had insisted on buying original artwork from local artist exhibitions, rather than mass-produced prints – my only real contribution to the decor.

I dumped my travel bag on the new square, chunky kitchen table, and a quick search of the phone book disclosed the necessary address. After a sandwich and a mug of tea, I set out on foot for Charnwood Gardens, off Lockerbie Road.

It was a pleasant enough afternoon: the oppressive temperatures of last month were long forgotten and a more normal Scottish summer heat sat in place. Although heat and summer are not always found together round these parts – like beer and moderation.

The walk over made me realise how enjoyable it was to

be back. I'd only been away a few days but I had missed seeing a familiar face like a swimmer misses water. However, it was worrying to think that the company of Chiara wasn't enough for me. After all she was a woman who could stop a Dumfries man in mid-drink – I'd actually witnessed it. At some point I would need to figure out what was wrong with me and put it right.

But, at this moment, it was more important to find a way of taking on the Waltzing Man case. I needed to be hired. It didn't feel right to be snooping away at a stranger's death: so it depended on finding someone wanting my help with the enquiry. It depended on who was at my destination – Mr. Chamberlain's house.

A large, shiny-black, expensive looking car sat like a hefty blancmange on the runners by the side of this semi-detached modern house. A good start. The curtains were half-closed in mourning, but the doorbell played an inappropriate electronic, chirpy tune. I had to wait a while for an answer.

When the door opened, a stern, belly-protruding, heavy-breasted man looked down at me. He wore a white shirt, open broadly at the neck, and black trousers with black socks – thin enough to show clear outlines of his long white toes. He would be close to sixty. The top of his head was bald yet he'd reared enough white tufts round the sides to keep his overall hair average respectable. From the height of the top step, he peered over the rims of his small-framed spectacles. 'Yes?' It was an English accent and not welcoming. He waited impatiently for a reply, his right foot tapping off the linoleum of the entrance, as though I'd taken him away from some very urgent business.

'I was a friend of Mr. Chamberlain,' I said, producing a brief, friendly, yet, hopefully, solemn enough smile. 'I was wondering if you needed any help – with anything.'

A woman's voice called out from inside the house, 'Who is it, Reginald?'

The man shouted back to her, confirming his well-bred English accent. 'I don't know. Some person who says he knew our father. I'll get rid of him straightaway.' He had managed to meld 'some person' into a sneer.

He turned back to me, and stared – no doubt thinking he had said enough to set me on my way. He had underestimated my resolve. I stood my ground and unfurled another smile for him. It had little effect but, as he stepped back to allow room to close the door, a dredge of politeness halted him. 'And what is it you want – really?'

He took in the full length of my appearance, and didn't seem too impressed – even though, under Chiara's guidance, I was much less scruffy these days, and had a jacket on.

'Exactly what I said: I want to offer my help and to pay my respects as well.'

'Respects can be done at the funeral – whenever that might be – and as for help, we don't need any: we have it all under control. My father was a very tidy man.' He squinted at me, 'What sort of help did you think you could offer?'

'Have the police found out who did this terrible thing yet?'

He shook his head and, momentarily, a wave of sadness flowed into his distant eyes. He twitched and began to close the door once more. I stepped forward and braced it with a straight arm. 'My name is Johnstone, Jin Johnstone. I want to say that I'm very sorry for your loss. I spoke to your father quite recently – up at the old hotel.'

At first he was taken aback by my advance, then, as he stared at my hand, his irritation grew. I pulled my arm away immediately. It hadn't been the right thing to do, not the right tack: it was bound to frighten him off. Perhaps I was trying too hard to justify my early return.

Stepping back, I added, in a serious tone, 'I don't mean to make this difficult for you. I *do* want to help. I have experience in this sort of thing – unfortunately.'

'What are you?' His sneer had returned; his grip on the door had tightened.

'As I said, I help – that's it. I might be able to find out who did this to your father, find the person responsible. Don't you want that?' Now would have been a good time to pull out a CV from my pocket.

'I think we'll leave all that to the police, if you don't mind.' Then he asked, warily, 'Are you a private detective, or something? Only I didn't think they had them round these parts.'

I turned towards the car and flicked my head in the direction of the sticker in the back window – it said Chamberlain Electronics. 'You work in an electrical company?'

He moved forward, slightly, following my gaze. 'There's a world of difference between electrical and electronic systems,' he replied haughtily. I was put in my place, and he added, with satisfaction, 'It's my own company – built it up from nothing.'

I gave a suitable nod, before trying again, 'It's just that I thought I could find the killer – and bring him to justice.'

He looked scathingly at me: eyes narrowed.

'I've been in the papers,' I put in, immediately regretting the remark.

'You want money? Is that what you're after?'

I shook my head franticly. 'No, not at all. Not unless you *want* to pay me, that is.'

The corners of his mouth wilted into a scowl. 'And you imagine you can do a better job than the police?'

'Not a better job – but I might be able to go at it from a different direction. Talk to people who aren't so keen, normally.'

'What are you implying: that my father was up to something illegal? I don't think so. How dare you.'

'No, I didn't mean that… But if I could have a word inside…'

'Definitely not. We don't need your help. I don't expect to see you here again. Good day, sir.' He gave a firm farewell nod as he closed the door.

I slumped off. So that was that: no job, no investigation, and now there was no real need to hear about the case from Asa in the pub tonight – other than through plain curiosity.

*

I take my Aunt May and Miss Welch, an old lady I met a few weeks ago, to the supermarket each Monday. So, when I turned up on Miss Welch's doorstep, she was surprised to see me: her face frowning, deepening the many lines she'd collected on her long stay on the planet.

'You've got the wrong day,' she said sharply, resembling a five-foot tweed-skirted, blue-jumpered, purple-permed, small, angry hawk. 'It's not Monday, is it?' She held the pleased gleam in her eye at catching me out. It was one I was used to seeing.

'I know it's Friday, Miss Welch,' I returned, pleasantly. 'And how are you today?' I cracked open a grin, like my mouth had a ring-pull. 'It's a lovely day,' I added, in another attempt to wipe the widening glower from her face.

'There's rain on the way,' she retorted.

Over the weeks, I had expected Miss Welch's frosty manner to thaw with familiarity, but it hasn't – not so far. Despite this, she is always ready – coat and shoes on and fastened – for the shopping trip, but I get little more than a nod in my direction as she makes for the car. Nevertheless, I have witnessed, from a distance, my aunt and her share a giggle or two as they trawl the aisles of Tesco, pushing their trolleys side by side, sharing in the two-for-one offers.

Something occurred to her, 'Oh, is it to do with May?'

'My aunt? How do you mean?'

'She's in hospital. Didn't you know?' The question was delivered as a ticking off.

'No, I didn't. Nothing serious, I hope? When did she go in?'

'Tuesday night. She phoned me yesterday – but wouldn't say what was wrong. Maybe it's nothing too serious – but she *did* miss last Monday's shopping, didn't she? That wasn't a good sign. She's going to be in all week, she said. Do you think she expects me to go and visit her? I had to tell you that she wouldn't manage this Monday coming either. So that doesn't sound good, does it? She seemed quite certain on the fact.

But she also mentioned she might ask a neighbour to pop round to your house to let you know as well. What's that all about anyway, eh? Why doesn't she just phone you, instead of pestering me and having all this round-the-houses business?'

'It's probably because I've been away for a few days, Miss Welch. But, actually, it's more likely because she doesn't have my phone number.' I dropped my head slightly – and resented the movement.

Miss Welch found room for another frown on her forehead. 'You're her *only* relative – the last one,' she stated forcefully. 'She should be able to get in touch with you at all times – just in case. None of us are getting any younger, you know. And how did she expect *me* to get in touch with you, come to that?'

Miss Welch was right: maybe I have been taking this telephone business too far. I moved on, 'I was wondering if you were busy today.'

'Busy? I'm always busy. What is it you want?'

'Are you waiting for anyone just now?'

'My visitor has left – not so long ago.'

I knew she meant her cleaner, who comes twice a week. 'I have a job for you – kind of detecting work – if you fancy it.'

*

I drove her over to Charnwood Gardens, telling her, on the way, everything I knew about the deceased – it wasn't much. I parked the car down the street, out of sight of the Chamberlain house.

'I was a very close friend of his,' Miss Welch confirmed with a nod.

I returned the gesture. 'Yup.'

'Fine.' She struggled to free herself from the seat and the car, and then turned back to me, the door open, 'What was his first name again?'

*

It wasn't too long a wait. The radio said a wet weather front was approaching right enough, bringing days of rain. In Dumfries it arrived five minutes ago. Miss Welch's bent, stiff walk on thin legs eventually reached the car – the collar of her light green coat had been turned up against the elements. I jumped out and opened the door for her. She sat down heavily, lacking control over the movement.

By the time I returned behind the wheel, she had untied the knot under her chin, and was pulling the clear plastic hat-hood type thing from her head. She gave it a good shake before stowing it in her large brown handbag.

'Any luck?' I asked, wiping the splashed beads of rain from the gear stick, and running a drying index finger across the radio.

She emitted a throaty chuckle. 'I have to say I quite enjoyed that.' She cast a side-way glance in my direction, before pulling her reserve back into place. With a more serious face, she went on, 'I have something for you.' She dug into her handbag and held up a book. 'The son, Reginald, wasn't too keen to let me in, so I pushed past him and met the daughter – I heard *her* voice asking who was at the door. She was a bit more hospitable – I should think so too, with me being a close friend and all.

30

The daughter made some tea but they weren't keen on telling me anything. So I brought them into my confidence: I told them I was their father's girlfriend. You should have seen their faces.' Miss Welch broke off into a wheezy snigger.

At first I was shocked – she had overstepped the mark – but, after a moment, I couldn't help but join her in a chuckle.

After a hankie had been dragged harshly across her nostrils a couple of times, she went on, 'They couldn't take it in at first. I had to repeat it – that I was his girlfriend. I think it was the word 'girl' that threw them really. Anyway, they were doubtful and asked why they'd never heard of me before, why their father had never mentioned it, but I managed to skip over that by saying we'd decided to keep it a secret as we weren't sure how people would take it – especially them.'

Miss Welch sent out another throaty laugh. This time she didn't rein it back in and allowed her creased smile to linger on her face like a large crack down a new-build house. She set off again, 'Then I went into a few details about how often I used to stay over. I said I couldn't remember if I'd left anything behind after my last visit and enquired if they'd found anything of mine lying around – like undergarments. They were fairly squirming in their seats by now, so I hit them with the same of the questions I'd asked at the start – and this time they were only too willing to change the subject and answer them.

I persuaded them to let me take away this: it's his diary for the year. There might be something interesting in it – a clue, maybe.'

She handed the book over. I weighed it in my hand, keeping my eye on her, thanking her for her efforts. I wouldn't be underestimating her in future. I wasn't too happy about the amount of lies she had told, nor the changes made to her remit but, perhaps, I had that coming: having set up this feeble fishing expedition. It hadn't really been a good idea and, again, there was a smell of desperation about it.

I was aware of the silence in the car, so I asked, 'And they just let you have his diary – a private document belonging to their father? What about the police? They must have been in the house already – didn't *they* want it?'

'Take a look at the cover.'

I did: it said **The Twenty Best Walks in South-West Scotland.**

'That's a wee bit elaborate, don't you think?' I muttered. 'Why would a man who lived alone need or want to disguise his diary like that? He did live alone, didn't he?'

Miss Welch shrugged. 'Well, that would be one question I couldn't ask. There were some other things I couldn't cover either, you know – like where the bathroom was. Just as well I had that last minute visit before I left my own house. Very lucky, and that's not always been the case of late.' She fastened her seatbelt and waited for me to drive off.

I made no move.

She sighed and added, 'The Chamberlain boy, Reginald, mentioned the diary: he had just started reading it. So it seemed like a golden opportunity – and I grabbed it.'

'You stole it from them?'

'Of course not. I'm not some common criminal.' She stared with keen eyes, daring me to make a reply.

I knew when to keep quiet.

She went on, 'Actually, it did cross my mind, there and then, but I didn't think I would be able to outrun them.'

I had a brief image of Miss Welch belting down the pavement, diving head-first through the open window of my speeding car, closely pursued by a podgy, puffing, stocking-footed Reginald. Perhaps she was picturing something along the same lines, for it took her a wee while to explain, 'They'd only uncovered it a short while ago, when packing up some books – but hadn't contacted the police as yet. Reginald said he wanted a look at it first, to check it over.

So I said I would very much like to do the same: peruse it before him, if he didn't mind. Just in case there were details in there: things that might be a trifle embarrassing.' Miss Welch smirked, before going on, 'That flummoxed him. So I asked how much he had read so far. He said he'd only glanced at the last couple of pages – apparently there is no entry for the last day. Lewis never reached home to write it up.'

Now she was on first name terms.

She added, 'According to Reginald, the previous day's entry was only on quite ordinary stuff – and a couple of poems. That's as far as he'd read.'

'Why would that be?'

'What?'

'You said Reginald wanted to check it over before handing it to the police. What did he mean by that?'

'I couldn't possibly say. I suppose he wanted to see if it was worth them having it – and to see if there was anything there to explain this terrible incident. Only natural, I would think.'

'Well, we'll need to give it back as soon as possible. I don't think the authorities will be too happy if they find out I have it – even if there's nothing worth reading in it.'

'No need to worry: I'll take the blame if it ever comes to that. But I'm sure I can persuade the Chamberlains not to mention my affair with their father.'

I didn't doubt that.

She went on, 'I told them I would return it tomorrow and I wouldn't censor anything until I had their permission.'

'I don't follow. And I still don't understand why they let you take it away, Miss Welch – not if the son was so keen to read it.'

'It was easy: I told them that their father liked to show me descriptions, kept a record of successes, marks out of ten – and sometimes drew diagrams.'

I shook my head.

She gave me a tut and a long look. 'Are you married?'

'No.' The answer didn't appear to surprise her.

'But I do have a girlfriend,' I added, slightly put out – and now with the added irritation of, once again, justifying myself. But, on the other hand, it was pleasing to know I hadn't been discussed much on the shopping trips with my aunt.

'That girl you were with last month, in my house, is she the one? Suffers from hay fever I seem to recall.'

'Right.'

'She was very pretty: makes me wonder what she's doing with the likes of you.'

'Sometimes I think the same thing.' I was used to her barbs – I could flick them away like dandruff off a collar. 'But I still don't get the diary,' I coaxed.

'Quite simple. I told them the diagrams were for positions.' She gave another tut after seeing me shake my head again; then she clarified, using very deliberate tones, 'When one gets older certain arrangements are not possible, not even worth attempting – not even with ropes and pulleys. I said Lewis, their father – good job I remembered his name at that point – used to discuss what was feasible and what was not with me, before we tried them out. Hence the planning and the diagrams.'

'Diagrams of what? Exercises?'

She gave a lengthy exhale. 'I've told you already. Surely you and your girlfriend have tried a few out: it would be rather dull not to. They've got all kinds of names – and numbers. And you can buy books nowadays to show you. I've heard you can get them in the library now. That would never have happened in my day – the books I'm talking about, *not* the positions, the couplings.'

Then it dawned on me.

She gave a precise nod. 'There you are – and their

reaction was much the same as yours. I can feel the heat from here. I asked to see the diary first in case it might be embarrassing for me – and for them. Then I could erase certain things before it was handed over to the police. I wouldn't want the world to know about my dear Lewis' bedroom antics.' She chuckled. 'Reginald was very quick to pass it over – like he was handling a bag of dog dirt. I didn't even need to go to the next level – asking if he'd seen any of the compromising photos we'd taken.'

She paused for a moment, staring blankly through the windscreen. 'I thought it was worth a shot. It might be useful.'

I drove off, needing something to destroy the visions in my head.

She started up again, absentmindedly gazing at the clasped, bony hands on her lap, 'People think because you're old and a Miss that you know nothing about it. I've a few stories I could tell, young man. I could have married on more than one occasion, you know.'

I made no response.

After several minutes, I asked her, 'Is there anything else, anything you found out?'

'Not a lot. Either the police don't know very much or they're not letting onto the family. But one thing I do know is why Lewis Chamberlain was dressed in an evening suit that night.'

'Let me guess – he'd been dancing.' I glanced from the road in time to see a pained expression dart across her face – I'd hit a bulls-eye.

'Right,' she replied, reluctantly. 'Lewis had joined a ballroom dancing club recently. It meets every Wednesday, and he always dressed up for it. The fact that no-one else goes to such lengths didn't seem to bother him at all.'

'It's all to do with his wife – when he danced he could feel her in his arms. And with the old hotel pulled down he would need somewhere else – the desire would still be there.' It would be interesting to find out if he danced with other women at the club or if he just waltzed around the floor on his own, eyes closed. I told her about the first time I'd met Mr. Chamberlain in his evening suit.

'It was only the second time he had been there,' Miss Welch added. 'He left at the end of the evening – ten o'clock – to walk home and was found shortly before eleven, lying on the pavement. Nothing had been stolen.' She shook her head sadly. 'That's all I got.'

'Did you mention me at all?' I asked, as we pulled up outside the front of her house.

'No, thought I'd wait until tomorrow. What was it you wanted me to say again?'

'If you remember I just wanted you to befriend them and then mention my name, saying you know I'd do a good job.' I added an unnecessary but touchy, 'That was supposed to be the reason for your visit. That was all I wanted, really.'

She didn't pick up on it, saying instead, 'Do you need the money? Is that why you're so keen to get work?'

'Not at all, Miss Welch, I've still plenty. But I *would* like to find out what happened to the man.'

She undid her seat belt and spent an age tying on her plastic hood – gearing up for the five second onslaught of tepid drizzle on the trek to her front door. 'Okay, I'll see what I can do to get you on the case,' she said. 'And Reginald's obviously not short of a few bob. He owns a company. Quick to tell me that, he was. How much will I say you charge?'

'Nothing – unless I get results. I'm sure that will appeal to him. And thanks for all your help. I'll contact you about the diary as soon as I can. And what about the police?'

'What about them?'

'If they find out you've been round to visit and fibbing, and they come knocking here…?'

'How will they know where I live? I was careful not to mention it, nor give my real name. And anyway, I'm old. You can get away with a lot of things when you get to my age: nobody's going to suspect an old bird like me doing anything sneaky.'

She opened the door, held her hand on the handle, and turned to me. 'Now, my number's in the book. You *will* need to phone first before coming round tomorrow – in case I'm busy. Shouldn't I have your number as well – to be on the safe side?'

'Thanks again for the help, Miss Welch.' I watched some raindrops running down the inside of the open door, gathering inappropriately on the ledge of the window, needing to be mopped up.

'Anytime,' she replied. 'It was good fun, really. If you need anything else, let me know.'

'I'll keep it in mind.'

She sat tight. The arm returned, met the other one, and became stoically crossed. The door stayed open like a form of water torture. I forced my phone number down onto a page of my notepad and grudgingly handed it over. There it goes again.

Once again Miss Welch checked her coat buttons were fastened securely and everything else was in place, before saying, 'I told Reginald I wouldn't be mentioned in his father's will as I have money of my own. He seemed to know about that – the will. I reckon he'd checked it already. Unnatural haste, I would call it.'

Finally, she left the car and the door was allowed to close. I waved, she didn't return it, or look back, as she scuttled up her path. I leaned over and wiped away the unwelcome water with my sleeve and drove off. It looked like I had a new partner. I headed straight for the town centre.

*

An hour later, with the car dropped off at home, and some food washed down with a cup of tea, I walked, collar up, head down, in the dreich, spit of rain round to Jill Gittes' flat, expecting her to be finished work, back home, and ready to take me somewhere.

As I waited for a response to the bell-pushing, a cheer of sun burst surprisingly from cover and spread a rainbow across the dark clouds. The sound of footsteps on the stairs inside made me turn back to spy Jill opening the door.

It was over a month since my last visit here and, judging by her face, she had lost a lot of weight in that time – luckily she had started from a full base. It appeared that the death of her husband had really hit home. Her clothes hung on her: a loose red and white patterned blouse drooping over a black skirt, and her head appeared smaller, narrower. The hair was shorter too, straight, and dyed jet black.

Jill's husband, Jackie, had been stabbed. He had died quickly: a brown-handled kitchen knife forced through his heart. I had known them both from school days yet, in some ways, Jackie's death did not arrive as a complete shock: he had always led a rather roguish existence, spending a great deal of time on the other side of the tracks. I was never really sure how he made a living but it was surprising to find out that Jill, a hair salon owner, wasn't beyond taking the occasional trip through the underpass as well: twenty-odd years of living with each other had made its mark.

'You wanted to see me?' I had contacted her from the train, telling of my earlier than expected return. I pointed out the rainbow, and, like a couple of kids, we took in its splendour for a few seconds.

'We're only seeing half of it,' I said. 'The horizon cuts off the rest: it goes on to make a full circle.'

'Really? I didn't know that. Does that mean they see the bottom half in Australia?'

I shrugged.

'So their rainbows are always U-shaped? That would be

wonderful, smiley – but weird.'

I gave another uncommitted response, wishing it hadn't been mentioned – but then spent the next few seconds mulling it over.

Jill's drawn face parted in a grin as she stared skywards, blinking against the occasional raindrops, and it was still there when she invited me inside the building. I followed her up the narrow steps to her flat above the bicycle shop.

One thing I wasn't going to mention to Jill was the new sim card I'd purchased this afternoon: I was now the proud owner of a brand new phone number once again. After it had been passed onto the boys and Chiara, everything would be back to normal.

The door to her flat was wide open and, before reaching the landing, her boyfriend, Don Gardiner, came into view through the banister railings. He was sitting on the soft cushion of the sofa, waving his good arm in the air. I nodded back a hello and kept on climbing. Jill led the way in, offering us tea. It was accepted swiftly.

'Still off work?' I asked him, sinking into a chair opposite. I'd visited Don in hospital a couple of times after the incident: the last time would have been a few weeks ago now though.

He waggled the arm held in the sling. 'Naw, I got this arm-wrestling Jill. She's stronger than she looks.' He gave a single, sharp 'ha' noise, sounding like a cork escaping from a bottle. 'Aye,' he continued, with a nod, 'still off. It'll be a couple of weeks yet they reckon.'

Don Gardiner's right arm, still bandaged, was fixed across his chest, the fingers exposed. Jackie's murderer had attacked him with a black-handled kitchen knife – a knife later identified by Jill as the one stolen from Jackie's bed-sit. Don had suffered wounds to his side as well. The fact that he had volunteered to help me capture the killer didn't stop me from feeling very badly about his injuries: the thought that he might have died that night was branded on my brain.

There was time to fill until Jill returned from her tea-brewing operation in the kitchen area of the room, so I asked, 'What about that jog you were planning? Are you going to manage it?' Before the incident, Don had been training to run in the London marathon. However it was evident his fitness had taken a bit of a knock: his normal lean frame was showing signs of change. Some of Jill's loss of bulk had not gone to waste and now sat round his – which, perhaps, explained his less than smart, roomy trousers with their elasticated waistband. His crew cut was longer also and so would probably go under another name. The only constant was the diamond stud in his ear.

'I should be running soon enough – when I get rid of this.' Again he waggled his bad arm.

Jill carried over three mugs of tea and we sipped in silence for a moment. All of a sudden, she said, 'Can we go now, Jinky?' And stood up.

'Sure.' I put down my barely touched cup. 'Where to?'

'I'm not bothered.' She flicked herself into a pair of black flip-flops and didn't speak again until the door of the flat was shut behind – she hadn't said cheerio – and we were clumping back down the stairs. 'I don't want Don involved – he's been through enough,' she said, finally. 'He thinks we're going out for a drink. I was hoping you would come over to Jackie's brother's bed-sit with me.'

That stopped me in my tracks. 'You want me to go and see Jackie's brother?' I didn't like the idea. Jackie may have been dodgy but he was never malicious. The same could not be said of the brother: I'd had some first-hand knowledge on the subject after meeting him in the toilet of The Whitesands Bar. He had accosted me when I'd been standing, minding my own business, and in mid-flow. It had been a rather uncomfortable, threatening and scary experience, from which I was glad to escape with nothing more than a damp patch or two.

And I knew Jill didn't like him one little bit either, so it was surprising she was willing to venture over: with Jackie dead, she had no real reason to stay in contact. 'Come on,' she said, 'I'll explain on the way.'

The rain had hardened and Jill pulled a miniscule umbrella from her handbag, pressed a button on its handle, forcing it to open with a floomp sound. 'Do you want under this?'

I tried a quick calculation of its surface area and gave up – maths was never a strong suit – but it would be safe to say there was barely enough space for one person, far less two. I should have brought my golf umbrella. 'No, I'm fine, Jill,' I mumbled as we started along the pavement at a reasonable pelt.

'He won't be there, Jinky. He's gone missing – that's what this is about. No-one's seen him in over a month.'

I kept up with her. It was a delicate balance between being close enough to hear but far enough away to avoid losing an eye on the treacherous spokes.

Seemingly unaware, or unconcerned, that the exposed left shoulder of her blouse was soaking up a vast amount of dripping water from her inadequate canopy, Jill went on, 'He must have disappeared soon after... after Jackie passed away.' She gave me a quick look: tears had formed in her eyes.

I laid a hand on her dry shoulder. 'It'll take a while to get over it, Jill. Just hang in.'

We continued on, Jill's flip-flops sounding like a slow-hand clap, and turned the corner. She stopped and pulled some keys from her hefty bag.

'I still don't get why you need to be involved,' I said. 'He's probably up to some kind of mischief. Are you sure he's not in jail again?'

'I'm fairly sure – and I don't know how he has managed

to stay out for so long.' She unlocked the parked car and opened the door. 'I've done a bit of asking around – hoped you might do a wee bit more, Jinky. You see I promised Jackie's parents I'd try and find out what's happened to Jeremy, find out why he's missing, pack up his stuff and take it back to them.' She gave a tired shake of the head. 'It's hard for them: first Jackie and now this. You wouldn't wish it on any parent.'

I slid into the passenger side. The driver's seat was much further forward. She squeezed in, saying, 'When you come down to it, it was never going to end happily, I suppose I always knew that. But I tried to block it from my mind. Really, the worst I thought was Jackie ending up in prison. He was never a bad person – you know that.'

'I know.'

She took in a deep breath and then out, her still generous chest pressing against the steering wheel. I thought I heard a stifled croak from the horn. She said, 'I've boxes in the boot to pack up his things – the landlord wants his stuff out and the room cleared.'

My heart sank: I'd had enough of clearing up after people. I didn't like it, I never would – and it was becoming too much of a habit these days. I didn't say anything, asking instead, 'So you're still in touch with the in-laws?'

She nodded as we drove away. 'They're nice people but getting on a bit now. It's too much for them to come down and do it. My daughter's coming over later to help as well. Let's hope there's not a lot of stuff to be gathered up.'

That was one thing on my mind: the other was why I was needed here at all, on this mission. She answered my thoughts, 'I wanted someone with me – for security. A man. And if everything's fine I'll call my daughter to come round to help with the rest. I don't need you to do any packing, or anything like that, Jinky.'

'Riding shotgun,' I muttered.

When she didn't reply, I sat and watched her drive. She was upright, her forearms resting on the wheel, almost cuddling it, her left foot, in its precarious footwear, never leaving the clutch pedal. After five minutes of jagged, twisting travel through the town, we parked in Queen Street.

She turned to me, 'Jeremy's over a month behind in his rent – that's why the landlord's not happy. As far as I know, no-one's seen him at his bed-sit, around town, or even in the pub in that time. It was the landlord who phoned the parents and they contacted me to see what could be done. Jeremy and his father don't get along – not surprising, of course – but they want to know what's happened to him. They stay over Edinburgh way now, in Penicuik; it's only right that someone finds out for them.

I have to be honest, Jinky, I couldn't care less about Jeremy and his stuff, but when the parents asked me, I couldn't very well turn them down. So I hoped you might help – see what you can find out around the place. And it's not as if any of us will be contacting the police about this either – that goes without saying.'

Jill pulled her phone up from the depths of her handbag. 'There's one other thing you could do for me. Maybe I shouldn't be saying this – but I'll be glad when Don gets back to work.'

'Something the matter?'

'I'm getting right scunnered with him these days: he's lounging around all the time, mooching off me. I know he's injured, Jinky, but he's always there. It's not fair. I seem to be feeding him all the time and he does nothing, hasn't spent a single night in his own house since coming out of hospital. It sounds selfish when I say it – but I'd like some time to myself. I don't suppose there's anything you can do about it, is there? Have a word, maybe, and get him moving? Man to man. I don't want to fall out with him or anything like that.'

So that explained the absence of the cheerio. I said, 'It must be just as frustrating for him, though: he was a fit guy. Usually they don't take to hanging about.'

Jill made a call, spoke a few words, and then gave a nod in my direction. 'Right that's fine. The landlord stays in the property and he'll be out to open the door for us.'

'And this has never happened before – Jeremy going missing?'

Jill shook herself as though she had fleas. 'I wouldn't know and I don't want to know anything about what that man does. The landlord says it's written in the contract: if any tenant goes more than one month in arrears, he can evict them.'

It was a brave landlord indeed who was willing to go against Jeremy. And I wasn't too happy at becoming mixed in with it either – nevertheless, at this moment, I couldn't very well walk away and leave her to go in on her own.

The front door opened and a beer-bellied, middle-aged, grey-haired, panda-faced man scanned the street in both directions. He wore a black t-shirt and jeans. I didn't know him. There was a key in his hand and the bulge in his right hand pocket was square shaped. We escaped the car to meet him – Jill deeming the very short trip worthy of her umbrella again.

He started without any introductions. 'I haven't been in there, mind. In his room.' He turned and climbed the stairs: it might have been an ascent of Everest with the effort it required. We followed in his less than fresh wake.

The landlord blethered on, 'I would need to get the police in to do that, to be on the safe side – and I didn't think you'd want *them* involved. But I have a living to make. Tenants must pay their way. It's six weeks now since I've had any money from him. I only need to wait a month – it's in writing – so I've been more than generous. If it's a holiday he's away on, then he should have said, and paid me a month in advance, at least.'

'When was the last time you saw him?' I asked.

He stopped on the landing, pulled me in on a stare like a hard draw on a cigarette but didn't reply. I held my tongue as well.

'This is a friend of mine,' Jill said, breaking the deadlock. 'He's helping.'

The landlord, showing signs of recognition, gave a heavy sigh of long-held cloudy air. 'Last time I saw Mr. Gittes was the day he handed over his week's rent and that was on Saturday, the 15th of July – I checked my books.'

We reached a door with a black two on it. There were three other doors on this floor, all with numbers – none of them the same.

Jill said to him, 'If there's a lot of stuff, I'll need to come back tomorrow and clear the rest away: there's only so much I can take at a time. Okay?'

He was right back in, leaning forward, 'No, it's not okay. I've told you already, I need the room emptied. Tonight. I've a new tenant coming in this weekend, and the place has to be gutted and cleaned before then. I've been telling you for a week now. I've a living to make. The cleaners will be here in not much more than an hour's time – so I need you to get a move on.' He lifted the bottom of his t-shirt to his face to wipe away some sweat, giving us a show of his white, saggy, motley belly.

Then he slid the yale key into the lock and turned to me. 'Normally he pays his rent bang on time, every week, so I didn't think I would have a problem with him. Here's his mail.' He pulled a small bundle of folded envelopes out of his back pocket, handing them to Jill, as he pushed the door wide open.

She stepped forward immediately, standing in the doorway, barring his entry. The landlord, sneaking a quick look round her, must have been satisfied as he took a step back to allow me in. From what I could see, it was tidy, right enough.

He said, 'I'll leave you to get on with things then.'

Jill held out her hand and, unwillingly, the man placed the

45

key in her palm.

The moment I stepped inside the room, a memory returned, an almost identical moment: the time I'd entered Jackie's room, over a month ago. Jill had asked me to accompany her on that occasion as well. We knew her husband was dead by then, and now an odd, shivering feeling ran through me – Jeremy was dead too.

Yet this room was very different. Whereas Jackie's bedsit had been ransacked, this one was extremely neat with nothing out of place. It was completely at rest, and, like a graveyard, it held a lingering unease. Jill closed the door on the landlord, and paused. It was musty – with a background smell of floor cleaner, paint and baby powder. She stood beside me, unmoving, perhaps feeling the same. We stood quietly, slowly taking it in.

It was a large room with a door at the far end, probably leading to a bathroom. The curtains were partially open, allowing in barely enough light. In front of the window stood a solid desk with a large mirror, and a solitary hairbrush on its bare surface. Its stool had been pulled out in front, and waited to be occupied.

In a corner, a large wooden, muscular wardrobe rested, then a chest of drawers, with a single bed along one wall: made up as tightly as any found in a hospital. There was a neat kitchen area as well: the drying tray on its side, with a stainless steel sink still attempting to sparkle in the dull light. Jeremy would not like us being here, but the odds of him turning up at this exact moment must be very long – especially if he was no longer alive.

I took in a lungful of the stale air and noticed a couple of notes on the floor, pushed under the door. I picked them up. They were from the landlord: reminders of rent.

'Wait,' Jill hissed, her hand raised to stop any further movement. She continued in a harsh whisper, 'What if he never left? There's something about this room.'

I answered in a hushed tone: it was impossible not to, 'I feel it too.'

'Jeremy. What if he's still *here*?' She nodded sharply towards the wardrobe, eyes extended.

I glanced across and then, quickly, to the bed, to see if there was space underneath to stash a body. The only other place would be in the bathroom. We stared at each other. I wanted to tell her it was too far-fetched, but couldn't. I shuddered. But from a weak start, I managed to impact some authority into the assertion, 'He can't be here, Jill.' I added, 'If he was, there would be a smell: it's well over a month now.' I gave a brief laugh – it wasn't a convincing one.

I waved to her to stay put and crossed the floor to the wardrobe. My heart beat hard as I tugged on the door. It opened easily, without a squeak – only hanging clothes.

Jill motioned with her eyes towards the other door. I inched closer and laid a hand on its handle. It was locked. No, it wasn't – it opened out the way. Clicked on a light. Nothing. Only one of the tiniest of bathrooms I'd ever seen: you'd need to back in like a reversing lorry, already hunkered down, to sit on the toilet seat.

We both released our saved up air and started poking about the room. 'There's not a lot here, Jinky: no need to stay long. Just go whenever you've seen enough.'

'I'll wait until your daughter turns up.' I wasn't going to leave her alone in a place like this.

'Could there be something here to explain his absence?' she said. 'You're better at this than me.'

I liked her continuing faith: she'd asked much the same question last time as I'd looked for clues to her husband's death. I hadn't found any then.

She went on, 'Don't worry about mucking it up: it's all got to be shifted out and I couldn't care less about any of it. I'll just be bunging it together.'

'Right, everything in the room needs to be checked, Jill, and that'll mean digging into every corner.' I wasn't thinking of finding any money – unlike in my Uncle James' house – this time it was possible there was something a wee bit nastier lurking under the floorboards or behind the furniture.

So far, the killer of Jill's husband has refused to give the reason for the murder. However, I have reached a few conclusions on the matter: either Jackie was killed as punishment for trying to set up his own smuggling enterprise, or it was retribution for not passing on a consignment of drugs mistakenly shipped to him. It could even be both.

Jill had told me Jackie would never deal in drugs – it was a step too far for him – yet, at some point, earlier this year, his behavior changed dramatically: suddenly he was frightened and concerned for his wife's safety. He moved out but was happy enough for her to take a boyfriend. He became entangled in drugs, involved in serious crime, and she needed protection.

Now Jeremy was missing. It's not too big a leap to suppose that Jackie disposed of the drugs by passing the consignment onto his brother – and someone found out.

It left one tantalizing question though: in the search for these drugs, why hadn't Jeremy's bed-sit been turned over like Jackie's?

As I rummaged through the wardrobe, I wondered if the police had been here doing the same thing last month: they might have considered Jeremy a suspect in his brother's death. It might be worth asking Asa about it at some point.

All the clothes were on hangers and wrapped in plastic as if each one had returned from the dry cleaners. It didn't look like any clothes were missing: the wardrobe seemed fairly full, and an empty suitcase sat underneath on a shelf.

'His toothbrush is missing, but his creams and lotions are still here.' Jill said, returning from the bathroom. She pulled open a drawer. 'Everything folded neatly. If he needed to lie low for a while you'd think he'd have paid the landlord well in advance.'

'If he had the money.'

'You'd think he'd take more stuff though – unless he was in a hurry.'

I opened the top drawer of the dressing table: it contained more face and body cream. 'There doesn't seem to be anything personal: like a diary, credit cards, or bills. Have you found anything?'

She shook her head. 'Not even any of the gloves he liked to wear to protect his hands.'

I pulled up the carpet and tapped the floorboards, checked under the furniture, and along the skirting boards – but without any success. Jill returned from the car carrying boxes and began to pack.

After a further ten minutes I'd given up. 'I don't think I'm going to find anything, Jill. Any thoughts?'

She stopped and took one slow look around the room. 'There is one thing that's strange: it's that hairbrush sitting there. I've never been here, of course, but I remember Jackie telling me Jeremy always used a brush for his hair. He would sit in front of the mirror and do it for minutes on end – like a girl with long hair – counting out each stroke.'

'That'll be the one then, Jill.'

'Yeah, so if he's taken his toothbrush you'd think he would have taken that one as well, if he was so attached to it.'

'It's not much to go on.'

'But that's not all, Jinky. Jackie said his brother was very particular…'

'I think we can see that…'

'He had other brushes: a small one for his beard and another, larger, softer one, and this is why I remember it, for brushing his skin. He did it every day before he showered, gave himself a good old rubdown. If you did all that, you would need more than one brush, wouldn't you? So where are the others? Or, why leave this one behind? And why not take plenty clothes?'

'I've no idea.'

I helped her empty the wardrobe. 'Look at this, Jill. He's got name tags sown into all his things – just like we used to do at primary school.' Now that was as odd as a rough skinned masseuse.

*

I was an hour behind my usual arrival time at The Bruce. Under its towering columns at the entrance, I shook the drizzle from my jacket, and entered into the babble of the bar. A yard inside, and there was a sudden yank of guilt in my gut. Normally walking in here produces as much pleasure as a Queens' goal – but not this time. I hadn't done the right thing. Even if Chiara was with her father at this very moment, and enjoying his company, it had been selfish of me to leave. The situation required some serious, drastic action – I might need to phone her later on.

As I wandered over to their table, Asa nudged Tread and said loudly, 'In the name of the wee man…'

I hit back, 'That's enough of the height jokes for one night, thank-you very much.'

Chisel looked up from his pint and smiled as I plonked down beside them.

Asa continued, unadmonished, 'If I recall correctly from the minutes of our last meeting, you made an apology about not being able to attend tonight as you were heading off for a few days with your woman. Frankly, we were a bit taken aback by that. In fact, if you had given the excuse of going to watch a Gretna home game, we might have looked upon it a touch more favourably.'

'Steady on, Asa, that's taking things too far. We have

standards, you know,' Tread blustered.

'You're right, Tread,' Asa replied, with a shake of the head. 'Sorry, I don't know what got into me there: that was a bit below the belt. So what happened, Jinky, why are you back? Was it, in fact, something to do with the bit below the belt?' His eyes narrowed.

'Has he got that trouble as well?' Tread enquired.

Asa went on, 'No, forget it, Jinky – I'll have a pint.' Tread and Chisel raised their hands, like classroom children, for some of the same.

As I stood up, noting they were barely half-way down their glasses, Asa stated grandly, 'This apparition in front of me might very well be a figment of my imagination, but if it can buy beer before it disappears – then all the better.' He finished off with a chortle.

'I'll drink to that,' Tread cheered, raising his glass. 'Here's to ghosts of drinking buddies – especially all ale-purchasing spirits.'

'We thought you wouldn't be making it. What happened?' Chisel said to me, on my return, a load of beer for them and a gafoni for myself.

'Where's Hoogah?' I asked.

'Good one, Jinky,' Asa cut in. 'Get the round in first then ask the question later – just in case he's on his way and you'd have to stump up some more. Nice move: one less to buy. I must keep a note of them all and write a book.'

'What would you call it?' Chisel enquired.

Asa rubbed his chin. 'What about – How to Get Around Buying a Round?'

'How to Jink a Drink, would be better,' Tread put in. 'Or, How to Jinky a Drinkie, might be even better.'

I hadn't seen any of them in a while – with the decorating and stuff – so it wasn't surprising there would be a need to make up for lost time. I muttered, indignantly, 'I'll get him a pint when he arrives – don't you worry about that. But do any of you know how much a new kitchen costs these days?'

'These days? Listen to grandpa,' It was Tread, of course.

'Feeling the pinch, are we?' Asa said, as he completed one of many similar tasks for the night: the empty glass making a hollow sound as it landed back on the table.

'Well, I'm glad to see you Jinky,' Tread cheered. 'It's never the same when there's an absentee.'

Chisel said, 'In answer to your question, Jinky, Hoogah has had a bit of an emergency. Didn't say what, though, but he should be in shortly.'

Tread asked, 'How did you get on in deepest England? What was her house like?'

'It was nice. I enjoyed the paddling pool the most.'

He replied, 'Paddling pool? That's swanky.'

After thirty-odd years, I'm still never really sure when he's being serious.

He went on, 'You didn't fall out with that lovely creature, did you? Even by your standards that would be the stupidest thing you'd ever do in your life.' He added a sly, 'Was it to do with, you know, as Asa said, the bit below the belt?'

'We didn't fall out.' I made the comment with more certainty than I was feeling. I should phone now – she still didn't have my new number. I took a sip of my gafoni.

As the conversation turned to the difference between cake, flan and torte, I stared at the three of them – my close friends – chuntering on. I saw them from a distance, detached. I watched their mouths move. I didn't hear them: their words blending and becoming the hubbub of the pub. I looked on, taking them in – like a stranger.

Tread Dunlop, with his freckled, delicate, fair face, bald head, and eyes lit by mirth. Asa Murdoch and his large, round head on his broad shoulders, ruddy cheeks, and mouth widening, ready to burst out into another enormous laugh. And

Chisel Woods, upright, slim, with his slender face and keen eyes, crying with laughter. I should have been joining in but I couldn't. I was remote, outside. This used to be the best place in the world but, for the very first time, I wanted to be somewhere else. I was forty-three; I'd done this since I was eighteen. Right now I needed to be with Chiara, to be able to hug her tightly, to make sure I never let go of her ever again.

And if they looked in my direction, they would see nothing out of the ordinary: a slightly scruffy man with hair greying round the ears and an average, unremarkable face. Just like Miss Welch earlier, I sometimes wonder what Chiara sees in me.

Asa poked me in the arm and I jumped. 'What's wrong, with ye man? You look as though you're in a trance. You've hardly touched your drink. Are you feeling okay?'

I shook myself from inside to out and produced a weak smile. 'I'm fine. Tired, probably, from the journey up. And still on English time.'

Asa said to me, 'Did you hear what Chisel was saying? The old swimming pool is to close before the new leisure centre opens up. There's going to be a gap of months, so no public pool for the whole town. Now that's downright daft. You'd think they'd wait until the new one was up and running first, wouldn't you? Typical, isn't it?'

'What's it to you anyway – you never go? In fact, aren't you still banned from the time you belly-flopped off the diving board and they lost half the water?'

'I remember it well,' Tread added, absently looking skyward, his chin resting on hand. 'There were toddlers paddling at the deep end. Great days.'

Asa did his usual: continuing as though no-one had spoken. 'So we've decided to have one final swim in the old place on its last night – for old time's sake. We all learnt there, didn't we? Are you in?'

'I'm belly-flopping in,' I replied with forced enthusiasm. 'When's it to be?'

'Don't know yet,' Chisel answered. 'But I hear the new one's coming along a treat, or going swimmingly, I should say. It should be an improvement overall.' He stood up, heading to the bar.

I turned to Asa. 'I heard about the Waltzing Man's death. It was in the paper, even down in England.'

He pursed his lips and frowned: his face squashing together like a tomato in cling-film. 'Let me guess, that's what brought you back early? Tell me I'm wrong.'

'Or did you just miss us too much?' Tread added, wrapping an arm round me, pulling me closer, pouting. I fought him off.

Asa leaned towards me, 'Doesn't mean you need to have anything to do with it, you know. There's no real connection to you, is there? Just because it happened in Dumfries doesn't mean you have to be involved.'

'I know, I know. What makes you think I'd want to anyway?'

Asa gave a sigh. 'Don't tell me, I know that look: you've been poking your nose in already, haven't you?'

'I went round to his home to pay my respects,' I replied, huffily. 'Met his kids – they're older than me, mind you.'

'Can't you just leave it be, Jinky? We're more than capable of dealing with serious crime in the police force.'

'I know, Asa.'

'You keep saying that.' He squinted at me and rubbed his chin with his free hand – the other clinging onto his glass. 'You offered your services, didn't you – to the Chamberlain family?' He shook his head sadly. 'You asked if you could help to find the killer because the police are not very good at that sort of thing and you've had the practice. Now, come on, tell me I'm wrong.'

'You're being a bit harsh. I don't see it that way.'

'Really?'

'Really. But I've told you before – an extra pair of hands always helps.'

'What about cooks in the kitchen?' he retorted.

'Or the extra cost in manicures,' Tread added, with a nod of the head. He went on, 'And if you're a defender it's not so good either: twice as likely to give away a penalty. But maybe not so bad if you're a goalie though…'

'Someone stop him, please,' I muttered.

Chisel returned with beer, and Tread filled him in on the conversation. 'So you're going to be looking into the murder, Jinky?' the newspaper man said – I had read his report in the local paper.

I shrugged. 'Actually, no, it doesn't seem likely. They said they didn't want me – The Chamberlains.'

If that was the case, why had I roped in Miss Welch and why did I still have the diary? It was as though my head was telling me one thing but my body was doing something else.

Asa burst out into an immense laugh and clapped a hand onto my shoulder. 'That's just the way it should be. Good for them. Leave it to the professionals.' He caught sight of my face. 'Never mind, Jinky, I'm sure something else will turn up, some other job. In fact, I heard some leaves have started disappearing from the trees down in the Dock Park. Could be worth looking into.'

This might have been a good time to slip in my knowledge of another disappearance: that of Jeremy Gittes. The authorities would be unaware of it.

Tread broke in, 'Disappearing leaves – job for the Special Branch, that.' He added, to cover the moans from around the table, 'Maybe we should go and see what the problem is with Hoogah: the night's wearing on. Ah, talk of the devil…'

'Who are you calling a devil, Tread?' Hoogah replied,

standing before us in a smart blue shirt and v-necked jumper, dark trousers and brown shoes – no waistcoat. His style had changed with his new haircut. There was a bandage on his right hand.

'Let me guess, lads,' he said, 'you've just been the victims of one of Tread's jokes – I felt the backdraft of the groan the moment I entered the bar. It was like a shock wave. Drink anyone?'

'Just got some, ta,' Asa replied, 'but I'm sure Jinky won't mind getting one for you.'

'It will be my pleasure,' I said, standing up.

Tread tapped the side of his head. 'He's not quite right tonight, Hoogah. We think he fell out with his girlfriend – or fell out of a tree.'

'No, I didn't,' I responded. 'A beer, is it, Hoogah?'

'Will you be needing any help getting the drink to your mouth tonight?' Asa asked, nodding in the direction of his bandaged hand. 'What happened anyway?'

Hoogah shook his head. 'I should manage all right, Asa, thanks all the same. I might be a bit slower with the left, but, then, that might mean fewer trips to the bathroom – so, overall, things could even themselves out. Or to put it another way: I think I'll be fine.'

I headed off to the bar and was served by Andy the barman, giving him a generous tip – it's always a good idea to keep him happy and willing to pass on any messages from people wanting to get in touch.

'Did I miss what happened, Hoogah?' I asked, on my return, handing over his drink.

He held up his bandaged hand and inspected it. 'Bit of an accident. It's nothing serious – just a bit raw. I burnt it.'

'Cooking?' I asked, innocently. In Hoogah's world, if it's not microwaveable, it's not eaten.

'Well, if you must know, it was on my door handle.'

'How do you mean?'

He gave a shrug. 'There's nothing much to explain. I arrived home, went to open the door, and the handle was red hot. It burnt me.'

'No, I think you'll find there's quite a lot to explain in that one,' I said, feeling the first grin of the night. 'What handle do you mean exactly?'

'The front door one.'

'*Your* front door handle?'

He nodded back.

I said, 'You're telling us that your front door handle was red hot when you went to open it?'

He nodded back again. 'That's what I said.'

'Malfunction, was it?' Tread asked. 'Have you got a heated one? The wife was after me to get the same sort of thing for the bathroom – heated toilet seat. But I'll be doing nothing of the sort if that's the kind of thing that happens. Think of the injury. You got off lucky, old son.'

I said what everyone was thinking. 'Finished yet, Tread?' And turned to Hoogah, 'How could it be red hot?'

'Obviously someone heated it up,' he replied, nonchalantly.

'And you didn't notice?'

'Well, it wasn't *actually* red hot. I mean it wasn't the colour, red – it didn't look any different to normal. But it was burning.'

'You think it might be the work of your ex-girlfriend?' I slid in.

'More than likely,' he muttered back, taking in a hefty drink.

When Hoogah had split up from his girlfriend, Lucy, she had taken revenge by chopping off his ponytail. It had hit him hard as he had been cultivating and caring for it since his late teens – twenty-odd years of love.

57

'No other girlfriends, or tiffs since then?' I asked, innocently.

'I've kind of gone off women – for the time being.' He rubbed the back of his neck: there was only skin there. 'Let's just forget about it, lads. Maybe that's the last of it this time.'

'I hope so,' I said, and turned to Asa. 'So what's the word on the Chamberlain killing?' He was bound to be in the know: working as a civilian on the computers for the police.

Asa sat back, 'No, no, you're not getting me to talk about it. Just leave it be. It had nothing to do with you from the start and if the Chamberlain family don't want you involved then there's no point talking about it.'

'I suppose you're right.'

'Of course I'm right. This is one to leave to the police.'

Chisel's phone sounded and he stepped away to answer it, after checking the screen.

'That reminds me,' I said, 'I've a new number to give you all.'

Chisel returned and remained standing. 'Sorry, lads, but I'm going to have to head off: something important's come up.'

'What is it?' I asked.

'Can't say right now – not really sure. Don't know if I'll be back tonight though: it sounds serious.'

I squeezed in a question, 'Is this from your secret source?'

He didn't reply, merely giving us a nod, and was gone.

'Must be something mighty important right enough to take him away on a Friday night,' I remarked. 'I can't remember the last time.'

'Who's this secret source you mentioned?' Tread asked me.

'His informant. D'you never notice how often he's at the scene of a crime: sometimes as quickly as the police? But he's never said who it is.'

'I'm never at any crime scenes,' Tread mumbled back

forlornly.

Hoogah started, 'Maybe we should ask him: remember our new code of no secrets between us…' His voice trailed off but his mouth remained opened, frozen.

Tread's jaw fell. Asa rose to his feet and stared behind me, his eyes wide with amazement. The pub had gone quiet: the chatter dribbling away to silence, producing an unnatural, eerie hush. Suddenly the place was a tomb. I squinted round.

A circle had cleared away on the normal busy floor by the entrance, leaving one person standing within. And everyone was gawking at the old, wrinkled man at the centre. He was breathing heavily, his eyes darting here and there in panic. His long white hair, flattened on top by the rain, spilled down over the collar of his black, thick coat, and his hand, caught in the air like a hesitant conductor, trembled. He was as out of place as a lover of football at a Gretna match. It was Onion Sanny.

I stood up, laid down my drink, and walked towards him. Sanny saw me and pointed. 'You,' he croaked.

I spread my arms and moved him on, like a shepherd with sheep, out of this man-made corral, out the door, and out of the pub. A chattering noise started up, slowly, cautiously, behind us, then the door swept shut snipping off the sound.

'Were you looking for me?' I asked when we stopped on the pavement.

Sanny regained some of his composure. His big, black bike rested against one of the pillars. He threw a leg over it. 'Aye, A need yer help.'

He pushed himself off and started to pedal. Briefly, I stood still, watching him leave. He gave a glance over his shoulder and an onward nod of his head. I rushed to catch up, running along the pavement by his side.

'Them polis hae it in fer me.'

'What?'

'They think a killed the man.'

59

We curved past Greyfriars Church.

'What man? Lewis Chamberlain, you mean?' I was jogging hard – but not very well.

'Aye.'

'Why would they think that?'

'A kent him. A met him recently too. We had words. A'm no fond o' the man. They're gan to pit the blame on me – A ken it. A want ye tae fin oot who did it. Fin oot who killed the man – it's the ony way. A'll pay ye – dinnae worry aboot that.'

'All you need to do is explain everything to the police – if you're innocent.' I was beginning to puff.

'A didnae do it, A'm tellin ye that noo. It wusnae me. A told them a didnae kill him but they dinnae believe me. They'll try an get more on me. Are ye gannae help or no? A'm no havin them polis pryin into ma affairs. No way.'

I was gasping. 'Of course… I'll help. But I'll need… to know a bit more… about you… and Mr. Chamberlain…and anything else… that's important.'

'Come roond tomorrow.'

I couldn't go on. I stopped, bending to haul air into my sore chest and lungs. He pedaled on, head high. Despite the pain, a small smile spread: Asa wouldn't be all that happy to hear it, but I was now on the murder case – officially.

*

I had taken one bite of my well-after-midnight sandwich when the phone in my pocket buzzed. The screen said it was Hoogah. It had to be extremely important: he wouldn't call at any time, especially this late, otherwise. I hadn't found sleep on my return to the house, instead choosing to make notes on the Chamberlain case. I laid them to one side.

'Do you have an ice pick, Jinky?' His voice was breathless, anxious.

'An ice pick? What are you talking about?'

He replied quickly, 'I need one right now. Can you bring

it round to my house?'

'If this is your way of inviting me for a nightcap, I have to tell you I don't fancy another drink – I was never really in the right frame of mind, anyway.'

'It's not that.'

'Well, surely you can have a drink without ice. I've been doing it since April. It can be done you know.'

'Hurry up, Jinky. This is important. Maybe a saw as well, or a hammer – something like that.'

'Are you all right, Hoogah?'

'I'm fine. There's no problem really. But I need you to hurry.'

It took me ten minutes, and three attempts, to create a temporary ice-pick: a six inch nail knocked through a piece of four by two, found in the cellar. And I gathered up a saw, shoving some rubber gloves into a poly bag as well.

Hoogah was outside his house, waiting by his front gate. His clothes were wet. It was raining hard and, according to the radio a few minutes earlier in my home, this front would be hanging around, bringing days of very wet weather. But his grimace had nothing to do with the soaking.

'I would have knocked on the door, you know. There was no need to wait out here. I *do* know where you live.'

'Not in the mood for it, Jinky.' He jerked a head towards his house.

I peered up the path. In the weak light filtering in from the street, his front door was hazy, wobbly and wavy. I blinked a few times and rubbed my eyes. There was no change. I couldn't put it down to the amount of drink consumed earlier: it hadn't been the normal Friday session, nothing like it. With thoughts of Sanny buzzing through my head and the absence of Chisel, I had little desire for more alcohol by the time I returned to the pub. The others must have felt something too – especially when Chisel sent a text to say he wouldn't be back at all – as their consumption dropped away like an Acapulco diver. We had left earlier than normal: even Asa had sunk precious few, freeing up his mouth to try and convince me not to take on this new job for Sanny.

As I gazed up Hoogah's pathway, it took a few seconds to work out what was causing his front door to be as blurry as Saturday morning eyes. Sitting snugly in the frame of the doorway, under the shelter of his overhanging roof, was an extremely large block of ice – about the size and shape of a large fridge/freezer. It was barring the way into his home. I moved forward for a closer look. Hoogah followed.

It was the same height and width as the door – measured to perfection – and its interior patterns were as beautiful as the cubes that used to float in my gin and fresh orange. I stroked its smooth, flat surface and noted some strands of darkened, melted ice running over the path like tentacles.

'Hoogah, the door handle would have cooled down by itself soon enough, you know. There was no need for this.'

'I don't find it amusing,' he replied dryly.

I put my shoulder to it and felt its chill through my clothes. It wouldn't budge: it was far too heavy.

Hoogah stood to the side, his hands on hips. 'I tried that,' he muttered. 'Can't get enough purchase on it to force it out. If I could only get behind it and push it away...'

'If you could get behind it you'd be in your house and then there would be no need to move it: it would melt away.'

He gave a snort as I handed him my tools – his face almost burying itself in the bag as he peered in.

'Have you reported this to the police?' I asked.

He shook his head, pulled out the saw, and started at the corner nearest the lock. 'Not so easy with the left hand,' he griped, mostly to himself, 'and not easy getting started. Cut me a nick to get the saw in, will you? If we can slice away a corner, I should be able to squeeze through.'

I picked up the ice pick and did as he asked, then struggled down onto my knees and started to whack away below him. It was tough work. I put on one of the rubber gloves to stop splinters and blisters.

'It's like sawing through glass,' he said.

I kept on chipping away.

'The police have more important things to attend to than this,' he said, after a while. 'In any case, it'll be melted away by the time someone shows up.'

'I doubt that – it's a beast of a thing.'

'Well, it's hardly life or death, is it? Not worth bothering them about and I wouldn't want anyone else hearing about this either. If it got out I'd be the laughing stock of the school for weeks on end. Fingers would be pointed and they'd make up some stupid nick-name for me – and the kids would be almost as bad. I can't have that: I'm starting to look for promotion.'

'Good for you, Hoogah. It's about time.'

'Aye, and I've got a toe in the door already – so to speak. I'm off on a conference this Tuesday with the Headmaster. Just the two of us. Two days at the sea-side, at Ayr. Good, eh? So I don't want this private life stuff messing up my job prospects.'

'Just the two of you? Sounds cosy.'

'I've been specially chosen from the school – so that must say something, eh? Could be the start of big things for me.'

'Good for you, Hoogah. I take it you don't have a key for the back door?'

'Gosh, Jinky, I never thought of that. Here's me sawing away at half past one in the morning, when I could be in bed.'

He stopped his work to look down at me, no doubt giving me his most penetrating stare. I saw the shadow of his face only – so it didn't hurt.

He went on, 'It's bolted and the key to the shed – where I keep my tools – is inside the house, of course.'

I continued to hack away at my bottom corner, trying to

stick to a rhythm, wishing I knew some songs of the chain gang. 'What have you been doing all this time then? We left the pub well before twelve.'

'Waiting for you. Okay, I may have had a carry-out supper on the way back, and maybe I tried to break into the shed by picking the lock – but that didn't work. Then I had a go at the back door and then one of the windows: there's a ladder in the back garden but it's not long enough to reach upstairs.'

'Look on the bright side then: at least you know your house is fairly burglar-proof.'

'Not really seeing the funny side of this yet, Jinky. And I've never been a fan of DIY at the best of times... I just want to get in and get some sleep.'

'I know the feeling.'

'Thanks for coming round to help,' he added.

'It's what I do.' I gave him a salute – but he probably didn't see it. I went on, 'We're assuming this is the work of Lucy again, are we?'

'It has to be. Surely that's an end to it now. I'm beginning to think of her as Lucy-fer,' he added, grimly.

'Talk of the devil.'

'Where?' he shouted, cutting off his sawing in mid-stroke. 'Do you see her? She's not here, is she?'

'Relax. It was a joke. I didn't mean to scare you.'

'I'm not scared of her,' he returned, indignantly. 'But you'd think there's only so much revenge a person can, or would want to, hand out. I figured it was all finished and done with a month ago when I lost my...' He couldn't find the words to continue – the loss of hair was still hitting hard.

'Are you thinking of taking on another one?' I asked.

'Naw. They're actually quite a footer – that's ponytails *and* girlfriends.' He added, 'And they take an age to dry after they're washed.'

'Which ones?' He didn't reply, so I went on, 'Not even

grow one out of spite – just to show her? You could make it double the length and grander and call it a horse-tail.'

'You're enjoying this too much.'

'Sorry.'

'Naw, I don't think I want to rile her any further: it doesn't sound like a good idea. Like poking a stick through the lion's cage at the zoo.'

'I keep telling you, that wasn't me, it was Tread.' The ice-pick was hurting my thumb, forcing a change of hand. I asked, 'What about all your waistcoats then – with your new style. Will they ever see the light again?'

He shook his head. 'Probably not. I'm doing things differently now – they might need to go to the charity shop. I'm going to see one of those women in Barbours to help me. I decided that today.'

'How do you mean?'

'Personal shopper: she'll tell me what suits me and what to buy.'

'Sounds fancy. So you'll be wearing suits?'

He carried on with barely a pause, 'I'm going for a complete change of image.'

'Getting back to Lucy – are you sure all you did was stop seeing her? Is there something else you're not telling me?'

'You were there when I did it, Jinky – when I broke it off. I haven't seen or spoken to her since. That's well over a month ago – honest.' He had the sound of a frazzled man.

'I believe you. But what if I do some investigating all the same? You're not overlooked here but your neighbours might have seen or heard something tonight. Why don't I go round and ask them in the morning? You never know, someone might have reported it to the police already.'

I could see he wasn't keen on my idea by the short, swift shakes of his head. 'What's the point: we know who's doing it.'

'Just to be sure.'

'No, leave it, Jinky – it's not worth the bother.'

I went on, 'How would she have managed it anyway, and at this time of night? It's quite an undertaking.'

'I've thought about that. Her brother's in the building trade. Maybe he got one of those lorries with the cranes on them – the kind they use for delivering paving slabs and the like.'

'And where would you get a block of ice this big? I could find out if you want? It's been made specifically. They would remember who ordered it I'm sure.'

'There's no point. Let it go.'

'She must be keeping an eye on you, Hoogah – checking on your movements, picking the right time for the delivery. Are you sure you haven't spotted her around?'

'Nope. But it's hardly difficult to figure out where I'll be on a Friday night, is it?'

'But earlier with the door handle – maybe she disguised herself.'

Hoogah stopped. I moved out of his way as he attempted a squeeze through. He could reach the door and was able to unlock it but there wasn't enough space to allow his body through. We returned to work.

'A lorry and crane would make a lot of noise,' I said. 'It could have been done with a van. They drive onto your runners at the side then use those wheels they have for shifting pianos and roll the block into place. With two people it could probably be done in a minute or so and without any great fuss.'

I thought for a moment. 'If someone *has* reported it and the police *do* come round, why don't you say we're making an ice sculpture to surprise your wife in the morning. An anniversary, or something. That might allay suspicions.'

He nodded, 'Better to say girlfriend in case they check and find I'm not married and only have two ex-wives.'

'Right, good thinking.'

He went on, 'But what if they find out I haven't been taking night classes in ice-sculpting?'

'You're making fun of me now, Hoogah. It was an idea, that's all – to take your mind off this Lucy-fer business.'

The idea fell through my brain like a guillotine blade, slicing into a memory. I bolted upright and jumped back. First it was the heating of the handle and now this… Heat and cold. Fire and Ice. That's what this was: Fire & Ice. The Devil. Who knows where it might end?

'You need to report this, Hoogah,' I said urgently. 'I'm serious.'

'We've discussed that already, Jinky.'

'No, this is not right.' I pointed to the ice-block.

He stopped sawing and shook his head. 'She'll get fed up eventually. Once she reckons I've been paid back in full.'

'That's just it. This is Fire & Ice, Hoogah. I've come across it before. Have you heard of it?' I went on before he could answer, 'It's an ancient torture, but, more importantly, it started out as a means of ridding the devil lurking within anyone. I've searched the internet for this.'

'What are you talking about?'

'If anyone was suspected of having the devil inside, they were taken, stripped, tied and encased in ice. Then molten rock was poured over their heads. It killed the demon within.'

'And everything else, I should think.' He gave a short giggle before stopping himself. 'This actually happened?'

I returned a serious nod.

'So you reckon Lucy thinks I am possessed?'

'Something like that.'

He held himself in for moment – then burst out laughing. 'Aw, come on, you're losing it. When I saw The Exorcist I'm sure they didn't heat up a door handle and dump a block of ice on the front step. If they had, it would have made things a lot easier – although it wouldn't have made for much of a film.'

'Look, this might seem funny to you now but I don't think she's finished. There's going to be more. She's working her way up. Remember all the effort she put into your relationship. She worked at it for months on end. She's – what's the word – besotted by you.'

'I do take a bit of beating,' he said, straightening, lifting his chin, pretending to fix a tie in place.

'You have to take this seriously, Hoogah.'

'Not easy to do, Jinky. So what do you think is next – burning down my front door?'

I nodded. 'Yes, that would fit, another fire, more serious. It's possible. And then it would be something cruel with cold – a greater ordeal.'

'Naw, Jinky, your imagination's getting the better of you. These things don't happen round here…' The grin on his face froze – remembering my suffering from earlier in the year.

We returned to work: we weren't going to mention it.

'Just be careful, Hoogah. That's all I'm saying. Do you want me to stay the night, just in case?'

'I'll be fine. You get home and don't worry about me. I'll be safe enough. I'll buy an extra smoke alarm in the morning.'

'And make sure your existing alarms are all working. Will you do that?'

'Okay.'

Finally, there was enough of a gap and he squirmed his way through. I gathered up the tools. 'Do you want me to come inside with you?' I asked. 'Check the place out?'

'It's fine, Jinky, really.' He had another thought, 'Do you think this thing will be melted by the morning?' I saw his distorted face peering through the ice.

'It's almost 2 a.m. Hoogah – I would very much doubt that. And the forecast is not for much heat – mostly rain.'

'It's blocking the way to the letter-box – how's the postie going to manage?'

'I think that's the least of your worries. Can't you at least check the house quickly and give me the thumbs up if everything's okay?' I said.

I waited until a bandaged hand slid out from behind the door and a thumb pointed upwards.

'Night, Hoogah.'

'Night, Jinky. Saturday tomorrow – or today – you can always have a long lie.'

I heard his door lock and turned away, plastic bag in hand.

*

He re-tied one end of the rope to my wrist and the other end round the railway track. He did the same to my left hand. They were tethered to the rails but could fall inside the tracks now. My fingers were crunched into fists with tape wound round so they looked like black stumps at the end of my arms.

'Just so you can't untie the knots.'

I heard him walk away.

There was silence: he was gone. I burst into a ferocious frenzy once again, fighting against my new shackles, hauling fiercely at the ropes: maybe he hadn't fixed them as well this time. I twisted and turned and lunged, tugging with all my might. The pain from the shredding skin was hard and harsh, but I couldn't let up. I had to keep on and on: until all energy bled away.

I had a shard of glass sitting uselessly in my mouth: it could cut through rope. If only I could free it. I pulled my right hand towards my face and twisted, contorting, stretching my body, lengthening my neck. My bound fist scraped across the tape.

Rub the gag. Rub it away.

I tried again and again – like a cat washing its face. There was contact but not enough. No matter how hard I tried, I was merely grazing the tape. I couldn't scrape it clear. I tried the

69

other hand but it was worse – and time was wasting.

My lips were parted, caught before the yell. I tried to puff air out of my mouth: I filled my lungs, ballooning my chest and blew. I waggled my jaw, pulling my mouth in different directions to force the tape away. It wasn't working: it gripped too well.

I slumped back against the sleepers and hummed as loud as I could, sending out the shrillest note possible. It might attract attention. This was a bridge: someone must cross it from time to time, even at this late hour. My stomach and throat ached with the effort, and it wasn't nearly loud enough. No-one would come to help. No-one is going to venture down to the tracks on a whim, on a noise that could be an animal.

What did The Tramp say? In old films they laid their victims across the tracks. I remembered a film where men walked the line, checking the rails with hammers, hitting and listening for its ring, making sure there's no problem. Maybe it still happens. Someone might come along. Isn't that what a linesman was originally? There might be equipment doing that job now: like a pulse, like sonar through the metal, searching for faults. A system to detect blockages. What if a tree falls across the rails somewhere, what happens then? Does an alarm go off? Is it sounding now? I could be flagged as an obstruction: they could be on their way this very minute. They'll rescue me. How long will that take?

I can't wait.

I pulled down on the ropes. There *was* some movement. I pushed my right fist against the tether and the rope slipped slightly along the rail. I tugged it back. A fraction forward, an inch back. Push it forward, pull it back: rub the rope against the hard rail. Make it fray.

I tried the other hand: it was working as well. Was it better to concentrate on one side only? Which one was more likely to break? Rub them both back and forward, back and forward. I had both hands moving further now, flapping as though I was about to fly.

But it was such a small movement and it was so tiring: my shoulders and arms aching in no time. I breathed with the motion and changed the rhythm: bringing one hand up as the other travelled down. That made it easier – a balance. Now my feet were moving, sliding as well, up and down, breaking the fibres. Crossed over at the ankles, I could push down with my right foot and pull up with my left. I was dancing a jig – like a goal celebration for The Mighty Queens.

Seconds passed and nothing happened: my efforts became less and less. The rails couldn't be rough enough: they were too shiny, slippery. There wasn't enough friction. It wasn't working: the rope wasn't going to break. I had to rest: sweat coated my skin, my muscles were sore and my limbs were now heavy, so very heavy.

Slide the rope. Slide all the bindings in the same direction, push them down, move along the track, out of the shelter of the bridge, out of its darkness, out into the open – and someone might see me. Slink out of the gloom.

It was working: I was moving along the track, shuffling an inch at a time, the rope slipping forward a fraction. But I was heading in the direction of the train – travelling feet-first to meet my enemy. I wanted to change direction, to move away, to distance myself from its threat, to have more time. Yet, it made no sense: the coal train lumbers through town but I could never out-crawl it.

I urged myself on, disregarding the decreasing distance. The station is this way. I had to make for it: there might be people there. Why would there be people at the station? No-one would be waiting: there are no passenger trains at this time of night.

I shuffled on, tiny movements at a time. I can clear the shadow of the bridge and someone will see me. Millimeters of movement, bringing me out into the open.

What about the points? The track must split somewhere – even if it's only into a siding. I might be able to slide there and move *off* the main track. It's a chance. There aren't any sidings at the station. I know that for sure. I have to go in the opposite direction. I needed to stop and back up.

I changed, dragging the bindings, heading away from the train. It felt better: a relief. Soon I would be out from under the bridge on the other side – and, headfirst, onto a new set of rails. I kept on. This was better.

The movement stopped. The rope had caught. It wouldn't slide. It was stuck. I raised my head. I was at the spot where the rail fastened to a sleeper – and the rope couldn't pass. I moaned and sagged against the ground. I should have known it had to be attached somewhere. I'd moved about a foot from my starting position. I was still under the bridge: still trapped.

I was fumbling in fog: thick clouds rolling into my brain. I needed to think. What was wrong with me? My body started to shake. Slowly at first: like the start of an earthquake.

The broken bottle top still lay propped against the side of my mouth. Could I push it through the flesh? Break it out all the way out through my cheek? Or was there another possibility?

I felt round with my tongue, to the smooth end where the cap fitted, and pushed my tongue inside. There was grit there: the taste of dirt. I pushed the broken, ragged edge towards the front of my mouth. If I could force the glass out, through my parted lips, there might be a chance.

The opening between my teeth wasn't large enough. I maneuvered my mouth: my lips were held but I could engineer a wider gap by pulling back on my lower jaw. It wasn't quite enough: the glass scraped against my teeth. I forced it forward with my tongue, grinding away at the enamel. The noise was horrifying, a hundred times worse than fending off a hungover hygienist. For the first time I wished I didn't have such a winning smile: a space at the front would have been nice.

Small fragments of tooth splintered into my mouth. I burrowed on, rotating the jagged edge like a tunneling machine. My jaw, cranked back at an awkward angle, rebelled but there was no time to stop. The glass broke through, splintering fragments of tooth. Now it pressed hard against the back of my lips. I worked my tongue and jaw from side to side, sawing it further forward, working its sharp edges onwards. It cut in. I tasted blood and a pool formed in my mouth. I swallowed. The glass filed on through skin: the pain didn't matter.

The glass breached my parted lips and lay directly behind the gagging tape. This was all that mattered. My life depended on rupturing this gag. There was nothing else to try. The blood oozed. There was no time to stop. At least my tongue was strong: thanks to all the practice I'd had with Chiara.

Did my life really depend on this? I had one final play: lie low and let my feet slice away. The rest of me could be saved – as The Tramp had said. But it might be better to lift my head and have done with it all. When the time came, I would have to decide. One stage at a time: slash through the tape and see.

There was some give: the glass was moving further on. It had found a weakness, a crack, then a hole. It pierced through. The rough edge of the bottle top protruded from my mouth, wedged into the tape, like a short, wide drinking straw. I could suck in air. I pursed my lips out and thought the glass was visible in the dimness.

Don't push it all the way through. It mustn't be lost to the tracks: it has to remain firmly in place.

I pulled my hand closer and by arching my back, stretching, straining my neck, I could reach the tape bound round my right fist. Biting down hard to secure it, lips pouted, the glass extended a few extra, valuable fractions of an inch, as my tongue filled its neck for stability, the ragged edge scraped.

I rubbed my hand across my mouth, simultaneously nodding like a demented donkey. The glass cut, back and forward, again and again against my hand. Now I was a feverish cat washing its face.

A flood of sweat broke all over my skin: the shaking became worse. I was puffing hard and paused for a moment to rest my neck, slipping my tongue out of the bottle, shouting through the hole. It wasn't loud enough – and it was wasting time.

I returned to scratch away at my fist. How long would it take? The uncontrollable shuddering of my body was helping: keeping the glass moving. My neck was in pain: my arm and shoulder rebelling against the strain on the joints and muscles. But I couldn't stop again. There was no more time to rest.

There *was* some freedom. I felt my index finger spring free, then my thumb. It was enough. I could pick away at the knot on the rail. It wasn't easy. My fingers were frenzied, tugging, tugging.

Wait. Did he empty my pockets? I might still have my penknife. It doesn't matter: I'll never be able to reach there.

I picked at the knot, yanked at it. It started to ease. It was loosening. My arm broke free. How much time had I used up?

I reached down, checking for my knife, patting down the sides of my trousers. Everything was there – even my mobile. He'd left anything. I could phone for help. I could call the rail service and have them stop the train – that would give me all the time in the world. But I didn't have the number: I'd be stuck in directory enquiries. How much time would it use up to contact the police and tell them to relay my message? I couldn't spare it.

I pulled out my knife. I needed my mouth free to prise out the blade. I placed the knife carefully on my chest and tore away at the strip on my face, throwing it to one side. I should have done that straightaway. I could have been shouting for help seconds earlier.

I heard the tinkle of the glass as the discarded tape hit off the stones.

I bit on the knife, eased the blade out, then shouted loudly as it cut away at the rope at my left hand. I stopped yelling.

There was a tingling in the track – a singing noise ringing through. The train was on its way. I didn't dare glance away from the rope: there was no time to look for the train. The rope in front of me was all that mattered. The blade sliced through and my left hand broke free of its shackle.

I sat up. The track was empty. The noise was increasing. I started at my right foot. I could wave my hands and the train would stop. But they might not see me in the dark. The blade was taking an age to slice through the thick rope round my ankle. The noise in the steel of the line was howling now. My right foot snapped free.

One leg to go.

Through sweat-stinging eyes, I saw the train. It was curving round the bend. I could sense its power and overwhelming weight – and the sharpness of its wheels. There was a light shining out from the front of the engine. I saw my bare left foot dangling over the rails in front of me. I could wave now – the driver might see me in the beam. I should keep cutting. Which was better?

It won't pick me out down here.

The rails were whining. The blade gouged into rope. My whole body was shaking. I wasn't working efficiently. I couldn't think straight. It slowed me down.

You must cut. Cut!

I saw a light in the cab and waved. I didn't have time to wave: I needed to free my leg. It wasn't happening quickly enough. It was coming. The train was closing in.

I threw myself to the left, over the side of the rails. I was face down in the cinders. I tugged at my bound leg. It wouldn't budge from the rail: the rope held it in place. How much of my foot lay over? How much of it would I lose to the machine?

I couldn't tell. My toes were over the outer edge: I could feel them buried in the stones, but I couldn't sense where my heel lay.

The noise of the beast was unbearable. The stones at my face vibrated. I strained with all my might to pull my foot from the track, to keep it away from the edge of the rail and the vicious wheels of the machine.

The wind of the train blew: the thunder of its wheels boiled the track. I braced myself, waiting for it to smash across. I waited for the pain. There was nothing more I could do. Lie flat. My leg straining against the binding. I pulled and pulled and held.

The train hit. My leg sprang free. I spun away and rolled over, facing upwards. The train passed, plodding. There was no pain. The wheels had sliced through the rope, nothing more. I lay motionless, eyes closed, not daring to look, feeling the mass of each coal-crammed segment of the beast's tail vibrate through the ground, as it blew wafts of dirty, dusty air over my face.

What was I doing here? Concentrate. I listened for the sound of each coach passing and lost count after twenty.

The train faded; the ringing in the rails lessened and died. I turned over onto my front, bringing hands to my eyes. I cried until my elbows hurt against the cinders of the track, and my arms tired from the weight of my heaving head.

*

My mouth was dry. Water splatted against the back of my head. I hauled myself round, touching the shiny rail with the back of my right hand. I felt its cold steel as I rubbed back and forward. I held a small knife in this hand, and there was pain too – but somehow it was comforting.

Another drop hit me on the forehead. I shuffled

backwards and opened my mouth wide to feel the drops hit the back of my dry throat. I loved the thud of it. I remained.

I didn't know why I was here. I wasn't sure what to do. If I stayed here something might come to mind. There was throbbing in my wrists. I held them up but it was too dark to tell much. What had happened to me? I stumbled out from the shelter of the bridge to more light and into the rain. My legs wobbled, as though the muscles had never held me upright before. The stones under my bare feet dug in. This was a railway line. I couldn't understand why. There was rope round my left ankle. I sliced it away with the knife, conveniently held in my hand.

My left hand was just a stump. It looked black and dirty. It was tape – wound round and round. I cut at it as well. And there was some tape round my right hand as well. Why was it there? Why was I holding a knife – and not wearing any shoes?

My body was shaking. I closed my eyes and took in a long breath. My heart thumped, hard and fast. The smell of stale sweat was everywhere. I shouldn't be here. I was in danger. I needed cover: shelter. I was easy prey.

Staggering, bent to avoid being seen, I forced my way along the side of the track: sometimes over grass, other times over piles of strewn rubbish. I saw the old, empty Somerfield supermarket and further on a gap in the wire mesh fence. I pulled it wider and slid through. My jacket snagged. I was in the open, caught like a rabbit in a trap. I wriggled, struggled, thrashed. It wouldn't let me go. If I shouted out it would alert them, send them to me. I kept quiet.

My jacket ripped. I freed myself from it: pulling my arms out; then turned to heave it away from the metal claws of the fence. And there I was, breathless, in the disused, deserted, pouring wet car-park.

Unconsciously, I formed a crouching run, penknife held ahead, and sprinted round the edge of the space, seeking protection behind a small bin. There was a sound – my heart leapt. It was a car stirring, not far away. It revved and I slunk down into the paltry cover of the bin. The engine noise faded away.

My nerves jangled, dancing on needles. I couldn't stay here: I needed to find my way home. It wasn't far, I knew that – but I would be exposed on the journey. Still, I didn't understand why I was here.

I needed to phone Asa. That was it, that was the thing to do. My phone was in my trouser pocket. I called his number and let it ring and ring.

No answer.

I knew Asa. I knew how to work a phone – but I didn't know why I was here.

I tried the number again. Surely he would be at home: it was late, it had to be late. The phone said it was forty-three minutes past two in the morning.

There was a rough-voiced answer.

'Asa, I need your help.'

'Jinky?' There was a slur in the words. 'Do you know what time it is? What's this about?'

He had to know it was important – why else would I be calling? He had done the same to me before. I knew that. I remembered that.

'Where are you Asa?'

'I'm in bed – what do you think? What are you playing at?'

I sat down on the wet tarmac, my back against the rusty bin. It was overflowing with rubbish, unemptied since the closure of the supermarket. The smell provoked a splatter of memory – a man in a dirty coat.

'Hurry,' I said in a harsh whisper. 'You have to hurry. Please help, Asa. It's not safe out here. I think someone's after me. They're watching.'

78

'Who's watching? Where are you?'

'Somerfield car park.'

'Oh, Jesus, what's happened to you this time? Don't answer. I'll be there in five minutes. Stay where you are. Don't move from there.'

I couldn't stay. I needed somewhere better to hide and I saw it, by the boarded-up door of the old supermarket building: another bin, a big one, with four wheels. I ran to it: not directly, not across the middle, but round the edge of the car-park.

The space underneath was tight. I had to turn my head to the side to squeeze in. I jammed the knife back in my pocket and lay on my stomach and peered out, my left ear against the ground. It was dry under here. That was why I was down on the track – I was hiding. I should have stayed: it was safer than here. No-one would have thought of looking for me there.

I heard the car and the rumble of its wheels. Then its lights shone into the slanting rain. It toured round the parking space, and stopped, the brake lights facing me. They flashed and stayed on. The engine was running. A man got out: he'd left his door wide open. In the light spilling from the inside, I could see he was big. He rubbed his chin as he scanned the area. The windscreen wipers washed back and forward noisily.

He walked to the front of the vehicle, peering into the distance, helped by the headlights on full beam. He turned towards the car and made a gesture – a shrug. I saw Asa's face. He was here to save me. I started to scrape out of my hiding place.

I stopped: he had climbed out of the passenger's side. There was someone else in the car, someone behind the wheel: the brake lights were still pressed on. I shuffled back under. Why wasn't he alone? Why had he brought another? I thought I could trust him.

The door closed, the car turned, the headlights flashed across my face. I closed my eyes. It skidded to a halt. I heard a door thud shut. I opened my eyes and saw a pair of legs jogging towards me. The shoes stopped a foot away from my face. I heard grunting, and saw trousered knees on the tarmac, and then, even in the dimness, Asa's face came into view, turned sideways to look under, matching the way I lay.

'Jinky?'

'It's me Asa.'

'What's happened to you, man? What are you doing under there?' His voice was a weird mixture of annoyance, shock and amusement – like the voice of my primary school teacher when she discovered I had blue-tacked all fifteen of my coloured pencils, like stalactites, to the classroom ceiling above my desk.

He tried again, in his softest voice, 'Why are you hiding, Jinky?'

'Who's in the car?' I hissed back at him. 'Why aren't you alone? Who's with you, Asa? Who have you brought? Didn't I tell you to come on your own?'

'I don't think so.'

For some reason it took him a moment to continue, 'It's Rosie – my wife – in the car.'

I didn't reply.

He added, either as an explanation, or because he thought it was better to keep talking, 'I couldn't drive. Over the limit. My last drink wasn't so long ago. She had to bring me – didn't want to risk it. But I still don't get it, Jinky – why can't you come out of there? We'll take you home.'

'Rosie?'

'You know Rosie. You've known her for years – since school.' The last dregs of irritation left his voice. There was only kindness. 'We need to get you out of there. You need help, Jinky.'

'I'm hiding, Asa.'

'I know, I can see. What happened? Have you been

attacked?'

'I'm not sure.'

'Come.' He stretched his hand out in front of my face. I hesitated.

'You can trust me, you know that,' he said. 'We'll get you some help.'

'Can you see anyone about?'

'There's no-one – honest. You're safe. If there was someone, believe me, I'm in no mood to be messed with.'

I grabbed his hand and he pulled, dragging me out.

'I'm not getting in a car. I want to go home Asa – just with you. You take me. You said you'd take me.' I rose to my full height in front of him and let go of his hand. 'Just you, Asa.'

He turned and made a wave. He blocked the view of the car but I heard the engine stop, the clatter of the blades die, and a door bang shut.

He said, calling over his shoulder, 'Come over here, Rosie. So he can see you. Jinky's not feeling quite right. He needs to know who's driving. He's not sure.'

'I want to go home.' I muttered, low enough only for him.

'It's fine. It's fine. We'll see to it, don't worry. Everything's under control. You can relax now.'

The woman came forward and stood beside him. They clasped hands. She smiled. 'Jinky?'

I said nothing.

'Do you remember me?' she asked.

'Asa's wife, Rosie,' I replied.

'Then let's get you out of the rain,' he said – and then, suddenly, 'What happened to your shoes?'

I shrugged.

'He has to get out of them wet things, Asa,' she said.

He clasped a large hand round my shoulder and guided me towards the car. 'We need to take you to the hospital,

81

Jinky.'

The small stones under my feet were sharp. I halted. 'I'm not going to any hospital. They wear masks there. You said I was going home.'

'You're okay, you're okay,' he muttered. 'There's nothing to get worked up about.'

'What does he mean, masks?' she asked him.

He spoke to me, 'It's only during operations, Jinky. You'll be fine. There'll be no masks.' Then he turned to her, 'Maybe someone's been scaring him – in a mask.' He shrugged.

'That's it. I've seen them. They've been round my bed, looking at me. You can only see their eyes, staring. Their masks move when they talk, Asa.'

'Oh, in the isolation ward – is that what you mean?' He edged me closer to the car.

'I want to go home,' I said.

'Look, your hand's been bleeding, Jinky,' he said.

I looked at it for the first time. 'It's nothing.'

She tried to inspect my hands. I pulled them away. He held out his hands, palm up, I allowed mine to fall into them. I heard them talking. She said, 'It's not too bad. I think we should get him into some dry clothes first.' For some reason she pulled up the sleeve of my jacket and gasped. 'Look at the marks round his wrist. The skin's red raw. Bloody. What's happened to him, Asa? We need to get him some help.'

'He's been tied, Rosie. That's what's this is. Oh, dear God, this is serious. And his eyes – he's been drugged – the pupils are dilated. His pulse's racing. It's happened before, remember? We need to get him some help.'

I reared away from them and shouted, 'I'm not going to any hospital. They try and kill patients up there. They do it with needles. Inject them. I know all about it. I've seen it.'

He shook his head at her.

I turned away and started to walk from them. He followed me. 'Asa, you know what this is about. You just said it. He's drugged me before. He's back doing it again. He's after me. I can't be caught out here in the open. I have to go home. There's a bolt on the door – it'll stop him getting in.'

They moved quickly, one each side. 'You have to trust us,' he said, clasping my right arm, the woman holding the other. They pulled me to a halt. Then they led me towards the car. I didn't put up a fight.

'Who are you talking about?' he said.

'He never finished, don't you see? He locked me in my freezer, Asa. He drugged me. He wanted me to die. He's doing it again.'

He pulled at my arm. 'Listen to yourself, man. You're talking crazy. That man's dead.'

'Easy,' she whispered to him. 'Keep it nice and calm.'

I went on, harshly, 'How do you know that? Did you actually see him being buried? Did you?'

'He was cremated. I know it for a fact: I was there.'

I went on, 'It was High-Heid-Yin-Harris who told me he was dead. He could have been making it up – anything to keep me happy. They're all in it together. How can you be so sure anyway? Did you look in the coffin?'

We reached the car. He sat me down in the back seat, slipped my legs in, and slid in beside me. 'We'll call the police, Jinky. They'll be here in no time. What happened to you?' he asked. 'Why are you here?'

I shrugged.

'You don't know how you got here? What have you been doing?'

'I can't tell you – I don't know.'

'You remember all that other stuff.'

I shrugged.

'Well, what's the last thing you remember then?'

I stayed silent for a moment. 'I was in the kitchen with Chiara. The story of the Waltzing Man was in the newspaper. I was standing on a doorstep, talking to someone. He had white hair round the side of his head. I met you, Asa, in the pub. That's it – small fragments – here and there. Why can't I remember?'

'We'll need the police involved – you know that, don't you?'

'They don't like me. If Ed's there, he'll arrest me. He'll say there's nothing wrong with me. What am I going to tell them? I don't know anything. Do this for me, Asa – get me home.' I could feel panic rising again.

He rested a hand on my arm. 'Easy now.'

'Let's get him back to our house first,' she said, her head poking into the car. 'Heat him up. He'll catch his death. He can't be sitting around at the hospital in these things.'

She got in the driver's seat. She turned round to look at us. They exchanged glances. The engine started, the wipers swept back and forward. I'm wet, it's cold, I'm cold, it's wet.

The car drove off.

'We'll take you home – but not to stay,' he said.

'What are you talking about?'

'Give me your keys. I want to check your house. You still have them?'

I fumbled through my pockets, found them, and held them out in front of me, in the palm of my hand. Another flash – a dirty, smelly brown coat.

In less than a minute, we had parked outside my home. Asa opened his car door.

'I'm going in,' I said. 'This is *my* home. I want to rest. I'll be fine.'

His words were sharp, commanding, 'You wait here. Have you got that? I'm just going to make sure everything is okay inside.' He got out, clicked something on his door and shut it. Then he was at my side of the car, opening the door. I made to move across. He pushed me back, pressed something and slammed it shut. I yanked at the handle, the door wouldn't budge. I tried again, rocking the car with the effort.

She said, 'Child locks.'

I slumped back. They had me trapped. I would need to climb into the front. She would fight me off. I waited, weighing up my options.

The door opened and Asa slunk in beside me. 'Nothing. Everything's fine. It was locked and nothing looked out of place – except for a split piece of wood and some bent six inch nails sitting on the kitchen table. Do you know what that's about, Jinky?'

I shook my head.

'Well, whatever happened, I doubt if it happened there. Okay, Rosie, go.'

The car started up.

'Then let me go in,' I pleaded.

'You're not right, Jinky. You must know that. But I like what you've done with the place – a big transformation. About time.'

When we arrived at Asa's home they argued in the kitchen. Then Rosie brought some large, flannelette, paisley-patterned pyjamas and laid them on the sofa beside me. They took it in turns to phone.

He made me pee into a bucket.

Saturday 26th August

She woke me, her hand lightly shaking my shoulder. 'How are you feeling? It's getting late.'

I didn't know where I was. I looked up at her face. It was blurred. Her hair was light. It wasn't Chiara. I rubbed my eyes, eased up from the sofa, and my stomach muscles rebelled. I fell back, grimacing, clutching.

'Are you all right?'

I tried again, carefully this time, my head sloshing around, half-filled with muddy water. It made me dizzy and the room swarmed in front of my eyes. I held onto the couch.

'What can I do to help you?'

I nodded slowly.

'Do you want the painkillers?' she asked, hesitantly. 'Can I get you a cup of tea, or anything? Just say. Maybe I should have let you lie. Sorry. Are you feeling any better?'

My throat was rough, and as dry as an empty paddling pool. My head groaned, the skin encircling my wrists and ankles, under their white bandages, throbbed. The joints of my arms and shoulders rebelled, my teeth and gums were sore, and my belly ached. 'I'm a lot better. Thanks, Rosie.'

The words started as normal but by the end I was speaking like a ventriloquist: to stop the jagged cuts inside my lips yelping at the slightest movement. So I wouldn't be offering to buy bottles of beer anytime soon – no doubt another ruse for Asa to put in his book.

'Water, please, Rosie.' The tea might sting too much.

I knocked back a couple of the painkillers, left by the doctor, and cautiously padded through to the kitchen, keeping hold of the waistband of the oversized pyjamas, in case they fell down to the floor.

She offered me something to eat as well, set the table, and brought out napkins – the same colour as the walls. I chose porridge – it would slide down easily when cool – and she sat at the table, eventually, waiting for me to make the conversation – perhaps thinking I needed to collect my thoughts.

She was right: a series of pictures were forming. It was like picking up litter, a little bit here, another piece there, until the whole course of last night's events ended up dumped into one lucid, coherent, black plastic bag.

But the returning memories dragged in dread, like rotten driftwood on the tide, and fear firmed inside and rotated in my gut. I looked up from my untouched bowl – the steam still rising – and Rosie's eyes switched away quickly. I saw her mouth bunch as she held back, waiting for the right moment to talk.

Then anger flooded through me: The Tramp had been within inches of destroying my life. He had shown such dreadful, ruthless callousness – and, yet, amazingly, there had been a drip of compassion too. I couldn't figure it out.

He had no right to do that to me – to anyone. How could he think he had? I needed to fight. There would be no hanging back this time, no waiting for the police to act. I would search him out, hunt him down. It was the only way to stop him: I had learned that from the past.

Seven hours ago, while waiting for the doctor and the police to arrive, Asa had stripped me of my sopping clothes and bathed me under a hot shower. I'd hung onto him, exhausted, barely able to hold myself upright. I heard him gasp and curse when he discovered the marks round my ankles. He asked me again what had happened.

I pleaded with him to allow me to rest – I just needed to rest. I had nothing to tell the police. I could remember nothing. 'What difference will a few hours matter now?' I had said. 'Let me sleep, Asa. I can talk to them in the morning. Things will be better then.'

When the doctor arrived, I was asleep on the sofa: it was the most comfortable place in the world, and Rosie was shaking a snoring Asa out of the confines of the armchair beside me.

The grinning, big-bearded doctor had breezed into the house, apparently vaccinated against misery. He was disconcertingly large and his huge girth, wrapped up in a heavily padded anorak and high visibility vest, sucked the space from the room – Rosie had to squeeze her way out as he set about examining me.

For the early hours of the morning, he was an incredibly cheery soul and laughed heartily given the slightest opportunity, yet he managed to give my condition a great deal of dignity. A good man to have in a crisis.

He did all the usual things with a cold stethoscope, took some blood, gave me a jab, and dressed my wounds. They talked in the kitchen for a long time and when Asa returned, looking a touch more comfortable, he had two uniformed policemen in tow.

He did most of the talking: explaining where and how I was found. I was unable to offer much. The policemen left saying they would take a tour round the car-park and Asa mentioned to them that he would have a word with Ed at the police station, at the earliest possible opportunity.

*

Now I watched Rosie across from me at the kitchen table. She was staring at the tea swilling in her mug. She saw me taste the porridge and smiled. It was still too hot. As I waited, I tried to gather up clues about my attacker, going over every piece of conversation available. It wasn't leading me anywhere – for the moment.

'Asa still sleeping?' I asked, finally, my lips barely moving.

'He's away, Jinky. There was a phone call from his work at eight this morning: you should have seen the face on him. He said you've to wait until he gets back and he'll see to you then. You've not to go anywhere – I had to emphasise that to you. And he wants you properly examined.' She gave me a long stare, before asking, warily, 'Is that okay?'

'Fine.' I needed to apologise about last night, for giving her such a hard time – but the painkillers hadn't kicked in yet and I didn't want to talk much.

'Don't worry – you weren't yourself,' she said. She gave me a maternal smile and patted a hand against my arm, swiftly taking it back and changing the subject, out of necessity. 'Asa never heard the phone, mind. Just as well I bought that cattle prod last month – or he'd never have made it out of bed. Useful thing.'

I gave her a puzzled expression.

'It's a joke. I'd never use one on him.'

'They're illegal?'

'He'd never feel it.'

My brain signaled a smile but my mouth had other ideas, so I forced out, 'Why today – Saturday – for work?'

'Aye, it's never a good sign, is it? But he didn't say what it was about.'

I finished off half of the porridge and we tidied up together despite the protests from my body and Rosie – but I needed to keep busy. It was painful and awkward drying the dishes whilst making sure the pyjama bottoms remained in place, but, I suppose, I wasn't in too bad a shape – all things considered. It was tolerable. And the dark force of revenge, driving me on, helped mask some of the aches.

I would give Asa an hour and if he didn't show by then, I would take a taxi home – I wasn't going to risk walking the streets. I knew it wouldn't be a popular decision, but it was necessary to get moving.

After scanning me, head to toe, Rosie said, 'I'd give you something of Asa's to put on but they're far too big – and we threw out all his old stuff not so long ago. You're closer to my size. Do you want to try on a pair of my trousers?'

Before I could come up with a polite reply in the negative, she darted from the room, returning from upstairs with a nice looking pair of brown breeks. I gave them a go rather than disappoint – it was only until I reached home, after all. She turned her back while I pulled them on.

'I think they're fine,' she said, after asking me to do a turn, and picking off a couple of flecks of oose from the material. 'I'll get you something for the top half.'

I was rapidly becoming a replacement for the daughter she missed: the two of them used to shop together, trying on each other's things. In the end, the result wasn't too bad, and they were stretchy; although I couldn't understand the reasoning behind placing the trouser zip at the side, on the hip. I balked at the mention of underwear though, choosing a sturdy pair of Asa's Y-fronts instead. The only suitable footwear was a pair of wellington boots – which, in any case, might not be a bad choice over the next few days if the weather forecast turned out to be correct.

And that was me ready. Asa had forty minutes, or else I was off.

Again, we sat in silence – this time in the sitting room – as the rain made patterns down the window. Rosie sent him a text and the reply said he should be back in about half an hour.

'Look Jinky, I can't sit around, I need to make a start on the bedroom. I've got the hoovering to do. Our daughter's coming back from college tonight, so I need to sort it out. We've been using it as an office. It's only for the one night but I'd like her room to look nice and the way she left it. She's on her way to a pop concert, somewhere – it's the usual weather for them, isn't it? You can watch the TV if you want.'

The suggestion wasn't appealing. I wanted to keep myself occupied, as boredom rests like dust on a day. 'I can do something about the house – it's no bother,' I said, the painkillers had kicked in and I was happy enough to form the odd 'b' now and then.

Despite her protests, I plumped for some dusting – a payback – and she found the necessary items.

Rosie was upstairs when I heard the knock at the back door. If it was Asa, I hadn't heard his car. I unlocked it and opened up. No-one. I tugged on my borrowed wellies and plodded round the side of the house to catch the visitor before they left. It could easily be one of the pals sent to keep an eye on me. That had happened before.

I felt a jab at my back and a voice at my ear. 'Don't make a move. Don't do anything or this knife goes in, right through, all the way to the front. It'll be like a kebab with all your organs skewered on it.'

I could smell the foul, wretched rags he wore. I knew it was The Tramp. He'd returned and he didn't know all that much about human anatomy.

My heart pounded, my head clouded – for a moment I was stunned. How could he be here? He must have hidden behind the wheelie bin on the far side of the door – it was the only place. But how did he know I was here?

My brain settled and cleared like real ale in a glass. I didn't intend to let this man get away with it this time. If anything happened it would be after a fight. I wasn't going to stand back. Attack – at the right time. He wouldn't be expecting it. I had been passive last time. I had the advantage of surprise now.

He was saying, 'You survived in one piece I see. I'm glad. I was down for a look earlier on but there was no mess. No mass of blood. I took away the rope and anything else left behind. It's not good to leave litter on the track – or anywhere else for that matter. Am I right?'

I had never been asked my opinion on litter at knifepoint

– and I doubted if my view would sway him one way or the other – nevertheless, I would always have the same answer.

I took my time to reply, trying to force calmness into my voice: I wasn't holding out much hope for success. 'How can you be glad I'm not dead? That doesn't make any sense.' Actually, I might have achieved pass marks.

Keep him occupied, keep him talking. Even if my attack resulted in being stabbed, it will be worth it. I have to stand up for myself. I should have done it last night. I could call for help – but then Rosie would come. It's too dangerous for her. I mustn't let anything happen to her. I had to hope she was vacuuming at this moment and the noise of the machine was drowning everything out. But what if she looked out of the window? She mustn't get involved. I had to shield her. I needed to deal with this myself.

Could The Tramp sense I was about to retaliate?

Keep the arms slack: don't give anything away by tightening any muscles.

It has to be fast – give him no time to prepare. The moment the knife relaxes from my back. The briefest of lapses...

'Think of last night as a test,' he said. 'And you managed it. You passed. Some time you might tell me how you did it.'

'What are you talking about?'

'I have a job for you,' he whispered in my ear, grabbing my left arm, just above the elbow. He was holding his knife in his right hand. He spoke again, 'I won't hurt you if you do as I ask. You like these little jobs, don't you? That's what I hear.'

My brain was whirling. I repeated my last question, 'What are you talking about?'

'Work. I have work for you. I hear you can find people. There's someone I'd like you to find.'

Again, I didn't know what to say. I kept quiet, assessing.

'I want you to find a man for me. I have been looking for him but there's no sign. I'd like you to try. I hear you're quite good at it.'

Suddenly I was shaking. I didn't know why. It sounded as though he was sparing my life and flattering me at the same time – yet I was becoming more frightened. He would sense it. 'Are you going to pay me for this work?' There was no pain in my mouth; no pain in my skin.

'No, not quite. I don't have any money. But how much is your life worth? Surely it's a great deal more than your usual pay?'

'What if I say no?'

'I would prefer if you didn't.'

'What do you want with this man? Are you going to kill him – like you tried to kill me?'

'Now, now, you know I didn't really try to kill you. Maim you, yes. But it's none of your business what I want from him. Find him and I spare your life – that's the deal. There's only one sensible thing you can do.'

'I have no choice.'

'That's good – the right thing to say.' A clammy hand patted the side of my face.

'Will you leave me alone from now on?' This was the time to attack, the time to get back at him.

He went on, 'He's about six feet tall. Aged somewhere around thirty-five to forty. Darkish hair, short and it sticks up so it appears flat on top.' He stopped talking. I waited for him to continue.

'Is that it?' I sneered. 'Out of the whole of Dumfries I'm supposed to find this man from that description? He *is* local, I assume?' It wasn't the right time to get shirty: this wasn't a simple request, but I had rage dousing my fear. I added, 'There are hundreds of men with that description round here. Don't you have a name or anything?'

'If I did, it would be easy and I would have found him. One thing I can tell you is that he looks fit – no beer belly – so that more than halves the male population. And he has a diamond stud in his left ear. You have until tomorrow night to find him.'

'That's never enough time. How am I supposed to manage it in little more than a day? How long have you been looking for him?'

'A while.'

'And I get twenty-four hours?'

'It'll be longer than that. Are you declining my offer?' I felt the tip of his blade jab in.

'If I find him, how do I let you know?'

'We'll meet.'

'And if I can't find the man, do I get more time?'

'That's not going to happen.'

A hand came round in front of my face. A grubby hankie waved. 'Open your mouth,' he ordered.

I shook my head.

I felt the pressure of the knifepoint in my back again and gasped. He rammed the filthy material into my mouth. I could taste its stench, his smell: the soiled dregs of his dirty pocket.

'Just in case you feel like shouting for help.' He slapped his gloved palm across my lips. It held tape and blocked the hankie inside. I was left with its taste within my sore mouth, and his germs crawling into my cuts.

I couldn't leave the moment any longer. It was time to attack.

He said, 'I want you beside the fountain in the High Street at 1 am, early hours of Monday morning – that's about thirty-six hours for now. Do you understand? If you don't show I'll come looking for you – and you know I can, and you know what I can do.'

The man was out of his mind: I could have the police waiting, ready to catch him the moment he shows. And that would be much, much safer. This wasn't the time to fight.

He added, 'One last thing – if you're thinking about a no-show, or going to the police, I will make you a promise: I will search out a friend – Hoogah, Chisel, Asa, or the other one – and then I'll come after you. So you had better get busy – for their sake. I want to be impressed by your efforts when we meet again. Put your hands behind your back.'

I felt a rope round my wrists. He made me sit down and began tying me to a drainpipe, working from behind. 'This is just as a precaution,' he muttered. 'I don't want you following me, that's all. I'll not make it too tight: I wouldn't want to spoil the work of the bandages and it shouldn't be painful. Actually, I'll tie it further up the arm out of the way of your wounds. How's that? I'm sure someone will find you soon enough. It wouldn't be a good idea to be wasting your time sitting here when you've work to do. You're safe this time – I don't want anything to happen to you until you find this man for me.'

He left me sitting in the rain at the back of Asa's house. I thought about hauling at the drainpipe – I was sure I could pull it from the wall but that would give Asa the expense of repairing it. I sat and waited patiently for Rosie to come looking, or for Asa's return.

Had The Tramp really offered me a job? Did he expect me to work for him – the man who wanted me dead, or seriously injured? If he *was* crazy enough to show up tomorrow, I would make sure the fountain was surrounded, no escape. As soon as he appeared, he would be caught and his danger eliminated.

As I sat in the rain, his disgusting hanky filling my mouth, an odd feeling of relief poured through me: I wasn't in any danger for the time being. He wouldn't be after me and nothing would happen until our next meeting – and then it would be over. I would be free of him.

It had to be said, though, that the job he'd given me was very interesting – and curious. I'd found missing people before but this was the first time I had the answer straightaway. I knew where to find this person. I'd been given the easiest job in the world. The tape across my mouth stopped me laughing as heartily as the early morning doctor.

*

The wet had soaked through my white blouse, leaving it see-through, and the trousers had drawn up the rain from the ground like a very good sponge, but there was no still sign of Rosie or Asa. It was a matter of being patient.

Time had stacked its minutes up on end before the footsteps sounded. Chiara marched round the corner of the house. I was almost as shocked as her – but not quite. She jumped and gasped and dropped her car keys, all in one movement – then she froze, eyes wide.

I beckoned her forward with a jerk of the head and a lift of the eyebrows. She dashed over and bent down in front of me. 'What happened?' The panic in her eyes was patent.

I thought of my dentist: she asks unreturnable questions as she fumbles away with both hands inside the mouth. So I hummed a couple of short, sharp notes at Chiara, squirmed and tugged against the drainpipe to highlight my situation.

She picked away a corner of the tape, and held it between thumb and forefinger. She hesitated, building up the bravery to rip it from my face. I nodded quickly. It was a good, fast yank and I was very glad I hadn't been growing a moustache – but there was stubble. I spat out the filthy hanky. Something strong would be needed to take the dreadful taste away, but I managed to twitch out a wee smile for her. 'It's okay. No need to be alarmed. I'm fine. Everything's under control – and there's always a job for you at one of those waxing salons.'

Her eyes suggested puzzlement as she scurried behind, fidgeting with the ropes. 'Can't get them,' she yelled in my ear.

I recoiled. 'Take it easy. No need to shout. It's better if the neighbours don't get involved. There's bound to be a knife in the kitchen somewhere.'

I watched her run to the open back door, knock on it, and waver again.

'You can go inside: Rosie won't mind,' I said.

She wiped her feet on the welcome mat before entering, returning a few seconds later with a long-bladed, wooden-handled kitchen knife. 'Who did this to you? It's not some sort of prank, is it?' She hacked away at the rope. 'Only it doesn't seem all that funny to me.'

'Like on a stag night, you mean?' I shook my head. 'You don't need to worry – it's nothing like that.'

'Then I don't understand – who did this to you? And why are there bandages round your wrist? What on earth's been going on, Jin?'

The rope broke away and I dragged myself upright: the trousers clinging nastily round my backside. 'It's okay, Chiara, I'm not in any danger. Don't worry. He wanted to make sure I didn't follow him, that's all.'

'Who? Who are you talking about? Follow him where?'

'I don't know his name – but I will. Come on, let's get out of the rain.'

She looked to the sky as though registering the weather for the first time. I picked up her keys and handed them back, putting an arm behind her, guiding her into the kitchen. Unthinkingly, she accepted my help.

I eased out of the wellies, swilled some water round, spat it out, found a chocolate biscuit in a tin and munched the distaste away, adding a couple more painkillers for dessert.

We faced each other, a foot apart – the knife still in her hand, and the keys in the upturned palm of the other. 'I don't get it – who did this to you and what did he want?' Her face was wet with a mixture of tears and rain.

I had the dish towel from beside the sink – it was damp from earlier use but it would do to mop my head. 'He offered me a job. He's a tramp – or something like that. I've to find a man for him.' I threw the towel down and wiped away the damp from her cheeks with both thumbs.

She shook her head vaguely – unable to grasp any of my words.

I smiled. 'I'll explain everything, don't worry.' I parted her outstretched arms and gave her a cuddle, nestling my nose into the sweet scent of her damp neck.

'You need to change your clothes,' she said as she took a step back, trying to slide a brave face into place. We walked into the sitting room: the vacuum cleaner buzzed away upstairs.

'Do all your clients treat you this way?'

'No – and he won't be one after tomorrow night. That's Asa's wife, Rosie,' I added, nodding to the ceiling.

'Does she know what happened out there?'

I shook my head, deciding not to mention the daftness of the question.

'I'll go and get her,' she said immediately. 'You have a seat.' She took a couple of strides towards the only other door of the room.

'Better put the knife down first,' I shouted after her. 'Wouldn't want her to get the wrong idea. The daughter's coming back tonight, so maybe we should let her finish tidying first: it has to be done.' I gave a chuckle. 'There's no real rush now – I'm free in more ways than one. Better put your keys in your pocket.'

Chiara handed me the knife and studied my face. 'I still don't know what you're talking about. Why are you finding all this funny? I don't see what's funny.'

'I'll explain, don't worry.'

She left and I returned the knife to the kitchen, spread an old magazine on the sofa, and sat down, waiting, thinking. Perhaps, I should have gone upstairs instead, or, at least, introduced them to each other.

The machine stopped. There were voices. Then the stairs thundered and Rosie burst into the room. 'When did this happen? Who did this to you? Have you called the police, Jinky? And look at your clothes again... you'll catch your death. Don't sit on that: it'll put print all over my good trousers and through onto the sofa as well.' She tugged the magazine away from underneath, forcing me onto my feet, fussing around me.

'I've got another pair that might do you,' she said. 'Loose fit, blue. And what about a jumper this time, Jinky? A pale blue to match?'

I saw Chiara shake her head in disbelief.

'I'm fine,' I said, brushing her away. 'Just calm yourself. Everything's okay. Why don't *you* have a seat, Rosie?'

'It's all a joke, is that what this is, Jin?' Chiara said.

I gave her a grin. 'I'll put the kettle on. Go on, sit down. Both of you. I'll make some tea, maybe a biscuit – there are two chocolate ones left. You don't need to bother about the clothes: they'll dry soon enough. Are they polyester?'

'Cotton mix,' Rosie returned, indignantly. She turned to Chiara. 'Do you know anything about last night? Have you been told?'

Chiara shook her head.

Rosie looked at me. 'You didn't tell her anything – not even how you were found? You do remember that part, don't you?' She didn't wait for a reply, striding across the room, grabbing the phone. 'We need to get the police again.'

'What's she talking about, Jin? Why again? What's been happening? Tell me.'

I raised my hand to calm them down, calling to Rosie, 'Wait, there's no need for the police to come round.'

'We have to, Jinky.'

'It's okay, it's okay, I'm going there as soon as I can. I need to see *them* – to organise a plan for tomorrow night. Put the phone down, Rosie. I'll sort this out, don't worry. There's no immediate rush – we've time, plenty of time.'

'Let me get Asa, then – see if he's on his way back yet. He can go in with you. I think you should have someone with you.'

'I don't need him. I just want Chiara to run me home first to change into some proper clothes – no offence meant.'

Rosie said, still unable to settle, 'What about that tea? I'll get it,' and she rushed to the kitchen, closing the door before we could reply.

'I was going to do that,' I shouted after her, but it was doubtful if she heard. I stood in the middle of the floor and stared at Chiara, uncertain of what to say.

Then it started again: a roar, erupting in my head, racing through my body and limbs like a million stampeding bulls. My skin smarted and I started shaking: slowly at first.

Chiara asked, 'Aren't you going to tell me what this is about?'

I felt heat and a spiral of dizziness. I swallowed hard into my drying throat, pulling my arms tightly across my body, trying to stop the trembling. 'I will... but let's wait for Rosie... and that tea... she needs to calm down... She's been like a mother hen... all morning.'

'What's wrong with you?' She took a step closer.

What was happening to me? I couldn't control myself. I held up my hand to halt her, to keep her at bay: she must not see me like this. I tried to push through, I tried to hide it and stay light. 'And do you know... the first thing a hen does... after scratching the ground... for food?'

Her jaw dropped a touch; her eyes remained on me, unblinking, as she shook her head slowly.

'She takes a step back... to see what's been... raked up.' I tried a laugh. Nothing happened.

'You're not right, Jin.'

I fought to be clear, plucking out one word at a time from my blurring mind. 'I... am... fine.' I slumped down into the sofa, my head bowed, my hands pinned between my legs to stop the shuddering.

I sensed Chiara kneel before me, her hands touched my knees. I couldn't look her in the face. I glanced away. Rosie returned. She carried no tea.

'I've talked to Asa – he's leaving right away. Ten minutes,' she said. 'He'll take you up to the police station and make sure you get there safely... What's wrong?'

'There's... no... hurry.' I said – but I didn't know why there was no hurry. I wiped the sweat away.

'Are you all right, Jinky? You haven't told us who tied you up,' Rosie said, unable to stand in one spot. 'Is it connected to last night? Do you know?'

'What happened *last* night?' Chiara demanded.

'He can't remember,' Rosie said. 'We found him wandering in town at three in the morning, without any shoes. He didn't know where he was.'

They stared at me. I hid my hands behind my back this time – then they wouldn't see the tremors.

'Who tied you to our drainpipe, Jinky?' She asked, unable to let it lie.

My heart was knocking on my chest like a stranger at a door. It was taking longer to process the images gathered through my eyes.

'Are you feeling all right, Jin? He needs help, Rosie.'

I stood up suddenly, pushing her away. I found the words through anger. 'I'm fine. D'you hear? I'm fine. Now leave me be!'

Rosie shook her head. 'Is it delayed shock, or something? What can I get you?'

I dabbed my face on the sleeve of my blouse.

'How about some dry clothes, Jinky?' She didn't move,

staying still, gawking at me. Both of them still staring at me.

I fixed on Chiara, on the floor, on her knees. Something wasn't right here, something didn't make sense. I towered over her. I couldn't hold back the venom. 'How did you know I was here – at this house? How could you possibly have known that?'

She was stunned. She shook her head and glanced to Rosie before making a reply. 'There must be something wrong with your phone: I couldn't get an answer. I tried several times last night and again this morning.'

I saw Rosie shake her head too. It was a signal. They were trying to communicate. They didn't want me to know something.

I hit back, 'What's that got to do with it? What does a phone number matter? What's this obsession with phones everyone has? What is it!?'

'I tried to call you, Jin. Why couldn't I get through?'

I didn't want to answer. It annoyed me when I did. 'I changed my number.' I could remember that but not why I was here: like this. 'Why do you want to know?' I paced the room.

Chiara rose to her feet. 'Jin... why don't you rest?'

'How did you know I was here, Chiara?' I said harshly, moving to a corner, away from her. 'You still haven't told me that. Why aren't you answering? What are you hiding from me?'

'Jinky, there's no need to shout. What's wrong with you?'

'There's nothing wrong with *me*.' I tapped a finger against my chest and then pointed it at Chiara. 'Tell me now! How did you know I was here!?'

'Asa told me. I rang him this morning when I couldn't get hold of you. He gave me the address.'

'That makes no sense. Why would he do that? Why would you need *this* address? It doesn't make any sense.'

'What are you doing, Jin?' She turned to Rosie. 'He needs

help. Look at the way he's shaking. Can you get him a blanket?' And then back to me, stepping forward, coming closer, 'I think you should lie down.'

'I'll call the doctor,' Rosie said.

'Answer my question, Chiara!'

I saw Rosie freeze in mid-step, then nod to her – and I saw Chiara take a deep breath. She spoke deliberately, 'I called Asa from the car, Jin – I was back in Dumfries by then. I dropped in at the house. Then came over here.'

'How did you know his number?'

'He's phoned me before – remember? He set up a meeting for us months ago. Why are you acting like this? No, I shouldn't say that – something's wrong, I can see that. I just want you to sit down and be calm.'

I did nothing.

She turned to Rosie and there were tears in her eyes again. She could turn them on and off. 'I'm trying to understand,' she pleaded.

My throat was parched. I couldn't stay here. I yelled, 'What are you keeping from me, Chiara?'

She struck back, 'I don't allow people to shout at me!'

I made for the door, pushing her out of the way.

'Let me help you.' she pleaded.

'I don't want you!'

Rosie cut me off, standing her ground, barring my way. She placed a hand lightly on my shoulder. 'You have to go to the hospital, don't you see?'

I shrugged her off and turned back to Chiara, crying out, 'Why did everything start the moment I met you? Tell me that! What is it about you, Chiara? Why are you doing this to me? No-one ever tried to kill me before – and it all started the moment I set eyes on you. And it's kept on and on. It's you: you're doing this to me!'

'What are you talking about, Jin? You're not making any

sense.'

'Jinky, you're not well,' Rosie muttered, picking up the phone. 'I'm calling for an ambulance.'

I sprang, grabbing it from her. 'Later, Rosie,' I hissed. 'I need to find out everything – right now.' She shrunk back. 'What are you going to do next, Chiara – arrange another ordeal for me? Is that what you do? Is that why you're here – to put me through it all again? Does it give you some kind of pleasure?'

'I want you to sit down. Please, Jin.'

I paced back and forward.

'I'm going to be as calm as possible. I want you to be the same, Jin.' She was making herself sound reasonable.

I shook my head, 'I'm not talking to you. I'm telling you nothing. You've to tell *me*. I thought I could trust you. I'm not falling for it. I want Asa. There's no point crying. It won't sway me. I fell for it before. For almost six months I've fallen for it. I should have known someone like you could never go about with someone like me. It made no sense. Everyone said so. It was suspicious right from the start – but I ignored it, trying not to let it niggle away, niggle away.'

'Why are you saying this?' she sobbed and looked directly into my eyes. 'You trust me. You've said it. Somewhere inside your brain you know that's right. Get the ambulance, Rosie…'

There was a loud voice from the back door. I heard the thump of it closing and then Asa's head poked into the room. 'What's all the carfuffle?' He was out of breath. He looked at me. 'You all right?' He took in Chiara's presence. I moved towards him.

'He's not, Asa,' Rosie said. She started to explain.

I cut in, 'I need to get out of here, Asa. I need to be away from *her*. She's involved. We need to go to the police now.' My bare hand wavered, the veins raised.

In a flash I saw it. I knew who the man was from last night. I knew his name – it was obvious. Why had it taken me so long? He wore gloves.

'Asa I need to speak to you – alone. And I need to go now. I'll tell you in the car.'

Rosie grabbed Asa's arm and whispered something to him.

'Asa, I've got it,' I shouted at him. 'I remember last night. I know who attacked me. We need to leave now.'

He blocked my way.

'Come on, you need to drive me to the police station,' I said.

He didn't move.

'I'll go myself then.' I tried to push him out of the way. He moved to one side, grabbed me from behind, and held me in a bear hug. I struggled, my feet off the ground. How had they managed to turn him so quickly, bring him onto their side?

'Asa, listen to me: we can catch him!'

He held me firmly. I kept wriggling. The women had their hands to their mouths.

'Who's trying to kill you?' he said.

'Last night. The Tramp.'

'What are you talking about? What tramp?'

I had to sway him, bring him back. 'Listen to me, Asa. The Tramp is Jeremy Gittes, Jackie's brother. I was at his flat yesterday. Jill took me there. He's missing. No-one's seen him in weeks. He's been hiding away, trying to get at me. That's what he's been doing. Maybe he saw me at his flat with Jill. He wouldn't like that. He wears gloves. Don't you see? He wears gloves and he did this to me last night.'

Asa dumped me back onto the floor like a sack of potatoes. My legs wobbled. I turned to face him. 'It's Jeremy. The Tramp wears gloves. Have you ever heard of a tramp wearing gloves? At this time of year? Jeremy wears them when

105

he's decorating – to protect his hands. Jill told me that.'

'You're not making any sense, Jinky.' He gave a long sigh. 'Do you want to know why Jeremy Gittes is missing?' He turned to Rosie, 'Why weren't you watching him? He's been drugged again – can't you see? How could this happen here?'

She answered him sharply 'He said he was fine. I thought he was safe. You did too.'

'Did you hear what I said, Asa?' I shouted.

He shook his head and sat down dejectedly on the sofa. I wanted to tug at his arm, get him moving and out of the door. Why wasn't he doing what I wanted?

He looked up at me. 'What happened to you Jinky?'

I shrugged. I could remember nothing of this day.

'Do you want to know where *I* was this morning?' He wiped a hand across his tired, red eyes. 'I was called to the station. There's been a body found.'

'Not another one,' Rosie gasped.

'Who is it?' I asked.

Asa replied, with a sigh, 'It's Jeremy Gittes. He was found in the ruins of that old hotel – the one demolished last month. The body was discovered yesterday, late afternoon. It took a while to dig it out.'

'Yesterday? It can't be yesterday. Jeremy Gittes attacked me last night, the early hours. He tied me to the rails, Asa. It was him. I'm telling you. What are you playing at?'

His voice was patient. 'At about four o'clock yesterday afternoon, workmen, digging out foundations for new houses, uncovered a body in the cellar of the old hotel. It took forensics hours to get it out, brick at a time. It had been there for a while – before the hotel was demolished last month.'

'Naw,' I shook my head. 'That can't be right. Why are you telling me these lies?'

'Listen to yourself, man!' Asa roared back.

His wife laid a restraining hand on his shoulder.

'Bring him some water, Rosie. He needs to drink – flush it out of him. Has he peed yet?'

Rosie returned with a glass. She handed it to me. I refused to take it.

Asa gave another sigh. 'At this moment we can't be a hundred per cent sure. But the body is the right size and height as Jeremy's. His wallet was in his pocket, and a library card with his name. The remains of his clothes had name-tags sown into the labels. A bit strange, that one – but Jill told us he does that with all his things.

The body's a mess from decay and, of course, from the building falling down on top – but we'll know for sure when the DNA test comes back. That won't be long. Drink the water, Jinky. Look at yourself, look at your hands.'

I ignored him. 'It's not right, Asa. The man after me was Jeremy – I'm sure of it.'

'How come you didn't tell me this before? And what's with the rails? What are you talking about?' He waited for an answer: I gave none. ' Let's get you to the hospital first, Jinky. You need a proper examination. You have to let me take you. D'you understand? Can't you see you're behaving the same way as last night?' He rose to his feet.

Chiara said, hesitantly, 'He was tied up outside the house, Asa. He said someone wanted him to do a job.'

'Did I?'

Asa and Chiara exchanged glances. The room was quiet. I heard the clock on the mantelpiece click through the seconds. I rubbed my head vigorously.

Asa said, 'The body in the hotel had been tied up. We've been round to Jeremy's bed-sit – the landlord hasn't seen him in six weeks. It all fits.'

He went on, 'Maybe I shouldn't be saying this until we're definite, but it looks like Jeremy might have been alive before the demolition started. It might have been falling timbers that killed him.'

I found one last piece of bile, pointing at Chiara. 'Get her out of here, Asa.' I slumped into a chair, my legs weak. 'I need to rest.'

Asa stood over me, 'Look at me, Jinky. Do you believe what I'm saying?'

I hesitated then nodded.

'You're not well. This isn't you. Something's happened. Were you injected with anything just now?'

'I don't know.'

He grabbed my arms. 'You need to come with me right now. Can you do that?'

I muttered, 'I don't want *her* anywhere near me.'

'She found you Jinky. She's a witness. It backs up your story. You'll change your mind. See the harm you're doing to her?'

Rosie gathered up my phone, wallet, and the rest of my things and stuffed them in the pockets of my ripped jacket – holding it out at arm's length for me.

Asa said to her, 'Rosie, can you nip upstairs and fill a jam-jar from the bucket he used in the bathroom?'

He led me out of the house, holding me in front of him, a hand gripping my upper arm. There was a flash of memory and a bad smell. I tried to ignore it.

'Jeremy was in prison years ago,' I said. 'You told me fingerprints are the last to leave the skin when a body decays, so why can't you use them for identification?'

'You're not trusting anyone, are you?

I stayed quiet.

'There's no fingerprints, Jinky. The hands are missing. They've been sliced off.'

*

The windscreen wipers swept across. The jam-jar sat in a cup holder by the side of the steering wheel and the liquid swashed to the movement of the car. He made me sit in the back – said he was my chauffeur. I knew he didn't want me to escape: I saw him check the child locks before setting off.

He spoke over his left shoulder as he drove, his eyes unwilling to leave the road, 'What was all that about? What happened to you to make you act like this?'

'I don't know.'

'Can't you remember anything at all?'

I didn't reply, gazing out of the window.

'And what about last night? When were you going to tell me about that? Rosie thinks you know what happened. Who is this tramp fellow?'

'Later.'

He allowed me to change clothes at my house, never leaving me alone, constantly rubbing his chin, watching over me like a grandfather clock. As soon as we'd entered the back door, I made him slide the bolt into place.

He told me to pee again. I didn't have a jam-jar. I found a re-sealable sandwich bag. I had to hold it in the car – it wasn't safe to put down. It might spill, he said, and then he'd have to buy a Christmas tree air-freshener and hang it from his mirror. He didn't want to do that.

We drove onto the A&E department. It was busy. I walked in feeling obvious, carrying my small bag like a goldfish won at a fair. I sat in a corner while he spoke to the woman behind the desk. I didn't recognise anyone. No-one paid me any attention, wrapped in their individual woes – but I couldn't be totally certain.

In front of me, held in a blanket, in the arms of its mother, a baby reared up and gave a pained, tired cry. Then it collapsed back down, its forehead banging against the mother's shoulder, its head too heavy to lift for long – and the howl died away. The weary-eyed mother cuddled in and kissed the back of its wet-hair head.

109

A name was called and a man, supported by friends on either side, his thick arms round their shoulders, limped away. There was blood on the trousers of his damaged leg and his sock was soaked in browny-red: strange that they hadn't arranged a wheelchair for him.

Asa brought me some tea in a plastic cup and a glass of water. I found painkillers in my pocket. He said it was fine to take them. The clock on the far wall clicked when it moved into the next minute. It was forty two clicks before we were called. I didn't check to see if anyone looked up, recognising my name, but hurried beyond this room.

As the time ticked slowly by, I improved – as though passing through a storm into calmer waters. My mind gradually opened up, becoming composed inside.

We were ushered into a curtained off, desolate space by a nurse. It held two chairs, a bed, and a wall cabinet containing medical supplies. We sat down, remained silent, cradling the samples on our lap. I had to hand it to Asa: even though the contents were no longer warm, and separated by glass, I would probably have been too repulsed to hold onto another person's pee. If our roles were ever reversed, it would have been a struggle for me – I thought about telling him so.

And now I could remember everything from this morning, and tacked onto the events of last night, it didn't form a pretty picture. It was embarrassing – at the very least. I would keep the information to myself for the time being, though: noise travels far through the thin material walls of the room – like on a camp site.

We waited a further fifteen minutes before a young, male doctor swept the curtain aside and stood before us, his stethoscope dangling over one shoulder of his white coat like a pet snake. It obscured his name badge.

As I was examined, Asa gave this doctor much the same spiel as the one last night – describing my injuries and my state of mind. 'D'you want to add anything?' Asa asked me.

I shook my head.

'This is very interesting. I'd like to speak to a colleague for a minute,' the doctor said, and left us for a further ten minutes.

It was a Dr. Omar who visited next. She was small, neat, with wide eyes and a wide smile. She might have been the same age as us but it was difficult to tell: her skin was smooth and her hair dark. She listened to Asa, asked a few questions, checked me over again, took some blood, changed my bandages and looked pleased as we handed over the urine – grasping them without the slightest hesitation.

There was nothing obviously wrong with me now, she said, finally – other than the superficial wounds to my skin.

'You should have seen him earlier,' Asa said, with a shake of his head. 'Didn't know what he was saying.'

'Blood tests will tell us more – and with the urine you've kindly brought in – but it won't be for a couple of days.' She turned to me, 'I think you will be okay but you should probably rest up.'

'Do you know what caused this?' I asked.

'It would be better to wait for the test results.'

'But if you could just give us something to go on,' I insisted. 'My memory has returned – but I won't hold you to it.'

The doctor nodded. 'Obviously my colleague thought I might have some understanding of this. There are a number of possible drugs you may have been given. Would you say any of these symptoms have been evident: an initial rapid heart rate, flushed skin, stupor?'

Asa cut her off, 'That's it, spot on. The flushed skin – and the sweating. And his eyes go all dilated and weird.' He demonstrated using his own eyeballs and a pair of swirling index fingers.

She turned back to me, 'Other signs may include dry mouth, confusion, panic, inappropriate or vulgar behavior…'

'Vulgar behaviour?' It was Asa again.

'Yes, something like cursing or becoming lewd.'

'*That* I'd like to see,' he muttered back.

She said to him, 'He might not remember but would *you* say his speech was slurred?'

Asa pondered, scratching his chin, making the noise of a damp match reluctant to light. 'I suppose he was a bit like that last night, but I thought it was because it was Friday night.' He gave the needless explanation, 'It's the norm around here.'

'This is all very interesting,' she said.

'But no slurred speech today,' he added.

She nodded. 'I may be wrong, but I've experienced a few cases like this before.' She asked me, 'Do you have anything to do with the Army?'

Asa burst out laughing. 'Jinky didn't even join The Cubs – thought they were too much of a para-military organisation.'

'And with the narrow, short-term memory loss,' she went on, thinking aloud, 'it fits quite well. I'm afraid we will need to contact the authorities.'

'The police?' Asa asked.

'Yes.'

'Don't worry that's where we're headed next. I work for them.'

I said, 'I feel fine now, doctor. But I was never injected with anything – if that's what you're thinking.'

Dr Omar continued, 'Well, if I'm right, the tests will confirm you've been a victim of some kind of incapacitating agent – perhaps a derivative of a glycolate anticholinergic compound. The effects wear off fairly quickly – depending on the dosage – and usually there are no long term problems. Although, I would have to stress that I can't be certain of any hidden damage as there are many different types around, producing an array of differing side-effects. You should be examined again when the results come through, and maybe have a scan.'

Asa said, 'I've never heard of that glycolate compound you said.' He added, 'I work on the computers for the police, storing the facts from crimes. This is a new one on me. Is it a new date-rape drug?'

'More sophisticated and much more expensive, but as I said, I cannot be certain about this – nor how harmful it might be. It depends on the amount of exposure and the type of agent. We'll know more in time.' She paused before going on, 'I have to say, though, this type of chemical is very rare over here. You see, it's primarily used by the military to confuse the enemy and so give an edge. It doesn't kill and it can be administered easily as it comes in different forms – and it keeps well in damp conditions.'

'How easily administered?' Asa asked.

'It can go through the skin, be taken orally, sometimes delivered in a spray, liquid or gas – there are many different ways.'

*

Asa let me sit in the front seat this time. I asked him to take me home first for some necessary food and to give him a detailed account of recent events – he deserved that at the very least. Moreover, his response would be crucial in deciding my next move.

There was no sign of Chiara.

I made tea and sandwiches, refusing his offer of help. He sat at the kitchen table, still keeping an eye on me.

'Thinking of doing some walking?' he asked, seeing the book, **The Twenty Best Walks in South-West Scotland**, and stretching for it.

I dashed over, mumbling something about climbing Criffel, and snatched it away to the safety of the window-sill. It was better if he didn't know about the diary: withholding potentially valuable information might not sit too well with his bosses. To divert his attention, I suggested that a piece of cake might be a suitable addition to our meal. He wavered, like someone on the edge of a precipice, before finally patting his stomach and deciding against it. Just as well – there wasn't any.

I sat down beside him. 'I remember everything now, Asa.'

'Everything?'

I nodded. 'As the doc says, it wears off after an hour or two. This time seemed quicker than the last – maybe I've become immune to it, or, more used to it, at least.'

I described my meetings with The Tramp, starting from the moment I first saw him on the corner of Queensberry Street, up to the point where Asa found the three of us fighting in his home today. He listened as he ate his sandwich.

When I finished, he started up, 'So he didn't use any powder this morning and you weren't injected with anything?'

'I'm certain.'

'Then I don't understand why you had this memory loss and confusion again.'

'Nor me.'

'I reckon some of the stuff in that envelope was a kind of homemade pepper spray – it can be done easily enough using a base of ground-up chillies. There must have been some of that drug the doctor mentioned mixed in as well.'

'It wasn't pleasant, Asa – I'm not sure I'll be taking on any hot curries for a while.'

Asa nodded gravely at this and finished off his tea. 'Do you think The Tramp is really going to do as he says – meet up with you tomorrow night?'

'I wouldn't put it past him.'

'But he must know you're not going to turn up alone.'

'I think he will. He's picked the town centre. That's a

difficult area to patrol: there are more roads leading to it than Rome. And he'll be wary – he spots anyone and he's off. He probably reckons the threat to my friends will be enough to stop me going the police.' I took the first bite of my sandwich and chewed for a bit. 'That's what I wanted to ask you, Asa – can I take the chance of going to them?'

'You have to – what else can you do?'

'I'll be putting everyone in danger if the whole thing falls through? Shouldn't we all get together to decide?'

He sighed. 'They'll say the same thing, I'm sure – and you can't tackle this on your own, if that's what you're thinking.'

'I know that, but remember how we caught Jackie's killer?'

'Hold on there, Jinky, you're not seriously suggesting we should do our surveillance bit again?'

'Why not? I still have the torches and the walkie-talkies.'

'No, definitely not. You have to go to the authorities and trust them to do their job. It's the only sensible thing – and by far the safest.'

I gave a sigh: I knew he was right. 'But before we go up there, can we try and make some sense of this whole business first?'

Asa gave a firm nod. 'Fine. So the obvious question to ask is – who is The Tramp?' He added, 'And why would he want to kill you?'

I had been thinking of little else. 'I'm not convinced he did, Asa – want to kill me. In *his* mind he might only have been trying to keep me out of the way, rid himself of the threat I posed.' I paused to allow him to make his usual scathing remark at my comment. He didn't. I went on, slightly taken aback, 'Even if I'd managed to stay low in the track, as he suggested, and avoided hanking on the train, I don't think I would have survived: probably bled to death from the injuries.

Although, I suppose I would have been free to crawl away after the train's wheels cut through the ropes.'

He asked, cautiously, 'Do you still think it's Jeremy Gittes? Is it based solely on him wearing gloves?'

I nodded. 'Kind of – I never got the chance to see his face properly.'

'I remember you saying, when you met up with him a while back, he had a lisp. Did The Tramp have one?'

I pondered on it for a moment before replying dejectedly, 'No, he didn't.'

Asa formed a grimace. I kept quiet. His eyes swept the room as he thought of something to say. 'Quite plush in here now – quite nice.'

I nodded back.

He went on, 'You know, when you think about it, there shouldn't be an S in lisp – it's not very fair.'

'And there's no P in bucket – but sometimes it happens.'

He continued with barely a pause, 'Have you been working on any new cases without telling me? Any grudges out there?'

'Nothing at all. I've been too busy decorating. I'll need a few jobs once this is over to make up for the money I've dished out.'

'Maybe it's your bank manager's way of slowing down your spending – he's hired the Bank of Scotland's enforcer.'

'Let's keep it serious, Asa.'

'Okay – but you started it.' He gave a watery smile before adding, 'So, The Tramp, when he finds out you're still alive, comes looking for you. But this time he offers you the task of finding someone. We're assuming it *was* the same man at my house, aren't we?'

'It was the same foul smell. It has to be – how many killer tramps can there be out there?'

'Why didn't he give you the job first time round?'

116

'I don't know. How do you work out what's going on in a madman's brain? He said I'd passed the test, so, maybe, that meant he thought I was up to it. I'll ask when I see him tomorrow.'

'Hold on, Jinky, there'll be no call for that. If we get the fountain surrounded, he'll be caught the moment he shows. You don't need to be there.'

'I think he'll want to see me first. The lure.' I paused for a moment. 'Tell me, Asa, how did he know where I'd be this morning?'

'Aye, that's a bit of a mystery. He must know we're friends.'

'Well, he does – remember he rattled off your names without too much thought. He knows who to come after. We can't afford any mistakes on this.'

'It means we can discount the first attack as a random incident, Jinky. He singled you out. He was waiting – might have been following you for most of the night.'

I nodded.

'You came back early from England and went to see the Chamberlains – anything else you were up to yesterday?'

As I took him through my meeting with Jill and the trip to Jeremy's bed-sit, one persistent thought kept hitting the back of my head like a jackhammer – if only I had stayed with Chiara in her house in England none of this would have happened. It had been a huge mistake. I had no idea where she was or how she was be feeling right now – but it needed to be sorted out.

I withheld any mention of Miss Welch though: partly to shield Asa from the slightly shady goings-on but, mostly, because enlisting her help had been downright daft and would have, almost certainly, brought on some justified wrath.

'As far as I can see, this raises a few other possibilities,' he said. 'Either Mr. Chamberlain's son took an instant dislike to you, didn't want you snooping into the family affairs, and somehow enlisted the help of a tramp to bump you off – we might be able to discount that one.' He emitted an 'umm' noise, before adding, 'Or, and this seems quite likely, it has something to do with Onion Sanny.'

'How do you mean?'

'Sanny's hired you to prove he's innocent of the Waltzing Man murder, so, if the *actual* killer finds out, maybe sees the two of you talking outside the pub, he might want to make sure you don't start poking your neb in.'

'Which would mean The Tramp killed Mr. Chamberlain and has set up Sanny to take the fall.' Again I was surprised by Asa – suggesting I was a possible threat to the murderer.

'It's possible.' He scratched his chin. 'What's all this 'take the fall' business?'

'Chiara likes watching old crime movies. And it's not too big a jump to suppose Sanny might have had a few run-ins with tramps over the years. Taking a step back, they're not all that different in lifestyle. Maybe there's a history there. I'll need to ask him. Come to think of it, I'm supposed to meet up with him today.' I checked the clock on the wall. 'I nearly forgot about that.'

'There is another possibility, Jinky, and that is it has nothing to do with Lewis Chamberlain but everything to do with Jeremy Gittes.'

'How d'you mean?'

'Well, what if it was The Tramp who dumped his body in the hotel. If he did, he wouldn't like you poking your nose in. Suppose he spots you at the bed-sit earlier in the day and decides you have to go as well.'

'But I didn't find anything there – and that doesn't explain why he gave me a job rather than something much worse. And can I just add that you still don't know for sure that the body is Jeremy's?'

'Only a matter of time – we'll find out soon enough. His

bed-sit will have been searched by now. I take it your fingerprints are all over it?'

I nodded. 'And Jill's. I'll need to tell them. Explain why I was there.'

'That would be an idea. Are your prints still on record?'

I shrugged. 'Wouldn't they have been destroyed by now – after the last investigation?' But, before he could answer, I launched into another niggle. 'You see that's what's puzzling, Asa – Jackie's place was ransacked but Jeremy's wasn't. It was perfectly neat. We have someone tearing Jackie's home apart, presumably looking for drugs – but not in his brother's room. What does that tell us?'

He screwed up his mouth as he thought.

I went on, 'If Jackie was killed for drugs then it's reasonable to suppose it's the same reason for Jeremy's death – *if* it is his body, of course. But why then leave *his* place untouched?'

'Maybe he handed them over – but was killed anyway.'

'And we know The Tramp possesses mind-altering substances... It has to be part of the same thing.'

'That could be the key: when we find out the chemical involved, we might be able to trace it back.'

I nodded. 'So, as you say, it has to do with Jeremy Gittes and not the Waltzing Man... Wait a minute, Asa!' I stood up, suddenly, from the table. 'All *three* deaths could be connected!' I started to pace. 'Why couldn't it be that? The Gittes brothers *and* Mr. Chamberlain.'

He shook his head. 'No, no way, not all three: we *have* Jackie's killer locked up awaiting trial, remember? He's been held for over a month now and he's admitted it. He couldn't have done Mr. Chamberlain.'

I had to concede that. 'But he could have put Jeremy's body in the hotel before he was captured, couldn't he? There was time for him to do that. What else is he saying?'

'Nothing, nothing at all. He's refusing to talk any further.'

'Pity.'

'I think it comes down to this new chemical, Jinky. It's valuable and somehow Jackie got a hold of it and was killed as a result.'

'That sounds about right.' We were silent for a moment. 'Do they know when the body was put in the cellar, Asa – the exact day?'

'Not yet. In fact, I can't see them being able to give a precise answer to that one.'

I popped some serious painkillers and tidied the dishes before giving it one last go, 'The three deaths can still be linked. What if he was working *with* The Tramp? The two of them at it together, searching for the drugs, and we've only got one half of the team?'

Asa refused to comment further and I let it drop, giving a hand-clap. 'Right, okay, let's see about getting this tramp caught and out of the way – that's the main thing at this moment, and then, maybe, the rest of the pieces will fall into place. Are you ready to roll?'

I left him standing in the kitchen while I picked out a couple of long-sleeved shirts and two new, unworn jackets from my wardrobe – bought recently with Chiara's help – bringing them through, dumping them into a plastic bag.

Asa waited by the door, taking in my movements. 'Why do you think he came back to free your hands on the rail track?'

'They weren't free – not exactly. But I don't think for one minute it was to help me escape.'

'Why do it at all?'

I had considered this. 'I think he genuinely believed the train would run over my feet but he wanted the rest of me untouched so I would survive. It was his way of taking me out of the game. We can ask him when he's captured.'

'There is one slight problem in that, Jinky.'

'What?'

'Even if the police do catch him tomorrow night, we have no proof he tried to kill you. It's his word against yours.'

'I'm willing to take that chance – he might even breakdown and confess. On his past record, there's no way to work out what he might do – at any time.'

Asa opened the door. 'What's with the bag of clothes?'

'I need to drop these off at the sewing shop in Irish Street.'

'Alterations?'

'Something like that.'

'The jackets are new – I noticed they still had their labels on.'

'And what about it, hawkeye?'

'Why would you buy them if they didn't fit properly? That, if you ask me, is a very girlie thing to do.'

'Just as well I'm not asking you then.' I felt my first smile in a long time and added, 'Asa, I'm sorry for all the bother I caused and what I said. I'll need to apologise to Rosie as well for the abuse.'

He flapped a hand through the air. 'Don't worry about it. Just say you mistook her for a referee – she wears far too much black these days. As it is, we knew you weren't yourself. But there *is* one person you have to say sorry to.'

'Chiara?'

'Right. Although…'

'What?'

'I don't want to say this, Jinky – but going back to how The Tramp found out where you were staying…'

'Go on.' I didn't like where this was heading.

'Only Rosie and I knew you were there, in our house.'

'What about the doctor – and the two policemen?'

'Okay, right, sure. But maybe we shouldn't discount the fact that I told someone else.'

'Who?'

'Your girlfriend, of course – when she phoned. And that would have been not long before The Tramp appeared at the doorstep.'

*

I dropped in at the sewing shop. I know the woman quite well now: she's had a lot of business from us, making new curtains and cushion covers. I drew a diagram on a piece of paper to show the alterations needed to my clothes, and, as a special favour, she said she would have them ready by five o'clock.

I returned to the car but hadn't managed to attach the seat belt before Asa started up, 'There's a madman on the loose and you're worried about sartorial elegance.' He gave a shake of the head.

'Come on, we're wasting time here. My usual jacket's ripped so I can't wear it now, and, for all you know, I might be getting a waterproof hood built into these ones – it's going to be essential if this weather keeps up.'

'This man The Tramp asked you to find – have you given it much thought?'

'I have. Why?'

'If you could track *him* down it might give a clue to who The Tramp is. What was the description he gave you again?'

'Brown, spiky hair, fit, and a diamond stud in his ear.'

'It's not a lot.'

'It's enough, Asa. I know who it is.' I paused to give him time to come up with the answer. 'You've met him,' I prompted.

'It's not Don Gardiner, is it?'

'Exactly. Jill Gittes' boyfriend. Odd, don't you think?'

'Almost as odd as a Gretna season ticket holder. You could talk to him: he might know something.'

'When I get the time.'

He turned the key in the ignition and the wipers started again.

*

We parked at the police station. Asa pulled out his phone and pressed some numbers. 'That's funny, she's not answering.'

'Who?'

'Your girlfriend. She's a witness. She should make a statement.'

'She didn't see anyone this morning.'

'But she *did* untie you – and that's important.'

'In case people don't believe me, you mean?'

'It all helps build a picture.'

He spoke on the phone for a short while. 'Rosie says she left shortly after us but didn't say where she was going. Has she been back to your house?'

'Not that I could see.'

*

We had another wait in a reception room. It must have been a strange experience for Asa to be on the other side of the counter. Ed asked me into the questioning room on my own. There was an awkward pause: Asa was burning to say something, but, in the interests of harmony, he decided to let it go.

The bare room was made from brick walls, painted over in dark green, and held a table with four chairs, two on either side. It looked like a bleak dining room. The TV set in the corner was the only redeeming feature. I'd made statements before but this was the first time I'd been here.

Ed was a handsome man with dark hair and good posture. He carried his slim, suit-bound frame to the table, pulled out a chair for me, and sat down opposite, opening out a folder. His chair made a screeching echo as it fought against the movement.

He was younger, by a few years, promoted here from Glasgow, and he had decided to keep his accent. Unfortunately, he didn't like me very much and had, at one time, threatened to have me arrested for meddling in police affairs.

As I took in his thorny demeanour, I pictured the diary sitting on my window shelf back home. It brought a chill through me – colder than the terraces of Palmerston Park on a bleak January night.

'We were coming to get you anyway,' he said, his voice ingrained with years of displeasure; however they hadn't managed to put any lines on his brow. 'Saved us the bother. I want you to have a look at this.'

He clicked on the TV. For a while my spirits were lifted enough to forget the diary: I thought he was about to impart some evidence, some help. It couldn't be about The Tramp – they knew next to nothing as yet – but it might have something to do with Onion Sanny. It was possible Asa had mentioned I was on the case when he was at work this morning. It would be a pleasant turn of events. Ed's boss, High-Heid-Yin-Harris, might even have whispered another word in his ear – he had come to my aid once before.

'This is some CCTV footage,' Ed said.

'Can we talk about the attack on me first?' I asked; then the image on the screen hooked in my attention. I couldn't quite place the street but someone was walking towards the camera. The man stopped, turned towards a building, grasped a large handle, heaved a door open and walked in. It was me.

'Do you remember this?'

I gave a vague shrug. On the screen I had been wearing a t-shirt, no coat or jacket, so it must have been taken sometime during the summer. And as Scottish summers are as short as Asa's temper, and sometimes as fiery, it narrowed it down to last month – when Dumfries had fizzed like an egg in an overheated frying pan.

124

'The date is Monday, July 17th, 8.53pm.'

'This year?'

He nodded. 'Just over five weeks ago now. I'll fast-forward a little bit here.'

Another man approached, opened the door, and entered.

'Do you recognise him?'

'He's not all that clear.'

'The person following you into The Whitesands Bar is Jeremy Gittes. Do you remember now?'

At that moment, with a gleam spreading across Ed's eyes, I should have twigged something was wrong. I didn't. I put on a smile to help with the thought processes. 'That's right, I was looking for him. Someone told me he drank there. We had, eh, a meeting in the toilet, actually.'

'The toilet?'

'Yeah, I was, you know, doing what you're supposed to do there, and he came in and started talking. At first I didn't know who he was: I'd never met him before, and he's quite a bit younger than his brother. And not much of a resemblance either.'

'What did you talk about?'

'Not a lot. I wanted to find out if he knew anything about his Jackie's death.' I shrugged. 'You've got to look at all the angles and gather as much info as possible.' It wasn't the best of comments: I saw Ed hackles rise at my little, condescending lecture.

He kept himself in check, saying, 'And *did* he know anything about his brother's murder?'

'He said he didn't.'

'Which sounds like you didn't believe him?'

I made no reply.

Ed stared at me, his eyes turning narrower and angrier. 'And then what happened?' He was straining to be polite.

I had a quick look round to see if our interview was being

125

recorded. There was no sign of a machine. 'Nothing much else. He left first and I left shortly after.' I wasn't going to tell him how much I'd felt threatened, and that I had wet myself and the floor during the confrontation and was forced to tug my t-shirt down as far as it would go to cover up the wet patches as I raced past the gawking regulars, nosying at the stranger in their midst.

Ed nodded, clicked the remote. 'Did you stay in the pub after your meeting? Did you see him again?'

'No, I headed straight out. And I didn't see him – but then I wasn't really looking.'

Ed stood up, circled the table once, studying me from all angles like the mechanic at the quick-fixit garage sizing up a faulty car. He stopped and looked down: Ed's slow headshake filled me with almost as much unease, but not quite. I stared at my bandages and slid a tongue round my mouth to check on the healing progress: it was going well, unlike this meeting, although the tips of my teeth were now like saw blades.

After a few drawn out seconds, Ed said, clicking on the machine again, 'Watch this – I'll speed it up. Here, that's you leaving the pub.'

I saw myself emerge onto the street, shaking a leg as though coaxing something down the inside of the trousers, then walking away like Charlie Chaplin. He froze the picture.

'There's no sign of Gittes leaving. None at all. We've played it through all the way up to closing time – and he doesn't show. What do you think of that?'

'Is there a back door?'

'It leads into a courtyard only – where the smokers go. What if I was to tell you he hasn't been spotted since? His acquaintances, the barman there, his landlord, and anyone else we've questioned – he hasn't been seen. He seems to have vanished. You would have been the last person to see him – until his body turned up in the cellar of the old hotel last night.'

'I thought you didn't know it was him for sure?'

He hit back with venom. 'How would *you* know?'

I back-tracked, 'The fastest thing around town, other than a postie in trainers, is word of a body being found. I just thought you would need to have tests done to make certain of the identity. And with this being the weekend, there would be a delay.'

'Okay, let's say we *think* it's him. Somehow, he ended up in the cellar, either that night or the very next day, because the day after that the hotel was pulled down on top of his body. Were you ever up at the hotel around that time?'

'Wait a minute, you're not seriously suggesting I had something to do with his death? Now that's not on. I came here...' I had been as slow as a horse drawing a barge through syrup.

'Answer the question.'

I took my time. But, unable to hold his gaze, I decided to look for new things on the back of my hands. Asking for a solicitor seemed a touch over-dramatic and, more importantly, might be a wee bit of a waste of money, so I went with, 'I went up to watch the destruction of the place. It was in the afternoon, I think. You'll know when it was exactly.'

'Why were you there?'

'Just as I said. There were others as well. And why not? It was a monument. People like that kind of stuff. It's history – or the destruction of it.'

'And had you been up there any time before that? In the days preceding the demolition, after your meeting with Jeremy?'

'It's possible. I can't be sure. Maybe once or twice – visiting Onion Sanny.'

Ed raised his eyebrows like Tower Bridge opening up for boats. 'You're friendly with Sanny. Now that's interesting.'

So he didn't know I had been hired by him. I said,

'Nobody's really *friendly* with him. He asked me to do one or two things.'

Ed leaned onto the desk in front of me with straight arms. He was looking down, bullying. Things weren't going well.

'How many murders are there in a year in this area?' I asked quickly – deflecting.

He shrugged back his answer.

I gave him the full force of my stare. 'And within a few weeks of each other we have two brothers dying. They have to be related.' I added, quickly, 'And I don't mean in that way.' I went on, 'You have the man responsible for one of the murders locked up for over a month.'

'What's your point?'

'Just that he could have done both murders, both brothers. Have you looked into that?'

Ed's face became as red as a strawberry and I felt a moment of satisfaction. He didn't say anything.

I added, 'Do you think Mr. Chamberlain's death is linked as well? Mr. Chamberlain ran that hotel years ago and Sanny stayed in the grounds of the hotel right up until it was flattened – is that why you suspect him?'

'Let's keep to the point.' He wanted to shout and fought to quash it, nodding back to the TV. 'What did you do after you left this pub?'

'That's a long time ago – I can't remember. Probably went home.'

'Then you better try and work out where you were in the days that followed.'

'Are you really trying to suggest I'm involved in this?'

'You seem to be in everything else,' he replied, flatly.

I stood up. 'Am I free to go?'

He hesitated, long enough to suggest he had a choice. 'For just now.'

I sat back down and slipped out a smile. 'In that case

maybe you can help *me*. I need you to catch the man who has been trying to kill me. It'll be in the wee small hours of Monday morning, in town centre. Can you do that?'

*

Asa was waiting outside sheltering under a tree. 'I've been advised to keep my distance from you, Jinky,' he said, immediately.

'No problem. I don't need a lift, I'll walk – a little bit of water won't hurt me. I'm fine.' It wasn't true: the pills were wearing off and I was sinking under the weight of pain and tiredness.

'They reckon I shouldn't be associating with you at all.'

'A word in your ear, was it? That's plain daft, Asa.'

'I know. Will you be okay on your own?'

'The only threat I have to consider right now is the one posed by the police – but I reckon it's all a ploy to scare me away.'

'Do they know about your involvement with Sanny?'

'I didn't go into detail.'

'There's been no sign of your girlfriend.'

I walked off, then turned back to him: he hadn't moved, still staring at me. 'I'm going to arrange for everyone to meet round at my house tonight at eight. Will you be there? I'll understand if you're not.'

He gave an uncommitted tilt of the head.

'Tell me, Asa, how long is CCTV footage kept normally?'

'A month.'

I set off. The pictures Ed had shown me were older than that. Either they had held onto them to keep tabs on Jeremy – or because they had been spying on me.

*

I reached Irish Street by a quarter to five, picked up my altered clothes and paid, leaving a generous tip, then returned home via the hardware store. I swallowed some more tablets. There was no sign of Chiara. It would have been surprising for her to be here, sitting, waiting, friendly. I'd said some terrible things. I may not have been in my right mind but I hadn't ranted at Asa or Rosie – well, not as much. All my spite had been directed straight at her – and that could never be justified.

Her phone wasn't responding. Had she changed her number? It would serve me right. I roamed through my apartment. Everything held a new, shared memory. That was the point of all the work: to destroy the memories of old and bring in fresh ones. If this was the end, if we never saw each other again, I would have to change the place again: I could never settle within these constant reminders.

I ended up in the bedroom. We have a wardrobe each. I opened hers – it was empty. In the bathroom there were spaces where her shampoo and creams used to sit, leaving behind faint, empty rings on the surfaces. My toothbrush was alone in the glass by the sink. Normally our two brushes are propped up, making a V shape: we prefer not to have our bristles touching. It might be the end of us. She could be on her way back to England. Had it come to that? I didn't have the experience to know.

And I didn't even know the whereabouts of any of her properties either – other than the Buckingham one. We'd always kept in contact by phone. Whenever I'd asked where she was, she would say near Derby, or Leeds, or, just outside York. I'd never pinned her down to actual places: I was never quite sure if I had the right, or if it would be construed as snooping. If she'd wanted me to know, she would have told me – isn't that the way women play it?

I called her number again – and there was nothing. She might be in her car at this very moment – lengthening our attachment, diminishing the need for Dumfries.

A bubble of hope filled me: she was simply getting her

own back at being unable to contact me earlier, and once I had learned my lesson she would appear at the back door. The bubble burst almost immediately: it didn't seem likely.

I searched for her door key – there was no sign. She had taken it with her. Surely *that* was a good sign. I was clutching at straws.

I paced the kitchen. Mr. Chamberlain's diary lay on the window sill. I picked it up wearily and held it in the palm of my hand. There was no time for this. It was a barrier. The Tramp would be caught tomorrow tonight: I could start searching for Chiara then. That's the kind of job I'm supposed to be able to do. There might be a chance for us if I could meet her eye to eye and talk.

I needed to find her properties: her name must be recorded somewhere in land or electoral registers. I would visit each one until I found her. I cursed myself for not taking up her offer of meeting her father when I'd had the chance. I didn't know where he lived, other than it was in the Birmingham area. Nor did I know his first name: although she may well have mentioned it at some point. I had been scared to meet him. I thought he would be disappointed by his daughter's choice – but maybe I'd just been too lazy.

I should sit down right now and phone every Mr. Preston in the Birmingham area. He might not tell me where she was – she might have warned him already – but, surely, he would pass on a message. She had to know I was trying and would not give up.

Why didn't I know more about her? That's never a good sign. I had asked occasionally, of course, but she'd always been evasive. Perhaps that sparked my behaviour this morning: the drug freeing up some deep frustrations? I suppose I always felt she was holding back on me – keeping something hidden.

I was wasting time. I needed to do something – and this damned diary needed to be returned. If it was Ed's idea to scare me earlier, then he had succeeded. At this moment, all I wanted was to turn my back on everything and run from Dumfries with one thing in mind – finding Chiara. But I couldn't: too many people were expecting something from me.

The diary burned in my hand. It should not be here any longer and it wasn't fair on Miss Welch to drag her out too late in the evening. I phoned.

'I haven't forgotten,' Miss Welch said, sharply. 'What's taken you so long? I expected a call this morning. I can't manage right now. This is a very bad time. I'm very busy. Why would you phone at this precise minute? Anything around five o'clock is most inconsiderate. You know this is my time for a cup of tea. And here's the cat in now – through the flap. Can you hear her? You've a note of my timetable: I gave it to you last month. Have you forgotten about that? Look, I need to go right away and see to her. Heaven forbid if she's kept waiting. Phone back in twenty minutes.' She hung up abruptly.

Mr. Chamberlain's diary, with its false cover, was hidden for a reason. Reluctantly, I flicked through it. The writing was small, with each page filled to the brim: some even had added lines written round the edges. It would take a while to go through it page by page. I didn't have time now.

What was I doing? Is this more important than searching for Chiara? Why bother with this book and why bother with Sanny? After The Tramp is arrested, I'm free.

There's a photo-copying machine in Tesco. I could put the diary through it – but that would take a while and it would be costly as well. I hit upon a much quicker and, more importantly, cheaper method. I brought out my camera, photographing one double page of the diary at a time, using the close-up setting.

*

Miss Welch was dressed, head to toe, in black when she answered the door. Even the plastic rain hood, she was tying under her chin, as she stood on her front step, was black. It seemed a touch overdone.

'Thought I'd better look the part,' she said. I wasn't sure if she actually winked then or if it was a raindrop catching her eye. She added quickly, with distaste, 'I've much better things to be doing than going out on a filthy night like this, you know. I should be in front of the fire with a good book.'

'I know, Miss Welch – and thank you again.'

The filthy night brought an early end to the light of the day and heavy clouds held the town down like a paperweight, leaving Saturday's pavements bereft of pedestrians. Again, I parked out of sight of the Chamberlain's house and handed over the diary. It took fifteen minutes for her to return to the car.

'Okay?' I asked.

'Fine. No problems. They were a wee bit surprised I was out in a night like this. I told them I was on my way to the hospital – so it was no bother. I'm sure they could have picked holes in that one if they'd thought about it – but they didn't. They were so very relieved to hear there was nothing untoward in the diary to think about anything else.'

'Did they say if they would be passing it onto the police?'

She chose not to answer, saying, 'Everything in that house is sorted and packed up, and my dear Lewis isn't even in the ground yet. What do you make of that?'

I started up the engine as she started up her next question, 'And how is your aunt doing?'

I did a three-point turn – which expanded into five. It bought some time for my reply and had nothing to do with my driving skills. But when the manoeuvre was over, I had no option but to answer. 'I'm not sure.'

'And why would that be?'

'I haven't had the time, as yet.' It sounded a touch pathetic: I was a grown up, I didn't need to justify myself to someone who was little more than a stranger.

'You're telling me you've been so busy since I last saw you that you haven't managed to visit your one and only aunt?'

'Something like that.' I could have, at least, phoned the hospital this afternoon to ask how she was. *And* I had been up there as well, for goodness sake. I could have dropped in for a minute after seeing the doctor.

'I find it very difficult to believe that you've been so occupied. You don't even work, and it's the weekend.'

There was silence in the car for the remainder of the journey – Miss Welch might have sensed she'd overstepped the mark. I parked in front of her gate.

'I did mention you to them, you know,' she said. 'They're not interested in hiring anyone. I had the impression they weren't too impressed by you.'

That was probably for the best anyway. I wasn't sure about the ethics of having two paymasters for the same case – that's if Sanny ever came up with actual money.

*

I knocked on the door of his caravan. I felt a touch better: the twenty minute nap at home had helped greatly. Sanny appeared, quickly. He did his usual trick of holding the door closely behind him, not allowing me to see inside.

'Ah, it's yersel,' he cried. 'Late for a visit.' There was a flicker of a smile across his stubbled, wrinkled face – either that or he was about to sneeze. He wiped his hands up and down the sides of his heavy, black breeks – there was still some moisture between his fingers. It would be interesting to know what he had been doing. Maybe it was just the washing up, but, somehow, I doubted that: his off-white shirt, no collar, held flecks of flour or dust down the front.

'I need to ask you some questions,' I said, 'if you're still keen for me to help you.'

'What sort o' things?'

'Why the police suspect you of murder of Mr. Chamberlain for starters.'

He studied me for a while, peered up to the heavens, then back to me cowering in my jacket. 'The rain's on for the nicht. Ye'd better come in, A suppose.'

I hadn't wanted to be here: I'd wanted to stay at home and find Chiara's dad, but now my heart started thumping faster than Asa can drink. His words, cast as casually as bread to ducks, almost made my legs buckle. I couldn't believe it: the sudden burst of excitement was immense. I was actually going to step inside Onion Sanny's den. I might be the first ever person. Wait until the boys hear about this. I might be able to put some of the rumours to bed.

His eyes were still fixed on me.

I stared blankly back at him, dazed. After all this time I was being allowed into the inner sanctum of his life. I would be able to find out what really goes on. I was heady, joyous.

He gave a nod of the head and slipped back inside, shutting the door firmly: perhaps to tidy up, clear a space. As long as he didn't put too many things away, I was more than happy to wait in the rain.

A few seconds later a door, further along, opened out towards me, barring a view of the interior. There were no steps up to it and it had no outside handle – it had barely registered in me. This new caravan was more like a mobile home: such a huge change from his old, small, battered one of before.

Sanny's head poked out and round the edge of the door. He looked in the opposite direction first, then round to pick me out. He gave a twitch of the head and I set off.

I heard his voice, 'In here.' I had taken my first step. Five paces and I would be there.

Would he show me how he makes his wonderful liqueur – and offer me two glasses of it? No more or less should be taken at a sitting, he says.

135

Second step – this was it. I was actually going inside. Does he keep a trained crow to collect worms for his fishing and another to dance on his roof as an alarm clock to wake him up in the morning?

Third step – I was level with the window between the two doors. The curtain was drawn across. A flicker of a lamp showed through a bare patch – but that was all. Does he keep his fruit under giant pyramids to keep them fresh, and his knives to stay sharp?

Fourth step – he had moved out of sight. Would he tell me the secret of guddling for salmon? They say he's the best. And how he catches rabbits with nothing other than guile and a pair of special mittens?

Fifth step. I rounded the door and gazed into the entrance: my head was level of the floor. I wasn't sure if I would be able to climb in, and Sanny was nowhere to be seen.

I grabbed onto the door frame, a hand on each side and tried to pull myself up. I wasn't strong enough – or tall enough. But I couldn't let it end at that: I eased back down onto the ground, took a few of steps back, ran and launched myself, headfirst, landing on my chest, grabbing the frame at the same time, straining, hauling, wriggling my way into the caravan like an oversized eel out of water. I managed to bring a knee up and propel myself across the threshold.

I was in a small room. An oil lamp sat on the floor in a corner. There was a window and a seat – which probably folded into a bed – and nothing else. The other door, through to the rest of the caravan, was shut. The room held that new-car smell. It had never been used. It was his spare room – his guest bedroom.

Sanny sat in a corner behind the door, his legs crossed, one hand on his knee, the other propping him upright. He had a bewildered look on his face. I slumped down across from him, gasping, trying hard not to show my disappointment.

He had lived for scores of years in a tiny place but the rules of the universe, the need to fill the void, did not apply to Sanny – he had no use for the extra space.

'Whit did ye want te ask me then?'

We were not much more than three feet apart. It was the closest I'd ever been to him. I could smell his clothes – they were earthy, woody, not unpleasant. Behind them lay a lighter tone, a hint of fragrance: a delicate scent of a rose, perhaps from his skin. Under the fall of his locks, clumps of black hair bunched in his ears, growing out at differing angles.

'Whit's wrang with ye man? Speak.'

I cleared my throat. 'First, I need to know why you're a police suspect.'

'Ye'd need to ask *them* that.'

'Do you have any idea?'

He fiddled with fabric of his trousers, pinching it up and letting it fall. His hands were clean but his fingernails held dirt.

I nodded at his silence and tried another tack. 'How well did you know Lewis Chamberlain?'

'Aye, A kent him lang enough.'

I waited for more, but when he didn't continue, I said, 'You're going to have to help me – if I'm to help you.'

'Why don't ye fin oot who did this tae him and stop botherin me with all these questions?'

'I need somewhere to start.' I gave him a pained expression and one more chance. If he remained unhelpful, there would be no point staying. It didn't matter that I was inside his caravan – there wouldn't be a guided tour of the rest.

'I think it's important for me to know why the police called you in, questioned you.'

Thankfully, he answered, 'A ken nothing aboot the murder. Ye'll need tae start frae the other end – no here. The line fae him tae me disnae matter. It's something else oot there that's got him killed.'

I shrugged. 'I tried talking to the son – that got nowhere. I can try his dancing club but I doubt if it'll be much use: he'd only been a couple of times.' I paused and breathed in deeply. 'If you really want my help, I need more from you. Give me somewhere to start: some other friends he had, the work he did when he left here, why he came back. Anything like that. You knew him years ago – he told me. He owned the hotel and you stayed in the grounds. There has to be something. Maybe arguments, scores to settle with people from the past – and they flared up on his return. Some information – even if it's only background stuff. So I can build a picture.'

'He said he owned the hotel? When were ye speaking tae him aboot that?'

I told him about the conversation I'd had with Mr. Chamberlain on the day of the demolition: he had spoken as the digger tore away at the building, hauling it to the ground. There had been a body in the cellar at that time, only a few feet from us, perhaps still alive and desperate for help. Yet, I'd sensed nothing at all. The air should have shattered with the man's desire to be saved, shock waves should have exploded, and the day should have wept from such a heinous crime: but we had stood, oblivious, merely fascinated by the spectacle. It was an unsettling and crushingly sad notion. It brought an involuntary shiver to me now.

Aware of my faltering voice, I finished off with, 'If there's nothing more you have to say, I need to get going. I'm not too hopeful about finding anything out. Give it some thought, if you can, and I'll come back.' I stood up.

'He never owned the hotel, Chamberlain. A'll tell ye that noo. He might have met his wife there, I daresay.' Sanny raised himself, shuffled round in the cramped room. 'Them polis kent a hud a row with the man. Take it from there.' He folded his arms in a final gesture.

I jumped down and walked to my car. I heard the noise of

the door closing. It would take a few visits to get him to open up – I couldn't expect anything different. It would need to be teased out like the last drink of the day.

However, I didn't have time to spare. I'd visited Sanny only because I said I would. It stopped me from finding Chiara. He had hired me to help him but, at this moment, I needed this job like a hermit needs a guest bedroom.

My golf umbrella lay on the passenger seat. Okay, I was disappointed with the meeting but I gave it a kiss on its handle all the same. Next time I'd ask to use his toilet and see his reaction.

*

Tread was the first to arrive, giving a chirpy rat-a-tat-tat on the back door, closely followed in by Chisel and Hoogah. They'd all been for a drink: it was on their breaths. I had a detailed map of the town centre, printed off the internet, sitting in the middle of the kitchen table, with coloured marker pens beside it.

'What's all this about, Jinky?' Chisel asked, taking in the new kitchen units. 'I like what you've done – but why bring us round here?'

'Who's for a drink?' I said.

They didn't sit down, standing round like awkward statues. Tread moved over to the sink, lifted up the tea-cloth, and gave it a shake, then opened the oven door.

'What are you looking for?' I asked.

'I'm searching for The Book of Daft Questions – I hear the new edition's out. You've obviously bought it and stashed it somewhere. Who's for a drink, indeed.'

'Right, if that's the way you want to play it,' I retorted, 'the beer's in the fridge, help yourselves. And before you go moaning about keeping it there and the need for real ale not to be too cold, blah, blah, blah, I've only just put it in, to take the edge away – and the fridge's switched off right now. I didn't think you'd want your beer at supermarket hot.

And, if you don't end up having enough to drink, then it's your own fault: I'll not be offering.'

Unfazed, Tread went on, 'I was expecting waitress service. Where is that lovely creature of yours with the poor eyesight? I hope she's in uniform tonight.' As was his habit, when talking about women, he licked his lips.

I could have given him a list of the various uniforms Chiara possessed. But that was confidential and our 'no secrets between the boys' policy didn't stretch that far – and neither did her uniforms. Also, Tread's heart might not cope with that kind of information.

At some point, though, I would need to tell them about my tirade, and, perhaps, ask for some advice in getting her back. They might know already, of course – Asa might have said.

'I'm not sure where she is,' I said. 'Probably somewhere in England.'

'Still down there, eh?' Hoogah answered. 'You must be missing her?'

'I am.' Asa hadn't been in touch with them then.

'My God,' Tread exclaimed, opening the fridge a touch and peeking in. 'Sorry, Jinky, didn't mean to break your house rules – but… would you look at this.' He turned to Hoogah, 'Have you seen inside here?'

'No, my super powers only go as far as ice-sculpting at the moment – but I'm working on being able to see through fridge doors in the near future. It could be handy – you can tell a lot about a person from what's in their fridge, I've heard.'

Tread opened the door fully and gave a gesture normally associated with magicians. 'Behold the glorious sight,' he trumpeted.

It was filled, head to toe, with bottles of beer. I'd even cleared out all my perishables, taking them upstairs to the top floor, asking Rodger the lodger to hold onto them for a few hours.

The boys stood with their mouths open, as though witnessing a miracle. Then Chisel said, 'I think what we can tell from *this* fridge is that the owner wants a very big favour from us. What have you got up your sleeve this time, Jinky?'

'Wait 'til Asa sees this,' Tread continued, unable to pull his eyes away. 'He's never going to be able to say anything about you ever again, Jinky. That book he's been threatening to write – How to Veer from a Beer – will need to be scraped now.'

'I don't think he's coming,' I replied evenly.

'Oh?' Tread's eyebrows arched high. 'In that case...' The tip of his tongue emerged like the head of a tortoise, evidently to help with the calculation going on in his head. It took a few moments of extreme effort before he said, 'Then there's about a gallon too much stuff in there.' He shook his head sadly from side to side, finding it all too difficult to take in.

Unfortunately, we'd used up far too many valuable seconds waiting for that outcome. 'It can keep,' I said.

'Keep? I don't think so.'

'Of course it can.'

'Are you sure? Has any research been done into that? There's certainly been none in this area.'

'What happened to Asa then?' It was Hoogah – his fingernails were dirtier than Onion Sanny's.

I asked them to sit down as they were making the place look untidy. And they did, Tread handing round the ale.

I started, 'I'm afraid I might have placed all of you in a bit of danger – not that I had any say in the matter, I might add.'

I told them about The Tramp, detail on detail: it lasted as long as two bottles of beer. At the start they butted in continuously, but, eventually, they settled and listened.

Sometimes their outstretched hands fumbled to locate their drinks, their eyes unwilling to leave my face in case they missed something important.

'So what's this map about?' Chisel asked, breaking the long silence after I finished talking.

'This is the place where The Tramp wants to meet.' I thumped my index finger into the centre. The three of them poured over the spot, in studious contemplation.

I left the room, returning a few moments later with a box: they were still in the same position. 'Come on, you know what Dumfries looks like,' I muttered, putting the box on the floor, and sliding it under the table with a foot. It would only distract them if it was left out in the open.

I went on, 'Right, what you need to know is that The Tramp has threatened to harm someone if I don't do as he wants. He mentioned each one of you by name.'

Tread gave a gulp – it pulled his voice up to a higher level. 'He knows our names?'

I nodded. 'Although he didn't say yours exactly – just called you the other one. But, you see, we have a slight problem, and that is to do with the police. They are fully stretched right now and I'm not convinced they'll be able to man the town centre fully to catch this him.'

Chisel said, 'You know they have to take this threat seriously – especially with bodies turning up every other day. This man could be the killer they are looking for...'

I cut him off, 'I'm aware of that and I don't doubt the police unit will be competent, but why not offer a little help? We can add some look-outs of our own.'

Chisel straightened, 'Right then, so what you are saying is that the old team is back in business?'

'I know it's a lot to ask...'

Tread looked decidedly happy. 'Can I have a codename – to make up for last time? What about Sir Veillance?'

'How long have you been working on that one, Tread?' Hoogah asked.

'Not long,' he replied, sheepishly.

I continued, 'If any one of you thinks it's too dangerous, I'm okay with that. We can leave everything to the police and see what happens. I just thought an extra pair of eyes here and there could be useful when they are a bit short on manpower...'

'Well, maybe that's what we should do,' Hoogah returned, 'leave it to the police.'

'Come on, Hoogah, we're doing this as much for ourselves as anyone,' Chisel came back. 'I, for one, don't fancy having a crazy man coming after me. This way we have some control over the situation. Is it to be the same set-up as last time?'

Now I lifted the box onto the table and pulled out the torches and walkie-talkies. 'I'm not so sure about codenames, Tread. I know you're desperate for one but it means remembering who is talking and that might lead to confusion – in the heat of the moment.'

Tread bowed his head in disappointment.

I went on, 'The batteries are new – replaced them today.'

'The police are okay with this?' Chisel asked, warily. 'They weren't too happy last time, if I remember correctly.'

I went with, 'The problem is the meeting place. There are an awful lot of ways into that fountain. He can come from either end of the High Street.' I took a yellow marker pen and drew on some arrows.

Tread showed no interest in the map, playing with his walkie-talkie instead, trying out his codename for size.

Hoogah took the plan on, picking up the pink pen, 'He could come up Bank Street, along English Street, or there's Queensberry Street as well.'

Chisel added, this time in green, 'Don't forget all the lanes: there's a stack of them. One at the mall, Dobie's Wynd, and the one running past The Globe, and another one there...'

I gave a sigh. 'You see, there are too many options. There's never going to be enough police to cover everywhere. That's why we need to be out there as well. And don't forget we need to remain hidden, completely out of sight, or else he's going to be frightened off. He has to get into the centre first and then we surround him. And even then...'

Tread looked up from his machine. 'Come on, Jinky, after the success of last time, this should be a doddle.'

'But you have to be fully aware of the dangers,' I urged. 'I'll say it again – I'll understand if anyone doesn't want to get involved. This is a very unpredictable, nasty person we're dealing with.'

'I think we'd all want to help. Am I right, lads?'

The two of them nodded back at Tread. 'There then, that's settled – so no more talk on the matter,' he said.

'And if we spread out...' Chisel started.

'No, it's not going to be that way – far too risky. No-one's to be on their own. I'm not taking any chances. The three of you will have to keep together. We must agree on that.'

'Where are you going to be?' Hoogah said.

'I'll be waiting by the fountain for him to show.'

'What about Asa?' Chisel asked me.

I gave a shake of the head. 'It's not fair on him – too many conflicts with his work. He can't be seen going against the wishes of the police. We can't put him in that position.'

Their faces dimmed to the colour of their beer. I went on, 'I know it means we can't cover as much as a group – but it's still going to help. It's better than nothing.'

Hoogah added, 'And we'd better not ask Jill's boyfriend, Don Gardiner.'

'Definitely not,' I replied. 'For one thing he hasn't recovered from the last time – but, more importantly, Don is the person The Tramp wants me to find.'

144

'Away you go,' Chisel blurted. 'Don Gardiner?'

Hoogah added, 'Why would The Tramp want *him* of all people?

'I've no idea.'

The quietness was broken by Tread's chair scraping over the floor. He had stood up for more beer.

'How much of the area are the police going to be able to cordon off?' Chisel asked.

'I'm not sure. I've to meet with them tomorrow to go over their plans. If today's anything to go by, I'm not too optimistic.'

'Maybe they could put a sniper on a roof – at Boots, maybe,' Tread suggested.

I ignored him. 'I'm not sure how seriously they're taking this: I have nothing to back it up. It's only my word that this is happening.' I gave them a quick recap of my conversation with Ed this afternoon.

'They can't possible think *you* have anything to do with Jeremy Gittes' murder,' Hoogah said. 'And you were away when The Waltzing Man was killed – so there's an alibi for that one.'

'Thanks for that, Hoogah.' A thought crossed my mind: I have an alibi only if Chiara is willing to state we were together. She would, wouldn't she?

'I've got it,' Tread pointed a finger, 'What about a giant net? It can be dropped the moment he steps into the centre.'

'And where are we going to get such a thing, Tread?' Chisel asked.

Unperturbed, he went on, 'From a fishing boat, of course. They have huge things. Although I'm not sure how you would attach it above…'

I went on quickly, 'The biggest problem is where to hide, still allowing him access and not scaring him off – but close enough to act, if needed.'

Tread clicked his fingers this time. 'I've got it. Marks and Sparks.'

'What about it?' I returned.

'Their window looks out onto that fountain. One of us could be in there, disguised, pretending to be a mannequin and then relay the information when The Tramp's sighted.'

Hoogah said, 'Don't be daft. Those displays are all for women.'

'Well, you're fairly trim, Hoogah. Shave your legs and you could pass for one of them models. And that vacant look you've been practicing for the last few weeks will come in handy too.' Perhaps the effects of the beer had made Tread a shade touchy.

'That's caused by women, Tread. And I for one will not be doing anything like that: I've had enough of hair loss for one year, thank-you very much.' His hand moved unconsciously to the back of his head and his missing pony-tail.

Tread detected the obvious signs of a man close to the edge. 'I know, I know, I was teasing. What we do is persuade one of them woman police to go into the window display. Do they still have the swimwear display on?' Lips were licked.

There was a rap at the door. We jumped.

'Anyone at home,' bellowed a voice.

I opened the door to invite Asa in.

Tread started the moment our visitor set foot on the new black and white squared vinyl floor covering. 'You're never going to believe this Asa...'

'Let me guess – he wants us to capture a possible killer again?'

'No, well, yes – but what I was talking about is the fridge. It's overflowing with beer. Enough for everyone, including you.'

'I thought you weren't going to make it, Asa,' I said.

He shrugged. 'I talked it over with Rosie – and I'm here.

146

What needs to be done?'

'Are you really sure?' I asked.

He nodded firmly.

I went on, 'We were just starting to work out where we should position ourselves – and now we have four, we can split into pairs. What are the teams? Do you want the red or the green marker, Tread?'

'Do you have a blue?'

They settled on Hoogah and Tread, and Asa with Chisel.

I continued, 'So it's the same plan as last time – we're not going to confront him. After he meets me, we keep tabs on him and relay the information back to the police and then they can make the arrest. We only become involved if it looks necessary.'

Asa asked, wearily, 'Do the police know about this?'

'Not yet.'

'They're not going to go along with it, you know. They won't want any interference from the general public.'

'I know.'

'When are you going to tell them?'

'On the night – if it all kicks off. If it looks like we're going to be needed. Same as last time: we're citizens, making a citizen arrest. If we're not needed, they need never find out. Chisel can do the talking to them – he's good at it and had the practice. Remember, at no time do we confront The Tramp. Is that clear?'

'Even if it means letting him go?' Tread asked.

'Yes, we don't want another injury, or worse.'

Tread waggled a finger in the sir. 'This time I've got it – CCTV. We can watch his approach on that.'

Chisel nodded. 'Now that's a good idea for once. The only problem is the police: they won't let us anywhere near the control centre. But, at least, *they* will be able to use it, which should help enormously. I wrote an article on this new system:

it was put in not so very long ago.'

I said, 'But how good are the cameras in the dark – when it's pouring with rain? And are there any blind spots?'

'We'll find out,' he replied.

'Well, I'll mention all that tomorrow at the police station. Actually, Chisel, before the meeting, I need a favour from you.'

'What?'

I hesitated. 'We need The Tramp caught, right? We can't risk him escaping and coming after us, right? So I'm asking you to arrange for a bit more help. We can't cover all the exits.'

'You want me to get more people?' Chisel asked slowly, unsure.

'In a way.' I went on, 'The call you took in the pub last night...'

'What about it?'

'Am I right in thinking it was to go up to see the body being pulled from the ruins of the hotel?'

'Could have been.'

'And this came from your informant: the one who seems to know what's going on.'

Chisel fidgeted under the gaze of everyone round the table. 'I'm a journalist. It's part of the job. We all have them.'

'Of course. But you've never said who it is – not even to us with our 'no secrets' policy in place.'

'Well, it's to do with work – not private lives. My work depends on keeping confidentialities.'

'I understand that. But I'm asking you to break it now. I want you to get your informant to help us. I really don't think Ed's taking The Tramp seriously enough. If the whole thing's taken too lightly, The Tramp might escape and then we'll be in trouble.'

'I still don't get what you think I can do,' Chisel returned.

'Your informant can tell Ed to put a proper surveillance unit in place.'

Asa cut in, 'How can he do that, Jinky? Don't be daft.'

'Because I know who your informant is, Chisel, and I need this help otherwise there's a distinct possibility we're all going to be in danger. I need the town centre to be as watertight as The Queens' defence.'

There was a pause as we watched Chisel's eyes flick from side to side and his mouth tighten. 'I'll see what I can do,' he said, reluctantly.

Asa scratched his chin. 'This is all very secretive, lads.'

'I'd like to keep it that way for just now, Asa, if you don't mind,' Chisel replied harshly.

Asa turned to me. 'Are you really going to wait at the fountain for this man to appear?'

'I have to.'

'He's going to ask you for that name – the man he wanted you to find. What are you going to do then?'

'Probably run. If he follows me I'll relay our route and we'll catch him.' I folded up the map and put it to one side. 'We meet up tomorrow night to finalise our plan.' I paused. 'And Hoogah, how come your fingernails are so dirty?'

He gave a sheepish look. 'It's because I've been barrowing soil most of the day.'

'In the rain?'

He gave a nod. 'All right, I'll tell you. Did you mention the ice to them, Jinky?'

'I thought you'd want the pleasure of that.'

He gave a quick account of last night's events at his house.

Asa said, 'Ah, so that's how The Tramp got you. I'd been wondering why you were out so late.'

Hoogah went on, 'I'm sorry about that, Jinky. If I hadn't called all this wouldn't have happened.'

I shrugged. 'Don't worry about it. It would have happened, I'm sure of it – just at another time, that's all.'

Hoogah nodded and said, 'The ice had melted by this afternoon – I used a hammer and chisel to break it up in the morning – but when I came back from my appointment at Barbours, there was a huge mound of top-soil dumped on my doorstep, completely blocking the front door.'

'Not again,' I said. 'But not as much of a problem, though.'

'Especially if you are a mole,' Tread put in. 'You could burrow to the door in no time.'

Hoogah went on, 'Well, this time I had a back door key on me – as a precaution. And if you think about it Jinky, this isn't nearly as bad as you feared. In fact it's been quite helpful for the garden. Good compost costs a lot of money, you know, so I've come out on top with this one. The plants will get the benefit. Anyway, I'm shattered. Do you know how many barrowfuls it took to clear it all away?'

We shook our heads.

'Well, neither do I, but it took over a couple of hours. Gardens looking great though. Raised up one of the beds while I was at it. But I was soaked through – and I'm dead beat.'

'And is this your new style from Barbour's? I think you've been short-changed.' I said, pointing at his t-shirt and jeans.

'Not short-changed, just didn't have time to *get* changed – rushed round here to be on time.'

'Or, at least to get to the pub on time, for a swift one before coming round?'

*

I opened the connecting door and climbed the stairs. It wasn't too late but I was flat-out exhausted and the boys had gone home. There was music coming from the top floor. I knocked on the door and Rodger opened it a touch. He seemed surprised to see me. Who else would it have been inside my house?

There was room in my fridge now, yet, amazingly, some beer remained. I hadn't touched any drink all night – didn't have the urge – sticking with tea. Rodger handed back my perishables. He didn't let me in. He might have had company. I hoped so: people shouldn't be on their own.

*

I lay on my side of the double bed, my hand in the emptiness of the middle. I wouldn't move across to her side: that was her space. But I *had* switched pillows and slept surrounded in her scent.

Sunday 27th August

*I could feel the carpet under my bare feet. I inched
towards the door. I was close now and the heat from within
emanated through the wood. I touched the handle. It was hot. I
held onto it. My skin burnt, the palms singeing. As I turned the
handle, my mouth opened to scream…*

Bolt upright in bed, sweat pouring, my stomach, limbs,
and skin aching in the bleak light of the morning, I saw the
empty side of the bed, flat and undisturbed. I'd spent a large
part of my life living alone but I'd never felt this lonely before.
I was one drop of water in the middle of hot desert sands. I took
a pile of painkillers and shuffled back down into my soggy bed.
This was a day that should have been put out with the bins.

Her smell was drowned; the damp pillow – turned
longways like a door – held *my* sweat and nothing else. I'd
been cuddling it. There was nothing of her left: not even the
indentation of her head. I shouldn't have touched her pillow: I
should have kept it to look at – like a photo.

I swept back the duvet, and on hands and knees, like a
bloodhound, rubbed my nose over the sheet on her side of the
bed. I didn't want her perfume: I wanted to smell her skin, her
real body – when the scent wears off. The sheet smelled of soap
powder only: she had spent just one night on it, days ago.

I picked the phone off the bedside table and tried calling
her again. There was no answer. I threw off my damp t-shirt
and drudged through to the kitchen. It had beer in its air. I
opened a window to allow in the noise of the rain and slumped
down behind the laptop – just in case she had sent an email.
There was nothing. I sat naked, reading some of her old
messages, bringing her closer to me. None of them mentioned
an address or even a town. All ended with: Love, Chiara.

I had to keep busy – the meeting with The Tramp rested

like a headstone at the far end of the day and I didn't fancy chewing on the hours like sticky toffee. The list of phone numbers for all Mr. Prestons in the Birmingham area took a while to write – there were sixty-nine of them. I delayed calling.

The pictures of Mr. Chamberlain's diary were there, sitting in a folder on the screen. I scraped some clothes over my flesh, made a cup of tea, some toast, and started to read them, enlarging each one to a decent size.

His last entry on the day before his death held no hint of what was about to happen to him: he had no inkling, no premonition of his life coming to an abrupt end. The page of his last day on Earth was completely blank – not even his usual morning entry. Was that something?

Other days held plans for the weeks to come – even the mention of a holiday. I started in January, trying to build up a picture of the man.

He wrote a lot. He seemed to like writing – every page filled with small, neat handwriting. Sometimes in between lists of groceries, he would make up a short poem, or a thought – mostly about his wife. He really missed her: his words made an impression in the paper as deep as a chasm. It made me hesitate about *my* feelings of loss: what was six months of intermittent contact with Chiara compared to this man's sixty years of devotion?

Usually he wrote something in the morning: describing the day ahead, then more after lunch, finishing with a summation at the end of the day. I made a note of anything that seemed interesting, weeding his diary for useful information.

Saturday January 28th 2006
My first morning back in Dumfries. I will walk the streets of the old town.
Didn't see anyone I knew. They're probably all dead now.

153

Forty years of changes, the High Street is pedestrianised, but nothing much is different. Strangely, after five minutes, I didn't feel as though I'd ever left. I don't know what I was expecting.

Wednesday 1st February

I'm going up to see if the hotel is still there. I don't have any hope – it's not listed in the phone book.

It's a mess: not much more than a ruin now. The windows are boarded up and it is to be pulled down some time soon. It is hard to think of all those years we spent there. It is sad how it's gone into decline. But I have an idea about visiting again tomorrow.

Thursday 2nd February

It is the first Thursday of the month – when the Market Dance was held. I'm going to recreate the first time we met. I don't care if I'm caught trespassing.

It was sublime. I could feel my dear wife in my arms as we waltzed round that battered old room.

Thursday 2nd March

Market Dance! It feels like forever since last month. At my age I should be happy for time to move so slowly. I'm not. I would happily die the next day for one, real, full night again with my dearest.

The hotel is still standing. I'm going again. This might be my last chance.

Thursday 6th April

Market Dance again. If Scotland win the World Cup someday, it will feel like this. The wind is bitter and showing no sign of dying away.

The phone call from my son last night was a complete surprise. I thought he might have invited me down to stay for a couple of days but he didn't.

Strangely, there was a man standing in the room tonight, watching me dance. I thought he was going to tell me off but he turned and walked away, apologising for disturbing me.

Now why would he have been in the old hotel at that time of night? Seems quite odd – but he did appear pleasant enough.

This was my first meeting with the Waltzing Man. Sanny had believed there were ghosts in the hotel behind his caravan and had asked me to investigate.

Thursday 6th July
Another Market dance for me tonight.
I think it's the right time to get what I'm owed – for my son's sake. I'll visit Sanny this afternoon.

Tuesday 18th July
I've heard the hotel is going to be demolished for certain on Thursday of this week. I've decided to go up tonight for one final time even though it's not Market Dance Day. I can't leave it any later in case they fence it off. The evening suit needs to go to the cleaners. I want to be extra sharp for this one, final dance.

What a shock. I almost died. Goodness knows why he was there. He ran off. I was too scared to stay. I couldn't dance. I don't know what to do.

Why didn't I think of it before? It was so obvious: Mr. Chamberlain was bound to have gone for one last waltz at the old hotel. He had gone two days before the demolition and stumbled upon someone up there – the murderer dumping the body in the cellar. It made sense. If only Mr. Chamberlain had gone inside and freed the man – if the victim was alive at that point.

This had to be the reason for Chamberlain's death. He was a witness and the murderer had come after him.

But why, then, had the killer waited more than a month to kill him?

Wednesday 19th July

I don't feel well. I keep seeing his face. Dreadful. I haven't been out for my paper yet. The sun is shining. It's going to be hot. I don't feel like it but Sanny's moving out to another caravan so I should pay him a visit. Find out what he has to say. I still have the doctor's happy pills from the funeral. I will need them.

I saw the man who startled me in the middle of my waltz all those months ago. He was helping Sanny move. A bit of a coincidence. I saw him in a van driving away with another chap. I tried to put on a brave face.

Thursday 20th July

Sweltering again today. Yesterday equalled the highest temperature recorded for this area. I am sheltering from it this morning and saving up my energy. Going up to hotel to face the demolition. I dread going near that place but I feel I owe it to the building – and it will be daylight this time. Besides, there are bound to be other people watching as well. I have to be fearless – I should be at my age.

It was sad to see the old building go – such a lot of memories. Met that man again and stopped to have a word. He seems to be everywhere I go. He didn't recognise me at first. I always like it when that happens. Now I think on it, I suppose I've always merged into the background.

I found out his name is Jin Johnstone.

I must make the effort to think about the positives of my life and not dwell on the past. I will phone my daughter tonight and ask how her husband is doing.

Two days before his death, Mr. Chamberlain wrote:

Sunday 20th August
Windy and cooler today. Decided to visit Sanny last night.
He did not want to honour our agreement. He was angry and
we did lot of shouting. Two old men bawling away like that – it
wasn't very dignified. We realised that when the police car
stopped. We quickly changed our tune – getting rid of them as
soon as possible. We wouldn't want them prying into our
business. Sanny told me to leave but I'll be back to see him
again. He won't be getting away with this so easily – I owe it to
my son.

I needed to go back and talk to Sanny again. This time he
had to tell me why Mr. Chamberlain had been visiting him and
what their argument was about. And if he remained awkward, I
would tell him I was off the case.

There was one small problem: the police needed to know
Chamberlain had witnessed the murderer stashing the body –
but I couldn't tell them how I knew. It was essential they
received the diary: I might need to enlist Miss Welch's help
again to ensure the family handed it in as soon as possible.

Where had he seen the murderer? Was it outside the hotel,
on his way there, or had Mr. Chamberlain gone inside and
heard something as he was about to start dancing in the room of
his precious memories?

The shock of something else rocked me. Why hadn't I
thought of it before? My hands were shaking as I pulled out the
phone. I looked up the number on the computer and called
through.

'Can you tell me if a Ms Chiara Preston has checked in,
please?'

'I'm sorry, we cannot give out that information.'

I changed my clothes, raced out of the house, revved the engine, and set off.

*

The knock on the door of room 43 sounded hollow. The room of *my* memories. It took an age before Chiara opened it. There was no hint of her usual welcoming smile yet she was more beautiful than ever in her white tailored shirt and jeans. She blocked the way inside.

'Back to the same room, I see.' I tried to sound jolly – my insides were hurting.

'It was the only one available – probably because it's the most expensive.' Her voice was blunt.

She was in her usual hotel, her usual room in The Cairndale. She hadn't left Dumfries: I was clinging onto that fact. 'I'm sorry, Chiara. Really, I am. I want to make up for it. Tell me what I have to do. I'll do anything.'

She didn't reply, her eyes unblinking fixed on my face.

'We can go for a walk,' I tried. 'Do you have your wellies? It's wet out there.'

'You're going to walk like that – in your best suit?'

'My only suit. I wanted to look smart for you. And, do you know what? I found a £10 note down the lining – there's a tiny hole at the bottom of one of the pockets. I blamed an Irish girl for short-changing me in the paper shop ages ago and there it was all the time: hiding in the lining.'

She showed no emotion or interest at my discovery. 'How are you feeling now?' she asked.

'Better.'

There was no invite in. I gave a brief account of what had happened at the hospital and the police station – keeping my voice as low as possible. She seemed indifferent to the news but didn't tell me to stop. I had to break off briefly when someone opened a door behind and walked the length of the corridor to the stairs.

'Are you going to allow me in?' I enquired after finishing. She didn't say anything.

I asked again about a walk. She turned and disappeared from view, the door slowly closing behind her. I thought about putting my foot in its way to halt it, to keep it ajar, to keep my path to her open: but it hadn't been a good idea on Friday at the Chamberlains' home and I didn't bother today. The door didn't shut completely anyway and I waited at its threshold. She had her coat on when it reopened.

We picked up her boots from her car – they were beside the boxes filled with her things. I drove off – no words were exchanged. She didn't ask where we were going.

The drive into the hills lasted forever. I thought of small talk, jokes, and dismissed them all. I used the time to rehearse what needed to be said.

We parked by the side of the road, the reservoir to our right, and fitted into our boots. I tugged an anorak over my suit as we walked to the gate, slid the rusty bolt back, and entered the field, up the hill, in the rain. The grass was short, still scorched and brown from the days of heat of last month. It was slippy. I hesitated in offering my hand: fearing rejection. We struggled up the knoll to where their regal majesties sit in their black glory – small puddles of rain gathering in their laps – and looked out to take in their view over the water to the hills.

These would be my most important words and I cleared my throat to banish the nerves. It didn't work: my voice was edgy, but I managed to hold her eye. 'Out of all the statues, Chiara, this one, the King and Queen, is my favourite. I've never told you that.' I went on quickly, unwilling to allow any silence to build. 'Did you know they had their heads cut off a few years ago? Someone hacked them away with a saw and dumped them in the reservoir down there. I don't know how anyone could do that. I came to see. It was terrible. I couldn't stay. It was like a massacre. They looked awful, eerie, suddenly out of place and pointless. Yet they're only statues.'

She stood still, staring at me. Then she cleared the dribbling rain from her face with the tips of her fingers.

'Their heads were found weeks later,' I went on. 'You can't tell looking at them now. I don't know how they managed to fix them back on so well. There's barely a mark; although you can feel ridges running round.' I stroked a finger against the King's neck to show her.

Chiara shuffled her feet. The rain had darkened and flattened her hair.

'Run your hand round *her* throat and you can feel it.'

She made no move.

'That's been me, Chiara. I have been headless, aimless, pointless without you. Do you see? I've tried to keep busy, but…'

She looked away, down the hill, to the parked car: perhaps signaling the desire to leave.

I kept on, 'You told me this reservoir is one of your favourite places. You discovered it by accident one day, with your father. I thought if I brought you here you might remember the happy times we had. We *were* happy, I'm sure of it. Only last month, over the hill from here, we had our picnic by The Visitation. We *had* fun, didn't we?'

I was running out of things to say; and my voice was leaking desperation. If she moved to walk down the slope, if she turned to walk away, I would have lost everything.

'When I went to the hospital I had my urine in a sandwich bag…'

She looked back at me, staring intently.

'It was part of me but it wasn't *in* me anymore, but they could still tell a lot by analysing the contents of that bag. It's the same with you.' I was stumbling in my brain. The words had sounded a lot better in my head on the drive up here. They had sounded clever. I should never try to sound clever.

'Are you suggesting I'm a bag – or worse?'

She had spoken. It was a start.

Keep going.

'I'm saying that you are inside me even when, eh, you're outside me.' It wasn't the point I wanted to make but I'd forgotten the point.

She shook her head. 'Wouldn't your story be better if you were holding a phial of blood? More dramatic? My blood is your blood.'

'Yes, yes, that's what I'm trying to say, Chiara. I've been running around like a headless chicken without you. My outward actions show my inside feelings – that's what I mean. I am lost if I am not with you. I don't know what to do with myself. I'm trying to say that I'm sorry. I didn't mean it, Chiara. Any of it.'

She looked away. Her silence had returned and was killing.

'How many times do I need to say I'm sorry for what I said? I've explained about the drug and I don't know why you didn't get the text with my new number. I don't know what else I can say.'

When she spoke again her voice was quiet and even, 'We came here in March. We drove to see John the Baptist. What did you ask me then?'

I would never forget: it came from another uncomfortable time. 'I thought you had lured me away from my home so it could be searched. It was too much of a coincidence. I wanted to know the truth. I wanted to know why you were with me.' I hung my head and felt the rain run down the back of my neck. I had a hood on my anorak – I wouldn't be putting it up.

She went on, 'You don't like coincidences: they are signs. That was one of the first things you said to me. I hear your voice in my head every time I'm confronted by one. They are everywhere. Room 43 was the only one free yesterday – you probably think that's a sign too.'

'Isn't it?'

She shook her head. 'Everything started to happen to you after we met – that's what you said. Before then your life was calm – no-one tried to kill you. There were no murders in your easy life – not until I arrived.'

'Again, I apologise for saying that, Chiara. You have to know it was the drug doing the talking: the hospital will confirm it soon enough. The urine. Asa made sure there were plenty of samples. I didn't know what I was saying, Chiara.'

'You didn't say anything that wasn't true.'

'What? No, I said a lot of things that weren't true.'

'You weren't wrong.'

'What are you saying?'

'Everything you said was absolutely correct.'

'But it's not *you* who's to blame.'

'All those uncertainties about me had to be *within* you – you wouldn't have thought them otherwise. Like your valued urine, if you like – within you and then released.'

'I should never have uttered any of it. I believe in coincidences now: they are echoes from another time. I should never have blamed you.'

'I *am* to blame for everything.'

'What?'

'I am to blame.'

I shook my head. 'I don't understand. What are you telling me, Chiara?'

'Your suspicions were right from the start.'

'No, don't say that.'

She began to walk away from me, back down the hill. I chased after.

'I don't think we should be together,' she said.

I raced in front. I couldn't see her face properly – huddled into her coat, the upturned collar reaching her cheeks, her hair stuck across her eyes.

'We *have* to be together,' I pleaded, and then I slipped, landing on my backside, sliding a few feet down the slope.

She stopped and looked down at me. 'I think I am a catalyst: something that sparks your life into chaos. It is better if we don't see each other – then you'll be safe again. I think it is for the best.'

She scraped some hair from her face. I saw the strength of her eyes. I lifted myself up and faced her. 'Don't say that. I never want that. Don't do this to me. I can't be without you.'

The King and Queen loomed over her shoulder.

'I've spent the last few days going round in circles,' I said. 'I can't function properly without you. I say one thing and do the other. And I'm hardly drinking, as well.'

'Jin, you never bothered with women before me. You can go back to your old ways. This will wear off.' The gentleness had returned to her voice. 'In the end, you'll be happier – you'll see.'

'I won't. This is different – it's always been different. I don't know why but I need you, Chiara. Tell me to give up everything else – and I'll do it. *This* is what I want. I thought you wanted it too. We put in all that work into the house so we could live there. Together. Only the other day you said you were selling up to move closer. It can't end now. What about love?'

'Love is an excuse for people to treat each other badly.'

'But I won't treat you badly, Chiara. You're on par with The Queens – honest.'

'That much, eh?'

I nodded vigorously.

Her mouth broke into the most glorious of smiles. I wanted a picture of it – to enlarge it to the size of a bed and curl up and sleep in it.

'And you're not worried about your safety?' she asked.

163

'What's so great about being safe when you're completely miserable?'

She eased herself down the slope. I followed on. 'The Tramp will be locked up tonight. He'll be no threat. It'll be over.'

'What are you talking about?'

There had been no time to tell her everything. I started to explain as we headed for the car. She listened. I found it difficult to concentrate – my trousers were sticking and mucky and I wanted to kiss her so much.

I threw my anorak in the boot, wiped some paper hankies across the back of my trousers, before getting in.

She said, 'And the other murder – the Waltzing Man – will that not lead you into trouble? It could turn out just as risky if you pursue it.'

'I won't do it. I'll stop – if it means you'll come back.'

'What about Onion Sanny – are you willing to let him down?'

'I can't be responsible for everyone and everything, Chiara. The police will get the answers. I might not be able to do much for him in any case. Look, if you asked me to move to Gretna and support the local team there, I would do it.'

'I think that's called upping the ante.'

I tried a Humphrey Bogart impersonation – her favourite actor, 'Whatever it takes, baby.'

She shook her head, a smile dancing again on her lips. 'Do you know what attracted me to you at the beginning?'

'I offered to buy you a drink? Asa says I don't do it nearly often enough – but he's wrong.'

'No, it was the fact that you looked out for people. I liked that you didn't always charge for helping. I will always like that.'

I didn't turn the ignition key. I looked straight ahead. 'Where are we now then, Chiara? Tell me what I have to do.'

'There is one thing.'

'Anything.'

'Are you sure?'

'Certain.'

'Okay then. If you agree to this, then maybe, maybe…'

'Just say it.'

'I have to make all the decision involving your work.'

I shook my head. 'I don't follow.'

'Take Friday – you asked me if you should look into the Waltzing Man case and I said yes. That's what I'm talking about. You have to run everything past me first and then accept my decision – whether it matches your own opinion or not. Do we have a deal?'

'You want complete control over me?'

'Yes.'

I reached out my hand – and we shook.

She went on, 'Then the first thing is to decide on whether you should meet up with The Tramp tonight.'

'I'm not sure that's a decision for me: it depends on what the police say.'

'They can't put you in danger without your consent.'

'You don't think I should – that it's too risky?'

'No, I think you have to.'

*

I'd been putting it off – I knew that. The moment Miss Welch told me that my aunt was in hospital, I should have been on my way up to see her – but I hadn't. I could say I hated hospitals and always did the most to avoid them – which was true but it wasn't the reason. Sadly, it appeared, I was more interested in helping other families than helping my own.

We walked into the room like a couple. There were three other beds, all empty – two had been made up, while the other, by the window, was untidy.

My Aunt May sat propped up in front of three bulbous

pillows. Her face was thinner: it dragged her wrinkles deeply down into her cheeks. She stared into space. The moment she saw us approach, she sparked into life, producing a grin wide enough to dam her furrows. It was the greatest welcome she had ever given me. Her dead eyes had transformed into sparkles in an instant. It made me feel all the more guilty. I introduced Chiara.

'And she is…?' my aunt asked me, with the audacity of age.

For a moment I didn't know what to say. 'She's, she's my girlfriend,' I stuttered. I wasn't actually sure if that was right: it felt I was on trial.

My aunt stared at Chiara, directing her words to her, 'We were never quite sure about him. I don't think he ever had one single girl all the way through his twenties – or even a married one, come to that.' My aunt showed great pleasure in her comment, tapping the side of her head to signify that she still had her marbles.

She went on, 'That's when men are at their most potent, you know, at that age. We thought he was still a virgin.'

I jumped in quickly, 'You're lucky to have a ward to yourself.' She had never talked that way before. It was completely out of character.

'That one died this morning.' She pointed to the unmade bed.

I looked over. It seemed the occupant still had rights to it: it didn't belong to anyone else yet. The same as if they had simply gone to the toilet.

'What are the doctors saying? What's the problem?' I asked.

'Pass me my specs, Jin, could you?' She motioned to the cabinet beside her bed. I handed them over.

She appraised Chiara like an art dealer checking the validity of a new painting. 'My, oh, my, this is a beautiful girl you have here, Jin. How did you manage that?' She turned to Chiara, 'We were never sure about him: thought he might have both feet in the other camp.'

Chiara nodded. 'Secret Gretna supporter, you mean?' She glanced in my direction and tried to wink. She didn't quite pull it off: it looked like something was stinging her eye.

I jumped in again, 'When are they letting you out, do you know?'

My aunt turned back to me. 'It's all being arranged. The doctor will speak to you about it. I need you to do something for me. They'll explain. I said you wouldn't mind. You do that – help people. That's what I'm told. Who'd have thought you'd be helping *me*. I never wanted it but now I'm forced.'

It was possible her association with Miss Welch might explain this acerbic change in her. I asked, 'What is it you want me to do?'

She replied, 'Did you never think it was a strange name – Jin? Although come to think of it, Chiara is quite odd as well. Is that how you say it – like the ch in chastity?'

'It was my mother's middle name: she was born in Argentina,' Chiara said.

That was something else I didn't know.

Chiara took on her comment, 'I thought his name was something to do with the drink.' She laughed.

'Are you implying, young lady, that his mother, my sister, was drunk on the stuff the night he was conceived?'

What was wrong with Aunt May? I cut in again, 'I thought it was a mistake at the christening or something. I was meant to be called Jim.'

Chiara added, apparently unperturbed by my aunt, 'Or they thought he was going to be a girl and his name was Jan.'

It wasn't a helpful comment. I hoped my face registered the fact. But Chiara went on in spite of it, 'Horatio Nelson's daughter was called Horatia. Do you see?'

I didn't and my aunt shook her head dramatically. 'He would never have been christened. Never. His mother wouldn't have allowed it. She was too scared.'

What was going on here?

She continued quickly, fixing me through her specs, 'But, in a way, you're right. You're right about the mistake. Your name is a corruption of two words: James and Sin. My sister, your mother, told me that.'

I wasn't sure if I'd heard her properly. 'What?'

She looked beyond me. 'Here's the doctor now, dear. Do as she says, will you? It needs to be arranged.' Her peculiar smile lingered like a smell of cabbage water in a cosmetic department.

The doctor led us along the corridor. Chiara laid a hand on my arm and whispered, 'What was that about – James and Sin?'

I gave an unconvincing shrug of a reply and continued walking.

We followed the doctor into a small room: her name was Milharti. She was younger than me and her smile was bright and full. She had as many teeth as years.

'She looks much worse than the last time I saw her,' I started. 'She's been getting very frail over the last few weeks. And she's been quite lewd today – that's not like her.'

The doctor nodded.

The news was not good. Recent tests had shown the illness to be in an advanced state. She would be transferred to the Oncology ward later today for assessment, but it had already been deemed impractical for her to undergo any form of invasive treatment. I was familiar with the procedure: the ward was where my mother had ended.

The doctor said there was still a good chance of my aunt getting home in the next few days providing an appropriate care package could be put in place and if the house was suitable. We discussed what was needed.

I would set up a bedroom on the ground floor, and as her house was identical to mine, there was a downstairs toilet to use. For her safety, she wouldn't be allowed up the stairs: they would be blocked off.

Then the doctor asked me some questions – mainly to see how much help I was willing to give – and we left her sitting in the small room, along with my mobile phone number.

When we returned to her bedside, my aunt was sleeping. I woke her with a light shake to her shoulder – any harder and it might have broken a bone. She gave us details of what she expected to be in her room and was adamant about having her own bed moved down. I couldn't argue with that.

I took her key, telling her I would do everything she wanted. My mother had never made it out of hospital to the home that was ready and waiting.

When we emerged from hospital, Chiara said, 'I can see you're not happy about this right now. It's not a good time, I know – not with tonight looming… Why don't we leave the house until tomorrow?'

It wasn't the moving of furniture that was bothering me. 'I'd rather do it now – while I'm able,' I replied.

*

I turned the key in the front door. We had been quiet in the car. When she asked again about my aunt's comment, I told her I didn't want to discuss anything about my name right now. We stepped in. This was going to be very difficult for Chiara: other people's houses make her extremely uncomfortable and stepping into an empty house always feels so much worse.

'Are you sure you want to go in here? I can get one of the lads to help later on when they come round.'

She took in a steadying breath of air: her chest lifting. 'No, we have to make a start and get the bed down ready for her: that's the most important thing. You can't be doing this

169

later: there are other important things to be seen to, don't forget.'

'Oh, I haven't forgotten.' The day was a large cage: no matter where I roamed its bars held me in, waiting. And they shut out tomorrow.

'Okay, we do the bed together, but then you go, Chiara. I can sort out the rest of the furniture for the room myself. There'll be things downstairs that can be used and I'll have it ready for the social worker's inspection tomorrow.'

I couldn't remember ever being upstairs in my aunt's house – perhaps when I was young – but the hairs stood up on the back of my neck as I entered her bedroom. I felt a panic. Chiara was breathing rapidly as well; although she might have been coping better.

We stripped the bed and hauled the mattress to one side. The place felt haunted. The frame clattered off each step on the way down. We didn't care. We hurried back up. The mattress slid most of the way. We shoved it into the room. Panic had overwhelmed us.

'I have to go,' I said. 'I can't stay here.'

She nodded an understanding. We left the bed in the middle of the front sitting room, and ran.

'You're getting as bad as me,' she said, with a valiant smile, as we raced along the pavement. 'I thought it was only me who felt like that in other people's houses.'

We reached our home.

'I don't usually – not as bad as that anyway. Maybe there's been a recurrence from the drug. That might happen – I'll need to ask the doctor.'

There was another possible reason and it was to do with my uncle, Aunt May's husband. *His* name was James.

She wanted to wash as soon as we entered our home.

'I bought new shower gel yesterday,' I said. 'I'd like you to use it. It's unperfumed. I want to smell your skin – if I may.'

She tapped a finger against her lips, her breathing had returned to normal and she slid the other hand over the surfaces of the kitchen – like patting a dog. 'In that case I have an idea but I'll need to visit the supermarket first.'

*

I heard the shower stop. I waited. It was more than ten minutes before she called me through to the bedroom. She was lying naked on the bed: splayed. The tray sat on the table beside the clock. The scents of citrus and sweet fruits hung, suspended in the room's air like perfumed humming birds.

She said, her voice as soft as a ripe peach, 'Let's see what you can do with all the practice you've had. This one is simple – and a good lesson for you to remember.

I will call out a fruit and you have to find where I've rubbed it on my skin – with your tongue. We'll start with lime.'

I was a bloodhound again, on my hands and knees. I found the lime on the point of her left elbow. I gave it a lick. It reminded me of a cocktail I once had at a barbeque.

'Apple,' she said softly.

It was in the palm of her right hand. I saw a pair of gloves on the floor by the side of the bed. Ever the one for thoroughness, she'd taken every effort to avoid contamination. I tasted the apple and looked towards the tray. It was a Granny Smith. I was surprised: she likes Cox.

Slowly she spoke and sighed as I licked and tasted. Pineapple lay in the crease at the back of her knee. I had to flip her over for raspberry: it was on her left buttock. The right one held the scent of melon – I kept that in mind.

I found each one in turn. There was a clearly defined path, a route-map. Her voice was becoming slighter, lower.

'Lemon… Pear… Melon… Orange… Raspberry… Melon… Sloe Berry… Raspberry… Melon Blackcurrant… Cherry… Raspberry… Melon… Sloe Berry… Cherry… Strawberry… Cherry… Sloe… Strawberry… Cherry… Sloe…

171

Strawberry… Cherry… Slower… Strawberry… Slower…
Strawberry… Strawberry… Strawberry… Strawberry… Slow.'

*

The rain was the wet kind, the clingy stuff that soaks
through in minutes. I stood in front of the fountain. I had my
umbrella up – the police said it was okay, but I had to hold it
aloft, my face visible. It strained my arm: I'd been here for a
long time.

The clock on the Midsteeple had practically stopped,
grinding to a near halt: it had taken half an hour for the last
three minutes to pass by. The High Street was deserted, its
cobbles glistening.

Four minutes to go.

I wasn't so sure The Tramp would show. Now I was here,
my certainty had diluted further: it *had* to be too dicey for him.
He must know I would go to the police.

Chisel had achieved something – Ed's tone had been
different today and they were taking no chances – I was wired
up with a microphone sticking onto the skin of my chest,
hidden under my long sleeved shirt. I had to tell them the
moment The Tramp appeared – always erring on safety, never
allowing him to get close.

The policemen, in their cars, were hidden away. I didn't
know where or how many: they wouldn't say, leaving us all in
the dark. My amateur back-up team of Asa and Chisel were
stationed in a car, along The Whitesands, and Hoogah with his
partner, Sir Veillance, sat in an engine-running motor in The
Cairndale car park. I had my walkie-talkie in my jacket pocket.
I might not need to use it: the police seemed to have everything
covered.

Ed had made a joke at the meeting when I'd asked about
taking a brolly. He said someone had hidden a gun there once,
taped to the spokes and, although his body had been searched,
the umbrella hadn't – and the man had pulled it out and shot. At

least, I think it was a joke: other people in the room had laughed. I couldn't see the relevance of the story.

I scanned each street in turn. It just needed the word from me and the square would be surrounded. There was still no sign.

I heard voices. Two people came into view, walking past the Midsteeple, arm in arm – a man and a woman heading for home. We had talked about this. They couldn't bar anyone from walking through – it wasn't practical and The Tramp would pick up on it – so if I spotted anyone I had to pretend to be passing through as well and not remain suspiciously stationary.

I headed towards them. She had her brolly up and he was attempting to shelter under it – but she held it too low and its edges bounced off the side of his head. He split away from her, walking out with the contact area. She shot him a look, and the twitch of her shoulders relayed her unhappiness at the distance between them.

They gave me a glance, the man offered a nod of the head, and a sharp 'Aye' – we were comrades of the night – and they continued on by. I slowed to a stop and waited, before doubling back, watching the couple's progress. They continued to walk on.

I returned to my original position between the fountain and the book shop and waited. It was after one. There were policemen sitting in their cars, possibly half a mile away, wishing they were in their beds. If The Tramp didn't show, they might not believe my story: they might think I had made it all up, and was wasting police time once again.

I heard a noise: a scrape like a file across metal. It sounded again. I edged towards it, to the corner with Bank Street. I jumped in alarm. In the dull light of a street lamp, The Tramp stood round the corner, in his big coat and hood, a long-bladed knife held out in front. He beckoned me with it.

173

'Go,' I whispered into my chest.

He looked exactly the same. The expectant smell of him made my stomach turn over. I should run now. The police will be here any second. There will be no sirens. Drop the umbrella and run. But something stopped me.

I saw the hole in the road where the manhole cover had been pushed to one side. I saw the gaping black chasm leading down into the roots of the town.

'This way,' he said. Only his mouth showed from the darkness of his hood. I couldn't see his eyes.

A million intertwining thoughts passed through. If I run, they won't catch him. He'll escape and slip back down into the depths. My friends will be in danger. He will come after them. How will I feel then? I have the chance to stop him now. I can end this. Where is Chiara to tell me what to do?

'Hurry up,' he shouted.

I walked towards him. Slowly.

'Drop the umbrella. Put your hands up.'

I did.

'Stop.'

I was three yards from him – too far to leap.

'Take off your jacket and throw it down.'

'My keys are in it.'

'Doesn't matter.'

I did as he wanted – and heard the walkie-talkie in the pocket clatter against the ground.

'Turn slowly – all the way round.'

I did.

'Put your hands out in front of you. Walk towards me.'

I could still run. I'll be faster than him. The cobbles are wet, slippery – I would need to be careful. I moved forward, hands out, almost in prayer. He threw a rope over. It was a noose. He yanked sharply, almost pulling me off my feet. The rope tightened round my forearms. 'I've a good hold of you and it's away from your bandages.' He tied the other end round his waist as though he was the anchor in a tug-of-war team. 'I'll go first and I'll be waiting for you at the bottom. Don't try anything stupid. I have a knife. Climb down the rungs when I shout.' He stepped down into the hole.

'Don't you want to know about the man?' *Stall him.*

'Later.'

'I can give you his name: I found him for you.' But I knew I couldn't utter the name – it would put Don's life in danger again.

'Later, I said. You wait until I tug on the rope. Don't try anything. If you try to escape, I'll be coming after you and your friends. Remember that.'

'Wait,' I urged. 'Don't you want to know how I found him – and you couldn't?'

'You're wasting time.'

He disappeared from view. I heard his boots grind against each rung. There was no sign of the police. I gave a harsh call into the microphone on my chest. Would they hear me underground? No-one had mentioned it. This might be the last chance.

I went on, louder this time, 'He's taking me into the sewer – top of Irish Street. I have to go. My hands are tied. He's tugged for me to go. I need to go down there. I don't see what else I can do.'

I eased into the blackness. A horrendous odour greeted me as my head left the street level behind. My hands clasped the slippy, smelly rungs of the metal ladder.

He was waiting for me at the bottom. It was dark. He flicked on a torch and shone it straight into my eyes and then onto the binding, making sure it was still secure, and back to my face. It wasn't easy to line him up – which hand was the torch in? If I lunged now I might miss my target. How easily will it be to fight with arms tied? This is not the time.

175

'Did you pull the cover over?'

'No. What difference does it make?'

'Get back up there and do it,' he rasped.

My body was heavy to heave up, difficult with the hands together. I felt hot. I poked my head out, thinking there would be a pair of police boots facing me. There were none. I dragged the cover over: making the black blacker.

He hauled hard on the rope – it pulled my hands away. I lost grip, my shoes slipped in the damp and I clattered the length of the ladder, flaying to grab on, my chin smacking off a wet rung, jarring teeth against teeth. More dentist work needed. I landed heavily. It knocked the stinking wind out of my lungs. The knife jagged into my side and I groaned.

He patted the pockets of my trousers. 'What's that?'

'My phone.'

'Show me.'

He stepped back to allow me to straighten. With difficulty, I pulled it from my pocket and held it out.

'You can keep it: it won't work down here. And that?'

I pulled out my penknife.

'Drop it. What else is there?'

I took my time, showing him everything I had. The manhole cover will be pushed aside any second now and help will come. He allowed me to keep everything else, but kicked the penknife away into the corners of the dark.

He rammed another foul cloth into my mouth and slapped tape over: I felt the sharp point of the blade against my chest: piercing clothing, perhaps drawing blood. 'So you can't spit it out. Now get a move on.' He shoved me ahead of him. The ceiling was low. I hobbled on, bent over, the sewer air filling my lungs. No-one had come to save me: there was no sound from above.

The stench was overpowering but it didn't mask the evil taste of the rag against my tongue. I covered my nose with the sleeve of my shirt.

'Down this one to the right. Hurry.'

He climbed down another long ladder first and then
pushed me on, to keep me moving. His torchlight was erratic: it
was difficult to see where we were going. We were paddling
through black water, bent, the tunnel no more than five feet
high. I held my hands out to one side to steady myself. The
brick walls were slimy. I touched mush with the back of my
hand. From the domed ceiling, slimy, weedy growths hung and
brushed against my head like oily fingers.

That was it, I'd missed my chance: the moment he'd
climbed down into the sewer I should have jumped in, feet first,
my entire weight landing on his head, knocking him down,
thumping into his exposed body, knocking him cold. I could
have overpowered him. That was then – and now it had gone. I
cursed.

We turned into a smaller tunnel. I had to bend further. I
was trudging through muck: my shoulders and head scraping.
We turned again, and again. I lost my sense of direction. Water
flows downhill: we were following it, towards the river.

For ages more, I struggled on, crawling sometimes, my
face inches from the dirt. If I slowed there was the jab of the
blade. There was no room in here for a fight. It would have to
wait. There would be a time.

'Into the left. Here!'

Another tunnel broke to one side. It was lower and I was
down again on all fours to pass through, my hands squidging
into mounds of filth – difficult to crawl with arms held
together. The police won't find us in here. They won't risk
sending anyone in: they won't have the right equipment. It will
take time to gather and arrange. I was on my own.

I crept on, breathless, forcing in large swells of soiled air
through my nose: my legs and back aching under the
awkwardness.

'Turn in here.'

It broke into a room, tall enough to straighten, but little more than an alcove. His torch beam picked out a mound of rubbish in one corner: newspapers, bags, a couple of bottles. I thought I saw a rat's tail as it dashed away.

'Turn round slowly.'

I was bent, hands on thighs, sweat dripping, breathing hard, exhausted. He flashed the light into my face and down my length.

'You're a mess. There's a method, you know, stops you acting like a human pipe cleaner.' His hood had fallen back, but his face was in darkness. In a moment he'd lit a candle and its light pushed the murk to one side. He stood, hood adjusted, like the Grim Reaper: the darkness of his face intensified. 'Pull the tape away. You say you've found him – the man I want?'

I nodded. He edged closer with the knife held out in front. I ripped away at my mouth and spat out the rag. It landed in the dirt.

'It goes back in your gob after you tell me,' he said.

I was pinned against the wall – frightened and brave at the same time. I tried to spit away the obnoxious taste but my mouth was completely dry. I said, 'Give me a moment more to rest.'

He stood immobile.

My body eased, the breathing slowed. I looked up. 'Nice place you have – although some pot-pourris wouldn't go amiss. Is that safe down here?' I nodded towards the naked flame. 'With all the gases?'

His voice was firm. 'I want to know about the man.'

'I found him, yes.' I'd faced madmen before.

The hood nodded: he might have been impressed. 'Who is he then?'

I straightened further. 'If I tell you will you leave my friends alone? They have to be left alone.' I spoke again before he could answer, 'Do you live down here?' Keep him off guard.

He delayed, as if deciding whether to answer or not. 'Sometimes.' His voice sounded weary.

'Are you homeless? I might be able to help.'

'I don't need your help,' he shouted back. Then he paused, reflected, 'Except for this man. Tell me where I can find him.'

'How do you stand the smell?'

He took a deep breath, his voice returning to friendly again. 'What's not to like? And I think you should know no-one's going to come looking for you: so there's no point in delaying.'

'But to sleep here…'

'It has its plus points: you don't have to go far in the middle of the night for the toilet.' He inched nearer and shouted, 'Now for the last time, *who is he?*'

Some of my courage ebbed away. My hands were shaking and my mouth stayed as dry as sand. He's going to kill me and leave me face down in the waste. Food for rats. My voice wavered, it was difficult to speak, 'I could make up… any name. How would… you know?'

My skin itched; it ran with perspiration. I had no option but to attack him. It was me or him. He had no intention of allowing me to go free. The shaking made it difficult. Draw in air. Easy now. No hurried movements. It has to be slow. My arms hung in front, tied. They wouldn't stop trembling. I have to do this now. He won't let me live.

Reaching under the left cuff of my long sleeved shirt with my right hand, I felt the popper with my fingertips and flicked it open with my nail. The knife slid into my palm. I'd practiced this again and again in front of my bedroom mirror.

The seamstress had made an upside down pocket, held shut by a stud, inside the cuffs of all the clothing I'd handed in.

The one in my jacket held my father's old switchblade – that would have been better, but it was lying in the street, a long way off, above head height, somewhere far away. This one held a modeling knife, bought yesterday, along with the batteries, in the hardware store. It wasn't as good – but it would do the job – it would puncture his foul body.

From the very start, as soon as my memory returned, I knew I had to be ready to defend myself. My protection was my responsibility: experience has shown that the threat never goes without a struggle. It had to be done.

'You can say any name,' he said, 'but if I find it's the wrong person, I will come back for you or someone else, someone you care about. Why would you want that on your hands?'

His hand with the knife was shaking. 'Give me the name!' he bawled at the top of his voice.

'What's to stop you attacking me as soon as I tell you?' That's right, he *could* do that. He could say I was free to go and then stab me in the back. He's not to be trusted.

He was breathing heavily now. 'You have my word. I will let you leave.' He untied the rope around his waist and let the end drop: his hands remaining outstretched. 'You see, I am freeing you and I will escort you from here. I wouldn't want to you get lost and have to drink the water to stay alive.' He gave an unconvincing laugh.

Could I believe him, this crazy man? Could I give him Don Gardiner's name? A man I hardly knew. A man I'd met only on a handful of occasions. What was the problem – if it saved my friends? Aren't *they* more important? Give it and this is over.

But it would be like putting him on a death list. The problem had to disappear. The Tramp had to disappear. *I have to use my knife.* I have to charge at him, take him by surprise, and drive my blade through his wretched heart. Two hands. It is good they're locked together: two is better than one. Drive it in hard and fast when he's off-guard.

I hesitated. I was becoming increasingly jittery: my body juddering. 'Tell me what... you want... from him ... what you... intend to do... to him.'

In the candlelight I saw his hood shake. His head poked forward slightly and his mouth was visible. There was sweat dripping from his beard. He shouted, 'That is between him and me! It's no-one else's business!'

It has to be done. Don't waste time. *Stab him.*

'As a... show of... faith... why don't... you give me... your knife. Then... I will... feel safe.'

He laughed. 'You want me to be defenceless?'

'You... give me... the knife. Then... I'll know... you won't... attack me... and... I'll be able... to leave.'

'You *will* be safe. I'm telling you. *I* don't end people's lives. But I'm keeping the knife.' He took another step closer and yelled, 'This is wasting time! Is that what you're after? Hoping the police will find us? It won't happen! There is no sound. Listen! You'd hear them long before they arrive. They won't find us. You're making me angry. I try not to be angry. Tell me what I need to know!'

He took another step. He didn't know I had a knife. 'Tell me!' he screamed.

I sank to my knees in front of him as though in prayer. He couldn't be trusted. My toes were curled under, ready to spring, my hands in front, pleading, turning the knife round, carefully in my palm, to blade first – all my force to be channeled into one, hideously thin, shard of metal.

Drop the hands. Feel the button on the edge. Slide out the blade with the thumb. All the way.

'Don't... hurt me... Please don't... hurt me.' Tears welled up and ran from my eyes. I was crying for the pain I would inflict. 'Please... let me... go... please.'

I couldn't do this. I couldn't plunge it in: to hear and feel it grind on bone, and slice through arteries, into his blood.

I looked up.

He said, 'You had your chance…'

I leapt straight at him, my legs springing. My hands lunging up and ahead of me. The power surged through this thin, thin blade. Only the handle stopped the knife travelling the whole way through his heart. He clattered backwards against the wall, his knife dropped from his hand, and then his torch. There was blood oozing through his clothes. He was silent, shocked.

Finish him off! Stab him again!

I grasped the torch. He was gasping, his arms across his chest.

Shove it in again. He deserves it. Look at what he has done to you.

My hand weakened. I let my knife fall. I heard it clatter. What had come over me? I wasn't meant to do this ever in my life. I wasn't here to kill anyone. I ran in panic.

I had no idea where I was going. I headed in the direction of the flow, splashing through, bent double, scrambling, turning into every opening big enough to fit. I couldn't stop to see if he was following.

I paddled through excreta. It splashed up. I tripped and fell, my head diving under the mess. I was coughing and spluttering. I saw a ladder and started to climb up. My grip was weak – one hand on the torch. My foot slipped. I fell to the bottom. Unbelievably, I expected his hand on my shoulder. It couldn't happen: I'd punctured his heart.

I dared to flash the beam back along the tunnel. It was empty. I climbed again. I knew I had time: I knew he wouldn't be after me. I stopped to rest: hoping the shaking would subside.

Where was I? My arms were tied together. What was I

doing here? It was a sewer – but why?

Find a way out! Free yourself.

I stumbled on. The pipe sloped downwards: the water was moving quickly – rainwater from the drains. It was clean water: it had fallen from the fresh air of the skies. It sought the quickest way out of the dark. The flow was strong: the torrent swept my feet away. I started to slide. No grip for fingers in the smooth tube. On my back, skimming down – like on the flume at the old swimming pool.

In a whoosh I was clear of the pipe. I was in mid-air, the rain hitting my face. I was falling. I smacked into the river and went under. The current was strong: it pulled me down. It didn't want me here. I fought to the surface, thrashing with my arms and legs. I was in the Nith – and it was running hard with days of rain.

I passed under the suspension footbridge; the river's power sweeping me out into the middle. I needed to find something to cling on to. I shouted for help. My head went under again and water poured into my open mouth. I was choking. Back on top, kicking with all my might, hands all but useless together. Still tied. Why were they tied? I dropped the torch.

It was better: I was gaining a rhythm with my legs. They were pushing me closer to the side. A flow of water suddenly caught and carried me, bashing me against a side wall. I fumbled and held onto a protruding lump of stone. I looked up. The wall was high: too high to climb out.

There is a way out down at the Dock Park: there is a patch of grass there. I could let go and hope to reach it. But I couldn't be sure: I might be swept down the middle of the river, never to find an escape.

The Nith tugged but my grip on the wall was firm. I pulled myself closer, tight as a ball, and found a foothold below water level. It was a small hole and I jammed a foot in. I yelled for help. I bit at the rope. It tasted bad. The wet had stretched it. I held it in my teeth and ease it out. It loosened.

For a second I was clinging on with one hand as the rope slipped over a wrist, then the other hand broke free and I flicked it away. Clasping with one hand again, I shuffled and pulled my phone from my pocket. Please still be working.

The phone lit. Modern technology. It was difficult to find his number. I clung onto the wall with one hand and a couple of fingers. I should have kept the voice activation system. I shouted at the machine, 'Asa!' I couldn't risk bringing it up to my ear.

He was stationed in The Whitesands – not far away. I knew he was there. I knew that, I knew lots of things: but not why I had been tied.

I shouted above the roar of the water. 'Help me. I'm in river... just below... the suspension bridge. Help!' There might have been a reply.

I shoved the phone in my mouth, unwilling to risk replacing it in a pocket. He wouldn't be long. I held on. There had to be a reason for this: I knew I had to meet The Tramp. He must have done this to me – and I'd escaped. Somehow, I'd broken free.

Asa's face was above me. He shouted something, I couldn't hear above the roar of the water. I couldn't shout back: the phone was in my mouth.

An orange ring landed beside me. I leapt for it and hung on. I was pulled against the flow, upstream. I clung on. They were high above me – both of them – pulling on the rope, dragging me to safety.

I reached a step. Asa yanked me from the water and I lay gasping on the wet cement like a freshly guddled salmon.

Monday 28th August

I heard her enter the sitting room but kept my eyes shut. One curtain was swept aside and her weight dented the sofa where I lay. 'Why don't you come to bed?' she asked, patting my arm delicately.

'It wouldn't feel right.' My lids dragged open over rough eyes and I saw her kind, courageous smile. 'I don't feel I can, Chiara. It's not fair for you to have to put up with it.'

'You've bathed, showered and bathed again – you're fine.'

'I don't feel fine. There's the taste of the dirt in my mouth, in the back of the throat, and the reek is everywhere. I don't feel clean enough.'

The stench was still within, coating the tunnels inside from nose to stale lungs. When the time came to kiss her I needed to be enveloped in her gorgeous fragrance, the blissful smell of her skin: I would not have it associated with this filth. I wasn't going to soil our bed.

And I had killed a man. I had destroyed myself as I had destroyed him. I had lost my mind: it wasn't up to me to decide who lived and who did not. I had no right. I had overstepped the boundary. I never thought I would. I had changed – for the worse. He had threatened me – that was all. I could have defended myself, attacked him, punched him, thrown him to one side to escape. Nothing more than that.

'I'll buy a paddling pool,' Chiara said, 'Every home should have one. Do you think that might help?'

I nodded. At some point she would need to know the truth about me: I hadn't struck in self-defence. It hadn't been a response of equal force.

'Your phone buzzed earlier.' She held it out.

'Still working? Didn't know it was waterproof.' Simple conversation seemed silly, pointless – but what else was there now?

I checked the message. 'It's from Asa. He says we need to talk.'

'Maybe they've captured The Tramp.'

'Maybe.' I knew he was dead – but I had told them I wasn't sure.

'Although, wouldn't he have phoned if they had, rather than send a text?'

'Hard to say: it might not be deemed important enough.' I gave a pathetic smile and she returned a kiss to the cheek.

'You smell good enough to me.' She raised her brows, playfully.

I hauled myself into a sitting position. I wanted to curl up and be left – but there was a new day to face. It would be expected. I had lost myself: I couldn't afford to lose the people who were willing to stand by me.

'I'll come with you to the paddling pool shop,' I muttered. 'I've missed my golf anyway today.'

*

I sat in my car, round the corner from the police station, forehead against the steering wheel. The radio was off and the rain pattered on the roof. I looked up and saw Asa's large frame coming into view, hurrying. He scanned behind him a couple of times as he rushed along the pavement. The car sunk on its springs as he entered. He grunted a sharp, 'Aye', without opening his mouth. I drove off. He bent to re-tie both shoe laces, his face hidden for a while as we passed police headquarters.

Hoogah stood in the playground in the rain, pupils milling around his feet. They were once us – not much has changed. The raggle-taggle plastic blinds in the windows of the school building looked the same. He nodded in our direction, marched over, and climbed in, saying nothing.

Tread looked out of the showroom window: he had been

keeping watch. He grabbed a jacket off a chair on the way out and slipped into the back seat. He held a new car smell on his clothes.

Chisel, talking to a man with a big camera, outside his office building, leaning against a wall, sheltered by the overhang, saw us, nodded, and made an immediate apology to the man. He squeezed in and was silent.

It was a squash for my wee car – the first words came from Tread, complaining about sitting in the middle at the back and having no room for his legs. His head filled the view from my mirror. No-one answered him – we each had a window to look out.

*

'The news is not good,' Asa said, both his big hands holding the coffee mug on the table, cradling it in the way of a woman. 'There's been a search of the sewer system but there's no sign of him.'

Everyone looked in my direction. They weren't sure how to approach me. They needed me to say something. I replaced my mug of tea on the table. Supping hot drinks in The Bruce – who would have thought?

'He's alive then?' There was a flush of relief through me. 'Was there a trail of blood to follow?' I asked, my eyes still cast downwards, not willing to fix on any faces yet.

'No blood found – none at all,' Asa replied. 'From the description you gave, we definitely have the right place. He wasn't there – and nothing to indicate the direction he took. We've lost him for now. He's able to get about. We know what that means.'

Hoogah said, 'Maybe he's too badly injured to come after us.'

I couldn't tell at this moment if they blamed me for the situation. I shot glances round the table – flitting from one face to the other. They were tired and drawn.

Hoogah pinched holes out of his napkin using a thumb and forefinger. Tread stirred the sugar into his cup, round and round. We hadn't discussed last night – I hadn't told them what I did, how I felt. There had been no time. Maybe I didn't need to now.

The police had arrived after I was pulled from the river – and the boys had slipped into the background, aware that their presence would not be well received. Through the next few hours I was questioned, examined, given injections and patched up. My memory returned, like walking backwards out of mist, and I told them they should be glad I'd had a bath in the river first.

The Tramp had not been seen by anyone else – not even on CCTV. They said I had walked out of sight, round the corner. It was only my word he existed at all. I saw doubt on their faces – the type given to alien abductees.

By five in the morning, I had told them enough and was allowed to go home. Chiara was waiting. She helped, she didn't fuss. Asa had phoned her to say I was all right and he must have given her a few details: she didn't ask what had happened.

She hadn't been able to sleep while I was away. It might have been easier if she'd gone in one of the cars. It wasn't my decision: that was our contract.

In the quiet pub, with its differing lunchtime clientele, Asa said, 'What we did find, however, were packets of some substance, in the corner of that alcove. At this stage we don't know what – but I've been doing a bit of research as to what it might be.' He took in a large wodge of air. 'There's one very likely candidate. It's called Bz or Buzz. It produces symptoms very similar to what you've experienced, Jinky: sweats, palpitations, short-term memory loss and so on. We'll know soon enough when the tests come back. Do you remember everything now?

'Yes.' They thought I would go on – I didn't.

'Are you sure you caught him, Jinky?' Chisel asked. 'Are you sure you stabbed him?'

I looked up from the table top – Asa must have told them about my statement to the police. 'The knife went in to the hilt. It was a new Stanley knife. How many inches does the blade extend?'

Tread shook his head. 'Maybe four inches, possibly five.'

'It would have done some damage. He deserves all he got,' Asa grumbled.

'Are you sure about that?' I asked, harshly.

'Of course, it was you or him,' he returned, showing surprise. 'Look at what he's done to you over the last few days. Come on, Jinky, you need to take it easy. Are you sure I can't get you a proper drink – it'll help?'

I shook my head. 'Look where it's got us, though. I'm sorry, lads.'

'Don't be daft,' they chorused – but not with good timing.

'What do they say about a wounded animal?' I asked, and answered it, 'Twice as dangerous, or something.'

'Your knife wasn't found. He must have picked it up,' Asa said.

I gave nothing more than a nod as we all took a sip from our mugs.

Asa went on, 'The air was saturated with that chemical – in that spot where you were held. If it's the same one I mentioned, it likes damp conditions and some of the bags were leaking. That's what brought on the memory loss and the way you felt: you must have breathed in large amounts of it.'

I popped a pill and took a sip of my tea and stayed watching the film floating and swirling round on its surface.

'Are you still on Sanny's case?' Asa started again.

I shook my head. It was an effort to speak: emotion bulging in my throat. 'No, I can't do it. I'll need to tell him this afternoon. He'll be fine: he might not think it but the police will sort it out.'

Chisel said, 'No-one's to go anywhere alone from now on.'

We all nodded.

'You might want to know this, Jinky: the DNA test is back. The body is that of Jeremy Gittes. We're still waiting for more results on time, or should I say, day of death.'

I might have been imagining it, but, for once, instead of talking me out of involvement in police matters, it seemed Asa was actively trying to draw me in.

'We didn't have a record of Jeremy's DNA – he was jailed in the Young Offenders long before such things existed – but we matched it up to a hair found on a brush. Fortunately, Jill had his stuff packed away in her car. We wouldn't have got much from his flat: it had been given a thorough cleaning by the landlord, and there's a new tenant in as well.'

'There is one wee strange thing – on another matter,' Asa went on, perhaps uncomfortable with the silence, by my lack of curiosity, or by the distinct lack of the usual merriment associated with this place. 'Mr. Chamberlain's son found a diary belonging to his father. It was hidden away somewhere and he's handed it in to us.'

'What's so strange about that?' Tread asked, scooping up the undissolved sugar at the bottom of his cup with a teaspoon and licking it.

'Every page was filled, right through the year, and there was a very interesting part about the hotel, round about the time the body would have been placed in the cellar: Mr. Chamberlain might even have seen the murderer run away. But the strange part is that a few of the pages have been torn out. Some missing days. The son says he doesn't know anything about it. I keep thinking something important must be written on those pages. It would be helpful to know what.' He looked straight at me.

I remained quiet.

Asa gave it one last shot. 'You know, Jinky, the old pool isn't closed yet: there was no need to swim in The Nith last night. Are we all still on for one last dip?'

At that moment I knew why The Waltzing Man had been murdered more than a month later. I knew why it had taken so long for the killer to get him: and it was all because of Mr. Chamberlain's evening suit.

I said, 'Out of curiosity, Asa, can you remember which pages are missing?'

*

'Hello. Where are you?'

'I'm outside, Chiara. Can you open the front door, please?' I had phoned – that's how bad it was.

I saw her look out of our house. I dashed from my car, parked on the street, and ran up the path and in.

'The rain's pretty bad,' she said, closing up. 'Is there any word when it will stop?'

'I haven't heard – didn't have the radio on.' It wasn't the rain: I was too scared to go round to the back door.

I told her everything Asa had said. 'It means you can't go anywhere alone,' I confirmed.

She nodded. 'And that goes for you as well.'

She made me a sandwich and we sat at the kitchen table with the overhead light on to scatter the gloom of the afternoon. Another burst of wind lashed rain against the window as we finished off our to-do list. Summer weather.

'You thought you'd killed him. You don't need to be so down, so hard on yourself – he's not dead.'

'At first I thought the same, Chiara, but now I know it makes no difference. It's what I *tried* to do that matters. I never thought I would have acted like that.'

'He held you at knifepoint, for goodness sake, *and* you had that chemical, Buzz, inside you. You're not at fault, you

191

can't blame yourself. It affected the way you were thinking – that's what these things are designed to do. It changed you.'

I reached out and placed my hand on top of hers. 'When I was ranting at you that was the reason I gave. You didn't accept it. You said I must be harbouring those feelings. Don't you see this has to be the same? Deep down, I wanted to kill him, shove my knife all the way through his evil heart.'

'Come on, Jin, this is different. Did you *really* think he was going to let you walk out of there?'

'He said he would. He dropped the rope.'

*

We stood in the rain, sheltering under my golf umbrella. I stretched out and tapped on Sanny's door. We stepped back. He was quick to answer.

Say it before he can make you change your mind. 'I'm sorry but I cannot help you from now on. I'm giving up.' This was my decision – the only one I could make. She had no say: it wasn't a case. There would be no more cases.

'Whit? Yer leaving me high and dry?' He paid Chiara no heed.

'Well, it's certainly not dry. I just can't go on. I'm sure the police will get to the bottom of it and if you're innocent, they will find the guilty party. There's been a development.'

'Whit dae ye mean by that, 'if am innocent'? A telt ye. An' yer havverin aboot the polis. They want nothing better than tae get into ma affairs. This is the excuse, the chance, they've always wanted.'

'I doubt if that's right.'

His head poked forward. 'Whit would ye ken aboot it onyway?'

'I know Lewis Chamberlain kept a diary and you're mentioned in it. He wanted something from you, something he felt he was owed, something his son has tried to keep quiet about. Anyway none of that matters now: it wasn't the reason for his death.'

Why had I even bothered to explain? And if I was off the case, why had I searched through the diary again before coming out here?

I turned to leave, Chiara held onto me tightly – perhaps alarmed at her first sighting of this strange man, her mouth remaining slightly open.

'Wait,' he called after me. 'If A tell ye the full story will ye help me?'

'I'm sorry I can't. The authorities can handle it. You have nothing to fear from them.' We walked away.

He shouted after us, 'A want ye tae sort it oot. If ye ken who did it that'll get them off me back.'

We stopped. I turned. 'I don't *know* who killed Mr. Chamberlain for sure. I only know the reason for his death.'

'That's a start. Tell them polis that – it'll tak it away frae me.' He paused and his next words were playful, 'A'll invite ye in oot o' the rain.'

He opened the door wide: the door to the main part of the caravan, the hub, where his secrets lay. I couldn't see in from where I stood: it was the wrong angle. I wanted desperately to move closer.

'But it will just be you – A cannae hav *her* in.' He pointed to Chiara.

I felt her shrink back.

'I cannot let her out of my sight,' I said.

He gave her a long look. 'Aye, A can see she's precious, right enough.'

'Why don't you go and sit in the car?' I whispered to her. And then loudly to Sanny, 'I'll stay out here, where I am, then I can keep a watch out, keep her in view.'

Sanny pulled the door behind him and stood on the top step – his feet were bare. I watched Chiara make for the car and ease inside.

193

'Chamberlain wiz efter me fer money.'

'You're wasting my time.' I took a backward step from him. 'How could he possibly think you had any money? He never came across as being daft.'

Sanny sighed. 'He's no daft. A hiv money. It might be aboot time to explain it all tae ye.'

'Only if you want to and I might still not take the case back on. You realise that? I'll tell the police what I know and that might be it, nothing more.'

He sat down on the damp step and started:

'I came up here as a young man. My father bought that hotel for me and sent me here to run it. I didn't want to but I was in trouble. I did a bad thing. So I knew it was better to get well out of the way. I arranged for Lewis Chamberlain to run the place for me and we even put out the rumour that he was the owner. Everything was done through lawyers. I had nothing to do with any of it – at any time. Even when the business folded, I couldn't have cared less. In fact, it suited me – no people around, only a few ogling kids from time to time. You'd be one of them, no doubt.

Then I got word that someone wanted the land. All of it belonged to me. For years I refused to sell. In the end they wore me down – the lawyers. Chamberlain heard about the sale and wanted a share. It was a lot of money. But he didn't deserve it: he was paid a good enough wage when he worked there, but he wanted more. He said he wasn't doing it for himself. I have a suspicion his son is in financial difficulties. Lewis Chamberlain threatened me.'

I couldn't find any words – I just shook my head.

'If I didn't pay him £30 000 he would sell his story, my story, to the papers. That's what he said. I refused.'

I kicked at the ground with the toe of my shoe and dislodged a stone. I stepped back to view it in detail – my mind blank. Sanny was waiting. Eventually, something arrived – it might have sounded cheeky, 'So him turning up dead was a bit of good fortune for you?'

'It doesnae matter, his son will come efter me noo for it.'

*

I threw my jacket into the back of the car and slumped in beside Chiara. 'A good talk?' she asked. 'What was he saying?'

I listened to my breathing – ebbing and flowing. When I was young I used to think we breathed back in the batch of air immediately expelled: there didn't seem enough time or force for it to go anywhere else but inside once again. So I couldn't work out why we needed to breathe at all: why let it go only to catch it again. Why not keep it in? Take it in when born, let it go at death – one big gasp. It puzzled me for years. I came to the conclusion that breathing in windy weather was a good thing: the old air would be whisked away, allowing a breath of fresh air. I've always liked it when the wind blows.

'I don't know… what it was about.' I shook my head like a dog emerging from the river.

'He must have said something.'

'I'm sorry but I can't tell you, Chiara. I'll never be allowed to say to anyone – that's what I agreed on. Call it client confidentiality. I might be back on the case.'

'It's the right thing to do – you have to keep helping. But don't you have to ask me first about this particular job?'

'Sorry, forgot. What do you think I should do?'

'I'll have to consider it – not easy without the full details.' She grinned. 'We'd better get moving on that list. Where's the best place for bed linen?'

*

I parked at the police station and gave my name at the front desk. I expected Ed or one of his team to come – instead I got the top man, High-Heid-Yin-Harris, no less.

'You got my message?' he said, unnecessarily. 'Would you like to come through to my office?' He turned to Chiara,

'Would it all right if you waited here?'

I gave her a shrug, I couldn't argue: this had to be one of the safest places for her to be on her own. I followed Harris through, still a bit surprised to be allowed his valuable time.

The lamp was on in his dull, north-facing office. He made himself comfortable behind his large desk and motioned for me to sit. He waited until two cups of tea in saucers were delivered, along with two chocolate biscuits – in wrappers.

He stirred his tea, even though no sugar had been deposited, and went straight in, still staring at his cup, 'The discovery of the drugs in the sewer this morning has turned this into a very serious situation.' He looked up, as far as my chest, adding quickly, 'Not that it wasn't in the first place – for you.'

He gave the same information I'd received from Asa an hour ago. I moved my face in a, hopefully, appropriate way to show it was all news to me.

'We have The Tramp now as our main suspect for the Chamberlain murder and every effort is being made to locate the man.' He added a few more details about the search to find him.

Harris stood up and turned his back on me to look out of the window. 'I'm sure we can trust you. This is a very delicate situation and I would like to think that you will be very discreet. In return, I can offer you my support whenever appropriate.'

He turned round, and for the first time looked me straight in the eye. 'Or not.' The words were delivered severely, with a raise of the eyebrows. 'Do we understand one another?'

I knew he had been talking in English but other than that I hadn't a clue what he was on about. I said with conviction, 'Definitely.'

*

The whole house needed cleaning. I'd managed to arrange it with a cleaning firm: four people for an hour and a half, arriving at four o'clock today. I might have considered doing it myself – but right now I was tired beyond belief – and, really, it was far too big a job in the time remaining.

'There's something I have to do before the cleaners get here,' I said to Chiara, as we unloaded the car, using the front door, always staying in twos.

I found the key in the back of the kitchen drawer and led Chiara through the house, upstairs, to the front room on the left. I unlocked the door and swung it open.

'This is going to be difficult for you, I know,' I said. 'If you can't do it then I'll manage myself. Leave if you can't cope – it's no problem. The cleaners can do this room last to give us time to sort it out.'

Chiara took a deep breath and stepped into my parents' old bedroom. I was glad she had stayed by my side – I wasn't really sure I could do it on my own.

'I don't understand. Why is it like this?' she said.

We stood two feet inside. I shrugged. 'I locked the door and left everything the way it was.'

She took another hesitant step forward, a hand to her mouth. 'At least there are no photographs staring back. I hate them.'

'My family never had a camera.'

I gazed round the room. I'd never really seen it before: I was never inside as a child. Never. The heavy purple velvet curtains were half-way open allowing in some light. My father had pulled them apart ten years ago and that's where they had remained. I clicked on the light: it made Chiara recoil.

His clothes were still over a chair, my mother's dressing gown lay across one side of the unmade bed. The place was untidy with more clothes on the floor, her face creams and lotions strewn over the dressing table, along with a hairbrush and hand mirror. Another full-length mirror reflected a blanket of dust on its surface.

'You didn't tidy up at all?'

'I never wanted to go in. All the other rooms are fine. They never had any mess. But I left this one alone. This is the way it was on the morning – when I found him.'

'But there could have been things of value in here: credit cards, money, that kind of thing.'

'I thought I told you about all that.'

'You said you found your father slumped at the kitchen table.'

I took her hand. It was cold. 'I wasn't staying here at that time – I had a bed-sit. My mother passed away a few weeks before so I arranged to take my father away on a short holiday – to help him get over it, and, I suppose, to bond. He'd actually agreed to go. I was surprised – we'd never been all that close.'

She nodded, seriously, perhaps thinking along the same line – Uncle James.

'When I turned up at the house, he had all his finances looked out, sorted into bundles on the kitchen table – everything I would need, including the will. He had burnt all unnecessary items. The smoke was still puffing out from the brazier in the garden.'

She turned to face me. 'He must have known he was about to die? That's terrible.'

'I'm not sure about that. Maybe he was just starting a spring clean and sat down to rest.'

'You don't really think that's the case, do you?'

'Isn't it better to go when you're ready? I think he was ready.'

'But why arrange to go on holiday with you?'

I shrugged. How many times had I thought about that? James and Sin – it altered everything. When was my father going to tell me? Was it on the holiday? Or had he decided never to say? I had some questions for my aunt in hospital.

'I'm going to get some big bags and shove everything

into them. Maybe take them to a charity shop. Do you think you can help: touch any of this stuff?' I asked.

'You'll have to go through the pockets: I couldn't do it.'

I wasn't so sure I could either.

She hesitated. 'Your father never tidied up either – after your mother died. All her things are here.'

'Maybe he found comfort in it.'

She looked at me. 'It's almost like you were expecting them to return, Jin, and you didn't want them to see any difference if they did.'

I shook my head. 'No, it was never like that, honestly. I moved back. I had all the papers to satisfy the lawyer and enough on my plate in sorting out my own apartment. I turned the key on the room and never got round to coming back.' I hadn't convinced myself – she wouldn't be convinced either.

*

They each arrived with their suitcases in their hands. It was half past six in the evening. I had managed a short nap.

Tread was first, accompanied by his wife, Elspeth – then Hoogah and Chisel together. And finally Asa and Rosie. All within a minute of each other.

They set their cases down on the floor in the hall before walking through to the kitchen, standing awkwardly in their coats – as though they were strangers. I introduced Chiara and still they stood. The house had opened its arms to them but they didn't appear to notice. I made some tea.

'Where's your wife, Chisel?' I asked as he approached me at the sink, looking out at the waterlogged earth of my garden.

'Spain – dropped her off this morning at Prestwick. That should be safe enough.'

'A bit of an expense: she would have been fine here.'

He came closer and whispered, 'She deserved it poor thing with the favour she had to do and all. Don't get me wrong

199

– she enjoys doing it all right. She's never been forced – don't think that.' He gave me a wink.

I hadn't a clue what he was on about – and that was the second time today.

I heard Asa refuse the offer of a beer from Chiara and turned quickly to see what it looked like and to capture the moment. Unfortunately, I didn't have my camera to hand. Everyone else had stopped talking too. Asa looked round the room – then he shrugged as deep as any Frenchman, and the low level chatter started up once again.

There was only space round the kitchen table for six, so Chiara and I clucked about, allowing our guests to sit. We had cooked them a simple meal of pasta with a side dish of salad.

'Okay,' I said. 'We need to have some rules for our safety. Number one is no-one is to be on their own at any time – that is obvious. Can anyone see a problem with that?'

Hoogah spoke first, 'I'm seldom alone at the school – and I don't intend to be at all now.'

Tread was next, 'There are always two of us on at any time in the showroom. I'll make sure I don't do any outside activities until all this is over.' I waited for the joke at the end – there wasn't one. He went on, 'And there's two of them in the sandwich shop, so Elspeth will have company. I'm a bit concerned with it being two women though.'

'We'll be fine,' his wife said. 'We have knives to hand at all times.'

I added, 'I could be wrong but I think if he's going to come after any one of us it's likely to be the people he mentioned. He said nothing about the wives.'

Asa started up, 'Well, I think I'm in the safest place – the police station. Rosie works Monday, Tuesday and Wednesday in the shoe-shop. There's always another there – right, Rosie?'

She gave a nod. 'Sometimes there's three of us.'

'What about when we get to Thursday?' I asked.

'Surely it's not going to last that long,' Asa replied. 'I think we'll catch him long before then.'

'And I'll be okay,' Chisel said, breaking into the ominous silence. 'If I'm out on a story, I'll make sure I take one of the juniors with me. A couple of them are sturdy lads, play rugby. So I'll be fine.'

I said, 'The police say they will patrol this area through the night. No-one else will be here during the day except me and Chiara. Can't do anything about that – but we'll keep together.' Finally, and with some relief, I saw Tread nudge Hoogah at my last comment.

'So,' I went on, 'I want you to make yourselves at home here until they catch him. That's the point of this – safety in numbers.'

I went on, 'Now for the matter of sleeping: I have three bedrooms upstairs, all with double beds and brand new linen. So the question is – do you, Hoogah and Chisel, our singles for this evening, want to share a bed? Either that or one of you sleeps on the sofa downstairs in the front sitting room? What's it to be?'

They looked at each other. I had the impression neither wanted to be on their own, but it wasn't likely they'd say so. Chisel muttered, 'I don't mind, but there'll need to be a line of pillows down the middle and pyjamas are a necessity.'

'Pyjamas? I don't own any, Chisel. Is this something you've always insisted on with your bedfellows? But I'm in favour of the pillows. In fact barbed wire would be better.'

'You will be wearing something that's for sure, Hoogah – top and bottom,' Chisel retorted.

'Fine.'

I said, 'We use the front door and I've had keys made up – it was one for each couple and one for you Hoogah.' I laid four keys out on the table.

Hoogah said, 'Actually, I won't need a key...'

'Not now you and Chisel are a couple,' Tread shot back, with a snigger.

He shook his head. 'Naw, it's not that. I'm away on this conference this week, remember? So I'll be up early tomorrow morning and away. You'll get the bed to yourself tomorrow night, Chisel. And don't worry, Jinky, no need for you to get out of bed, I'll manage to make myself something. It's an early start.'

I shook my head. 'No, you'll need to be seen to the car. And take a key anyway.'

'What conference is that?' Tread asked.

'Me and the Headmaster are going to Ayr – to do with work.' Hoogah gave a grin as he huffed on his nails, polishing them on his jumper.

'Fancy,' Tread replied, in an exaggerated voice.

Eventually the evening settled. We decided on other matters: such as the time for breakfast, evening meals, groceries and so on. No-one drank but it was comforting to be around friends. The old house had almost returned to the earlier, busy times of my youth, when it was filled with my aunts and uncles, and family friends staying over almost every weekend. Tonight could have been a party, except the cloud hanging over us reined us in.

Tread tried his best. 'Anyone for a game of adult twister?'

His wife's eyes rose to the ceiling.

'Not possible,' Asa replied. 'Not without alcohol and anti-inflammatories.'

'Don't worry,' Tread answered, 'there's only two colours so nobody has to bend over.'

'I'm just thinking, Jinky,' Asa asked, with barely a pause, 'are there locks on the bedroom doors?'

'Why?'

'Well, you said the whole house has been opened up, even the connecting door is going to be left unlocked – but what about Rodger the lodger?'

'Don't worry he knows you're all staying.'

'That's not what I meant.'

'What did you mean then?'

'He has the run of the top floor. I take it he has a key to *his* area.'

'Of course.'

'Then maybe we should have the same – for protection. It would be odd if he can lock his door and we can't. Do you see what I mean?'

'I'm not sure I do. If he wasn't there, would you want to lock your door? Because house guests don't tend to, usually. Or, are you saying you're worried about Rodger?'

'No, I'm not suggesting we need to protect ourselves from *him* – but I just thought…'

I dismissed it. 'No need to worry, every room has a key and I'll look them out.'

'Thanks,' Asa returned. He saw everyone staring at him. 'Just being careful, that's all,' he added, with a heave of his shoulders.

'Wait until you hear this,' I went on. 'We were in the library today and guess who was waiting to get in through the front door?'

Tread butted in, 'What book did you get?'

'If you must know it was on sewer systems.'

'Sounds like a great read,' Hoogah stated. 'I must think about putting that onto our book list at school.'

'Yeah, it's a Best Cellar,' Tread returned. 'D'you get it?' He spelled out the word – using an 'e' instead of the 'a', sadly.

Over the groans, I replied, 'That doesn't even make sense, Tread. Cellars and sewers are two completely different fish. And I've first-hand knowledge on both.'

Asa asked, 'Why would you want that anyway, Jinky? Didn't you get enough of a guided tour this morning?'

I held up my hands. 'Okay, stop, stop, it doesn't matter about the book. The question was – who was waiting for the automatic doors to open?'

Everyone felt it their duty to make a suggestion and their ridiculous guesses circled the table like the garlic bread.

'Right, you're obviously not going to get it – it was the library's boss. He can't get in now without someone to help him through the doors. Changed days indeed.'

Rosie asked Asa what I was talking about.

I went on, 'He had a bit of an accident, you see. He got his tail stuck in the door last week and three inches had to be loped off – it was that bad. Three inches off his tail, I mean – not the door.'

Tread again, 'Three inches? That's a lot.'

'I'll say,' his wife put in.

Asa explained to Rosie, 'The library has a cat, a black one – and it rules the place. Does whatever it likes – sleeps in the display cabinets, lies on the computer keyboards, the lot. You should go and see him some time. He's quite a sight.'

I continued, 'Well, because of his accident, they've had to alter the mechanisms for operating the doors. They had to raise the beams so the cat can't trigger them – so now he has to wait outside for someone to come along to let him in.'

'And who did you have to wait for, Jinky?' Asa shoehorned in.

Tuesday 29th August

For the first time in ten years I had the connecting door open to the rest of the house. But that wasn't the reason I hadn't slept well. My brain had been churning through many things.

I wondered if it actually mattered if Uncle James was my father: he certainly treated me well when I was growing up, sometimes better than my own dad. But, then, perhaps, that wasn't so surprising – if they both knew.

How does someone sit down and die anyway? What is the process?

Why is The Tramp so desperate to find Don Gardiner? What does he know about him – and how did their paths cross?

Would a word with Reginald Chamberlain, explaining my possession of a copy of the full diary, be enough to ease Sanny's problem? Would it stop him from blackmailing Sanny?

And which accent belonged to the real Onion Sanny? Was it possible for both of them to be authentic – the same way the accent of a singing voice can be completely different to the spoken?

Chiara stirred. 'What's wrong? Was it your dream again?'

'Was I that restless? Sorry. No, it wasn't the dream – too many thoughts and not enough answers. And does Hoogah have to make such racket making tea and toast for breakfast? No wonder he's been divorced twice.'

We lay on our sides, facing each other.

'Were you thinking about the Waltzing Man case?' she asked.

'A wee bit. But I don't even know if I'm on it now – you haven't told me yet.'

'When Don Gardiner was injured last month, he was stabbed by Jackie Gittes' killer?'

'This sounds like you've been doing some thinking as well, Chiara. Yes, when we caught the man his knife had Don's blood on it. No doubt about it. He had taken Don by surprise. Don was lucky not to lose his life. Where's this leading?'

'I was just wondering if there could there have been another person involved in Jackie's murder? The same person who put Jeremy Gittes' body in the old hotel? Could there have been two of them working together?'

I took it up, 'You think The Tramp might be his accomplice? I mentioned that to Asa before but he wasn't convinced.'

'And, because Don wasn't killed, The Tramp wants to finish the job.'

'It's possible, I suppose.'

'Don Gardiner might have seen something the night he was attacked.'

I shook my head. 'He's been questioned. Ah, I see what you are saying – he might have seen something but he doesn't really know it, something that didn't seem worth mentioning. Perhaps he caught a glimpse of The Tramp but dismissed it as not being important. The same reason Mr. Chamberlain was murdered – something he witnessed. I'll have to go and have a word with Don.'

'I think you mean *we* will have to see him – and that's if I agree.' She ran a finger delicately across my lips. 'Is your mouth still sore? Can it be used at all?'

The space in the bed between us started to fill. I hugged her – then broke away abruptly.

'What is it?'

'It's this one thing that keeps at me. Jackie was killed with a brown handled knife. We found another, similar knife in the rucksack of his killer. Part of the same set.'

'So?'

'So why was Don attacked with a black-handled knife? Why did the attacker have two knives on him? This was the black-handled knife stolen from Jackie's bed-sit. Why do that, why take another knife, if he already had a suitable one?'

'I don't know – as a back-up?'

'It's possible. For whatever reason, he felt the need to carry two weapons that night.'

But, then, I had done exactly the same before going into the sewer: one up the sleeve of my jacket, another in the cuff of my shirt.

*

We gathered round the table. I remember our family breakfasts vividly. Even through the week, there was laughter and amusement, as my aunts and uncles stoked up for the working day ahead, and I would sit and watch and be happy.

In contrast, the members of my new family were solemn. Another time and under different circumstances, I'm sure we could be just as jolly. Perhaps, when this is over, I should invite them all over to stay a night. Have a big shindig.

Asa said, plastering his toast with an inch thick layer of butter, 'Where is it Hoogah's away to again?' He had got up earlier, with me, to see our friend safely to his car. And Asa had looked very snazzy in his silk dressing gown.

'The sea-side, he said,' I replied. 'Although I don't fancy it much in this weather.'

'Still, it's a nice wee break,' Rosie added, before biting into her toast and marmalade.

'Two day conference. Lucky devil,' Tread mumbled. 'And he's got the headmaster with him so he's not going to be alone – not that he'd be in any danger away over there in Ayr.' He went on, indignantly, 'Jinky, are we having any eggs? Only I've a very full day and this toast is as cold as a check-out girl's smile. It's not enough for a growing man.'

'What kind would you like?' I asked.

'More like a groaning man,' said his wife. 'And I don't mean the good, bed-gymnastic kind of groans.' She turned to us all, 'How have you managed to put up with him all these years?'

'Same way as you, probably.'

'Knitting?'

I said, 'You haven't told me what type of eggs you want Tread.'

His wife continued, absent-mindedly, 'I used to try rumpy-pumpy, as it always made him speechless.'

Tread buried his face in his hands, his colouring firing up to match the ketchup on the table.

I enquired, 'Eggs, Tread? Once again – what type do you want? Wait a minute… wait a minute.' My tone caught their attention: they looked up. 'Where did you say Hoogah's conference is?' I asked.

'Ayr.'

I dashed to my phone beside the bed and dialed through. 'You've got to turn back Hoogah – something bad's going to happen.'

'What are you talking about, Jinky?' His voice turned into a whisper, 'I can't really talk: I'm driving. Nearly there, in fact.'

'Don't hang up. Is the Headie with you?'

'Of course he is.'

'Tell him you can't manage. At the very worst say you'll drop him off because you have to come straight back. Make up some story. Say I'm ill… or it's a relative. Anything.'

'What are you talking about?' He wanted to shout but in company could only keep to a hush. 'I can't do that. Is this about, you-know-who? Only I think everything's fine on that front: I'm well away from it over here. Sixty miles. I can't talk now. I need to put the phone down – it's against the law.'

'No, this is about Lucy. Don't you see it?'

'Oh, you're not still on about that Fire & Ice thing again, are you?'

'No, it's not that. But I've figured it out. She's been

208

building up to this. She must have known about your conference. How long has it been planned?'

'Before the summer holidays.'

'Think on it, Hoogah. First there was the fire in the handle, then the lump of frozen water, and then the mound of earth…'

He cut me off, 'Bye, Jinky, Keep taking the tablets.'

'Think of where you are going, Hoogah. Don't you see?'

He gave a cheery, 'Shouldn't be too late back tomorrow night.' And the line went dead.

*

We stood in the rain again, under the umbrella. It took a long time before the door was opened.

'Oh, hi there, Jill's not in right now. You can catch her at her salon,' Don Gardiner said.

'It's you we've come to see. Would you care to go for a walk?' I asked.

Don looked to the skies and brought a quizzical look to his face. 'I'd rather not. What's this about?'

'Come on the fresh air will be good for you. It won't be for long,' I urged. Chiara nudged me in the ribs.

'I think I know what this is about,' he said, with a nod and a slight smile. 'Jill wants me to get moving. Out and about, isn't that it? Don't worry we had a talk last night – and it's all sorted.' He rubbed a hand over his straggling hair. 'Well, I would normally but the police have said I should be very careful. So it's best to stay in until this is over. Did you hear about it – some madman's looking for me?'

'You're not worried by that?'

'Of course I'm worried.'

'Well, that's what we wanted to talk to you about. Can we come in and ask a few questions?'

He hesitated before pushing the door wider. I introduced him to Chiara.

209

'How did Jill take the news of Jeremy's death?' I asked, as we climbed the stairs.

'To be honest, she was relieved.'

*

Don had nothing more to tell us about the night of his assault. He was quite sure he hadn't seen anything, no matter how insignificant. The attacker had jumped him and fled. It was distressing for him and we didn't stay long – feeling badly about broaching the subject again.

From there we drove over to Miss Welch's house. This was going to be difficult: I had completely forgotten about our weekly trip to the supermarket yesterday.

'I tried phoning you,' she started, as soon as she opened up, keeking round the door, seeing me on her doorstep. 'What is wrong with your phone? I waited all afternoon. You could have at least let me know…' She paused after pulling the door wider, noting Chiara standing beside me.

I apologised deeply and offered to take her now – if it was suitable. She huffed for a while and then consented: her visitor had just left. I knew it was her cleaner again.

Surprisingly, Miss Welch was fairly civil for the remainder of the outing and even, much to my surprise, thanked me at the end.

We returned home with armfuls of groceries and, chores done, took to our bed for a rest before the hordes descended from work.

*

The noise at the front door made me jump. We all heard the scrape from the kitchen. We were finishing supper, and getting ready for bed. I rushed through into the hallway, Asa following closely behind. I hadn't picked up a weapon: safety in numbers.

When I reached the front door and looked back, there was a single line of people stretching to the kitchen – all peeking past each other, all anxious.

The door opened and Hoogah stepped in, a bag slung over his shoulder. Relief swept apprehension from the hallway and we broke into a bizarre cheer, with a few arms waving. A scunnered Hoogah added a portion of astonishment to his face.

'What's wrong? Why are you back so soon? What happened to the conference?' I showed him through.

He gave a nod in turn as he passed each person on his way to the kitchen – like a subdued royal on troop inspection. 'You were right, Jinky. Everything's completely…' he took in the walls and the ceiling of my home before adding, 'messed up.'

'Come on, I'll get you a cup of tea.'

'I'll need something stronger, much stronger.'

I pulled out my last bottle of Sanny's liqueur. There was less than a quarter left. I'd been saving it for a special moment. Unfortunately, this was a time requiring its power. I sat Hoogah down, Tread stood directly behind him, evidently not wanting to venture far from his recently vacated, and still warm, seat: perhaps feeling he still had claims to it. I poured the first of the two glasses of the amber liquid. And Hoogah started to explain.

The conference in the hotel in Ayr had been fine. It was held in a nice hotel near the front. It had been a long day but a perfectly acceptable one. At the end, Hoogah had taken a nightcap in the bar with the Headie – and they were getting along fine. By nine o'clock he had decided an early night was in order, said goodnight, and made his way to his room.

Once there, he had gone straight into the shower, but when he'd walked through, still drying himself, and switched on the light to the rest of the room, he spotted a lump in his bed. At that moment, the lump moved. A woman sat up, arms in the air, shouting, 'SURPRISE.' She was also without clothes.

Then the door of the room burst open and the headmaster

walked in. He came to an abrupt halt, with the three of them staring at each other. It was the headmaster who spoke first: demanding to know why Hoogah was in *his* room and what on earth did he think he was doing with *his* wife.

No amount of explaining from Hoogah or the Headie's wife could resolve the situation, with the headmaster becoming angrier by the minute. Hoogah, deciding on the fight another day principle, had grabbed up his things and fled the room, still dressing as he left the hotel. It had been a rather flustered drive back to Dumfries.

'And do you know the funny thing…' He was smiling now, as he approached the end of his second glass. 'The exact same thing happened to me about a year ago. Except on that occasion the situation was reversed: I found my second wife in a hotel room with another man. I didn't tell any of you about it at the time but that was the reason for the divorce.'

'Your second wife being Lucy's best friend?' I said.

*

It didn't take long for us to put the pieces together and come up with a possible scenario. Sitting round the table, we all managed to put in a thought or two; although some were immediately discarded. It would have been a good parlour game if it wasn't for the fact that Hoogah's promotion hopes were, more than likely, in tatters now.

At some point in the evening, the headmaster would have been informed of a room change and been given a new key. His luggage would have been transferred to this new room as well. When his wife turned up to surprise him, she would have been shown to this new room also – which, of course, was really Hoogah's.

It still raised a few questions. What had prompted the Headie's wife to make the journey and who had put the thought into her head that her marriage needed spicing up? Who had stage-managed a change to the Headie's room? And who had handed over the new key to him?

The answer to it all seemed to point to Lucy. A big, impersonal hotel, money, or something else, changing hands for favours, and it could be done. She probably carried out the same ploy a year ago to split Hoogah from his, then, wife.

*

My phone, sitting on the table beside our bed, buzzed and buzzed. It was after midnight, it had woken me, and it was the hospital calling. My aunt had taken a tumble – she wanted to see me urgently. I asked Chiara if I could go alone. She said she'd accompany me.

I dressed quickly in shirt and jeans, grabbing my jacket on the way, before chapping on Asa's door to tell him. He insisted on coming downstairs to watch us to the car. I gave him the thumbs up and drove off.

A nurse was waiting at the reception area of the ward. 'Sorry to phone you this late but she's been demanding to see you.' She led us through the darkened ward. 'She wasn't settling, seemed very nervous. She's better now – as soon as she knew you were on your way. Unfortunately, she got out of bed earlier, to go to the toilet we think, and fell. She was supposed to buzz for help – we always stress that. I don't think she realises how serious her condition is. Maybe she does now.'

Chiara grabbed my hand. I held it tightly. 'It must be difficult for her to accept her independence has gone,' I replied.

My aunt was in a room of her own. She had shrunk considerably since yesterday. There was a dreadful purple bruise down the right hand side of her face and a bandage round the top of her head. Her eyes were closed but her thin-boned hand gripped the emergency button.

The nurse tapped gently at her shoulder. 'Your nephew is here to see you.'

Aunt May opened her eyes slowly, like blinds being raised. She made an almost indistinct shooing movement with her hand, and the nurse left us alone.

'Look at me, what an old fool.' Her voice was rough with the gravel of exhaustion. 'I'll not be getting out of here now – I know that. They'll not allow me back to my home. These are the last walls I'll see.' Her runny eyes wandered round the room.

I opened my mouth to offer contradictory encouragement, but the raised movement of her hand stopped me.

'Listen to what I have to say – and don't interrupt. I have to tell you this now, while I can. There is a box on the top shelf of the cupboard in the back room, upstairs. The key for it is in the kitchen, in the drawer with the cutlery. I was going to destroy everything like your father did – but I kept some. He burnt everything he had. I was never sure if I would show them to you or not. Sometimes I think you have a right to know about your family and other times I think it would just cause harm. I was going to destroy that box. That's what I had decided on, finally. And then this happened. Now I can't. I could tell you to throw the box away and never look inside, but I'm not sure you could do that – you were always a very curious child. Sometimes you stuck your nose in too much. You might still have that tendency.'

Her eyes were closing, talking was an effort. Chiara reached forward and held her hand. I searched for something to say. 'When I found my father that morning, he had been burning things in the garden.'

The sound of my voice opened her eyes. 'Yes, he didn't want you to know. Go now and find that box. You would have found it anyway when clearing out my house. You'll be getting it, don't worry. Despite everything.

You decide whether to open it or not. I think you should destroy it but if you don't, come back tomorrow and I'll answer every question you have. That's why it is urgent. I need to sleep. I think I can relax now. Give me a kiss before you go.'

214

I was sure she was asleep before my kiss landed on her good cheek. Chiara did the same. We crept from the room. We didn't say anything. I expect we were thinking along the same lines: this would be the last time we would see Aunt May.

We cleared the ward and our footsteps quickened along the corridor. We were running down the stairs.

'Do you think this has to do with your Uncle James?' she said.

'Yes, I suppose it does.' There were two opposite flows within me: to find out and to never know. 'What should I do, Chiara?'

*

The key to the house was on my key ring. I slid it in the lock with difficulty: the key was reluctant to turn. I should have taken it as a sign. We rushed through to the kitchen, flashing on lights. I found a small key in the drawer and held it in shaking hands.

Chiara gave a nod.

We chased up the stairs, two at a time, and into the back room, throwing on the overhead light. Chiara bit her lip and her breathing was heavy. I was as bad: not only were we nervous of what we might find but it was a stranger's home, empty, and late at night. And this house unsettled me like no other.

The box she had described was there – except it was more like a small chest – sturdy, with metal ribs and a padlock securing the lid. I pulled it down from the shelf: it was lighter than expected, and sat it on the floor. We stared at it.

I knelt down, pushed in the key, and lifted the lid.

The first thing I saw was a large black and white photograph. It took a while to understand exactly what it was. I felt the blood drain slowly from my face like the sand in an egg timer. I pulled the photo out and held it for Chiara to take. For one brief moment I didn't want her to see it, and needed to throw it back inside and burn that box. My father was right,

Aunt May was right – but I'd seen it now.

What other, terrible things awaited?

Chiara clasped it and slumped down onto a wooden chair against the wall. 'Is this your Uncle James?'

I nodded back, vaguely.

'And that's your mother he's with? There was a lot more hair back then.'

I couldn't think of words. I nodded again, not knowing what I was nodding to, and turned away to look out of the window. My Uncle James was always good to me, spoiled me in a way, gave me sweets from his pocket: sometimes they were wrapped.

But this was vile.

I heard Chiara gasp and turned.

There was a knife at her neck – a long, sharp blade pointing under her chin. Her grip on the photo weakened: it drifted to the floor and finished face down.

'You should make sure you lock your doors at night,' The Tramp said. The room was bright but it wouldn't penetrate fully into the depths of his large hood: only his bearded chin caught the light. 'Now what would bring you here at this time, and so late?'

'How… how can it be you? I stabbed you. How can you still be alive? I put four inches of steel through your heart.'

The Tramp thumped the heel of his hand against his chest. 'Never felt better. You must have missed.'

I shook my head. Then the smell of him reached me. I made a slight movement towards them.

'Don't,' he shouted. 'Don't do anything. I would take absolutely no pleasure in harming this beautiful creature. What's so important to be out at this time of night, eh? Only bad people roam the streets. You should know that.'

He mustn't find out about the box. No-one should. 'What do you want?' I yelled back. 'You have to let her go.'

216

Absurdly, my brain showed images from earlier: the moment we charged through the front door of this house, as if deciding who was responsible for leaving it open would make the slightest bit of difference. We couldn't have been that careless.

'She will not be harmed as long as you do everything I ask. I want you to listen very carefully to me. I want you to take in everything I say. Are you ready to hear me?'

I nodded back feverishly.

'You have to comply – I think that's the right word – or else both of you will end up injured, or worse. And she will be the first and you will see it. I repeat: *you will see*. I take it you wouldn't want to witness that?'

Chiara's eyes darted to me and back to him: she was trembling, breathing wildly. I wanted to cradle her, shield her, transport her to safety. She shouldn't be put through this. It wasn't right, it wasn't fair. I felt an intense guilt.

I shook my head and brought my hands together in one movement and fumbled, slowly, for the pocket in my left sleeve. It held my father's flick-knife. The police had returned my jacket. They never said if they knew about the weapon.

'Please, just leave her and take me.' I'd heard those words many times – it wasn't made up, it was real, it was all I thought, all I wanted. Nothing else mattered. She had to escape untouched. I'd do anything for her to be free. Anything. I was unimportant. 'Please. You must. Let her walk out – now. Please. You can have me.'

'And you're quite a catch.'

Flattery or sarcasm: it wasn't something worth considering at this moment.

He went on, 'I do not want to harm her – so we *are* of similar minds. Remember that. I'm not planning to hurt her. But *you* could change it – and that would be silly on your part. *You* can force me. We don't want that. Am I right?'

'Right.' If I leapt he would defend himself – instinctively, he would defend himself. He wouldn't use his knife on her: he would turn to fight me off. That has to be the case – it's natural. I shuffled my feet as a decoy. The movement didn't alarm him. I felt the popper between the tips of the fingers of my right hand. One flick and the knife would fall into my palm. I'd practiced many, many times – and I'd done it for real before. It was almost one movement: the flip of the stud, the grasp of the handle, the lunge forward as the button releases and whips the vicious five inch blade, rigid and ready, held in both hands, and thrust on towards target.

I left the knife alone. It was a ridiculous chance to take. He was too close to her. If I witnessed his knife cut through her soft skin, if I saw the blade penetrate, if I was the cause of her death, I wouldn't be able to keep myself alive.

He fumbled in the bulging pocket of his coat and pulled out a roll of heavy duty tape. 'Now I intend to make sure she doesn't run off, first. Is that okay? You have to stay where you are, and there will be no problem. I promise that if there is no struggle, no fight, she will remain unharmed. Are we clear?'

He wanted me to confirm it: he stood motionless until I nodded back.

She flinched as he wound the tape round her wrists, hands behind her back, and round her ankles and the chair legs, finishing off with a stretch across her mouth – all the while holding the knife with intent.

'There that's done.' He seemed relieved.

I shouted, 'You want the name? I'll give you the name right now and you leave. Do we have a deal?'

'Ah, I didn't realise you were the one making the conditions tonight.' He jabbed the knife towards me and rasped, 'Just you listen to me! We *will* be leaving. We will be leaving in your car. It's outside. This lady will be kept here, though – as a guarantee of your good behaviour on our trip. Do you understand?'

He turned back to her and pulled something from his pocket. I saw her eyes flash in fright. I saw her cringe. It was a quick movement: he'd tied something round her neck. His hands had touched her flesh, contaminating the smell of her pure skin. An intense hatred erupted inside of me, far greater than I'd ever experienced before. It was roaring through my heart and gut. It was flaming, rampaging, seething around me. I wanted to kill this man. At this precise second, I knew I could do it in cold blood. I needed no more reason.

'This is a rabbit snare,' he said to Chiara. His voice was even, calm.

It was difficult to hold myself back. The fury jagged my muscles, stinging me to action. I kept my ground for her sake only.

He said to her, 'You mustn't wriggle, make any movement, or it will tighten and keep on tightening round your throat. Do you understand?'

She gave one frantic nod.

'Stop!' he commanded. 'Didn't you hear what I said? You must not *move* at all. But that was my mistake, sorry. Please be clear – do anything and that snare will choke you long before you can free yourself. I don't want that to happen. *He* doesn't want it to happen. What I want is that – is he your boyfriend? No, don't answer that. What I want is that he does exactly as I say, and this is my insurance.'

He looked over; he must have been able to feel the revulsion radiating from me. 'Okay, we leave now. We will go for a drive in your car – it looks a nice machine.'

I spat words at him. 'I'll give you the name and I won't tell the police you were here – if you leave us alone.'

Don't hold back, tell him. She is so much more important. She is everything. Why protect a stranger now?

'It's gone a bit further than that – as you probably have guessed. I don't care for people trying to stab me.' He took one

219

step towards me, one step away from her. I stood resolutely, defying him, judging the distance.

'Take off your jacket and throw it down over there.' He pointed to a corner of the room. I pulled my fingers away from the popper and did as he asked. I stood in shirt and jeans.

'Now empty your trouser pockets. Slowly. Put everything out on the floor where I can see them – in a line. Make sure it's everything.'

I laid my possessions in front of me and straightened, turning the linings of my pockets inside out.

'Where did you get that knife before? I checked your pockets last time!'

'I found it,' I said quickly. 'I fell on it in the sewer. It must have been flushed down there.'

'You're lying! It was brand new.'

'I don't know, then. Maybe it fell out of a worker's pocket. How am I supposed to know where it came from? It was there – that was all that mattered.

'Lift your shirt and turn round.'

I did as he asked. 'You see – there's nothing.'

'Lift up your trouser legs and then take off your shoes and socks.'

I did: exposing the bandages round my ankles. I threw the shoes to one side. He called me closer, told me to put my arms out wide. I took two steps towards him and stopped, standing like a scarecrow. He shuffled back: the knife returned to her throat. I neared them. The tip of the blade dented her flesh. I was so close but could do nothing. He started tapping down the sides of my trousers with his free hand, all the way down each leg, checking round the waistband.

'It was the same on the train track,' I said hurriedly. 'You wanted to know how I escaped – it was the same. I fell on a piece of glass. There was a cut to my hand. Remember? That's how it happened. I used the glass to scrape myself free. Do you

see? All these things were meant to be? The knife, the glass –
they are a sign. You should leave here now – or it will be the
end of you.'

He pushed me: a hard shove to my chest. I staggered
backwards, tripping over my wallet on the floor and fell. He
laughed heartily. 'You are a fool. Pick up the car-keys, put your
hands behind your back and turn away.'

I had no option: I couldn't fight him in front of her. I had
no certainty I would win. She was safe for the moment. Sense
quelled me. If I do as he says, she will live.

Where is Asa? He might wonder where we are, why we
haven't returned. He might be able to see my car from his
bedroom window: it is only a few doors along. He would see it
from the front door certainly – and be curious.

I squeezed my arms together as he tied them just below
the elbows and, with a jab of the blade in my back, we left the
room.

*

The Tramp held the knife in at my side as I drove. He had
taken no chances: tying my right hand to the inside door handle
the moment we reached the car. I'd complained that I couldn't
drive with one hand and in bare feet but it made no difference
to him. He told me to head for the river.

His odour was everywhere, inundating this small space.
How many Christmas tree shapes would it take to destroy his
smell? I took in his reek: it made me breathe slowly. It might be
a good thing – help me reappraise. Whatever happened now I
had to make sure he couldn't escape and turn back for her.
Crashing the car wasn't an option: it wouldn't necessarily bring
success, not at this speed, not with my hand fastened. I didn't
see a police patrol. They were supposed to be coming round
every few minutes.

'How did you find me?' It was difficult to speak, his
stench and the remnants of fury fought in my throat like

221

fighting cocks.

'I waited nearby. I come out at night – well, sometimes. I saw you leave and I waited for you to come back. It wasn't difficult. It's easy to hide at night – if you don't mind where. I was going to pick you off, one at a time. It was good of you to decide to keep together, in one house – saved me a lot of travelling around. Like hens in a hen house to a fox.' He liked the idea: it made him laugh.

We stopped at bottom of The Whitesands. It was a wet, bleak, empty place. I saw one person – so did he – on the other side of the river, walking away with his dog. We waited.

He slid a noose over my head. It was thick: it fitted like a scarf. He tugged on its end and it snuggled into my neck. He tied my hands behind my back. I let him – pushing my arms tightly together, shielding my weapon. Yet, it set off uncertainty. I tried to be calm again, to think rationally. I needed to use surprise. He wouldn't know I could cut myself free. His search hadn't reached the knife hidden in the cuff of my shirt: his anger had stopped him. He will think he is safe from me and he will become sloppy. At one point he will be careless.

I walked to the footbridge on bare feet but mercifully in a patch of fresh air. He followed, holding the end of the noose: the knife hard at my back. Someone should see us – even at this late hour.

'The suspension bridge. Interesting name – very fitting,' he mocked.

The rickety walkway – made from iron sheets supported loosely over cross-girders – clanged as I stepped on. The large chestnut tree growing by the side of the river blocked out the rest of The Whitesands: shielding us. The other bank was quiet, but there are houses: someone could look out of their window and call for help.

I walked on and the rope jarred and my head jerked

backwards: he'd wound the end round an iron strut. He called me to him, tied the rope tightly, and faced me upstream. The river was running fast below, wild with rain. I could make out the pipe in the wall where I'd been ejected like a torpedo only one day before. The river level reached it now; and further up the caul roared.

He stood behind. I knew what he was going to do. I knew about the suspension bridge now. I lost control. I was scared: my legs turned to tubes of runny porridge. I spoke rapidly, voice shaking, 'You... you don't have to do this.'

He was calm and cold. He wasn't waiting. 'Step up onto the handrail and down onto the ledge on the other side. Now!'

'If I tell his name will you let me go?'

'It's too late for that. Now step *up*.'

I couldn't keep my breathing in check: I shuddering with fear. 'I can't climb. I won't do it.' My fingers found the pocket in the sleeve. I couldn't control the shaking. The knife must not drop. He wasn't directly behind me – standing to one side. It would be difficult. He mustn't be allowed to escape. The blow has to be precise. I tried to line him up: picturing the angle of attack.

He was reasonable, persuasive, 'You have to – for your girlfriend's sake. She's depending on you. Do it now, step up, or I return to the house and leave you here, tied. You can't do that to her. It's not fair. You must know that.'

How would he leave me? Alive? I have a knife to cut myself free and the keys are still in the car. I could beat him back. Would *he* take the car? Can he drive? Or would he simply throw the keys away?

Play for time.

'I need my hands free to climb up.'

'Good try.' He shoved me up onto the rail, one hand under my armpit, his knife tearing into the fabric of my shirt as I moved.

I stood on top of the handrail. It was slippery. Someone might pass: a police car. They will see me up here. I'm obvious. My hands must be level with his eyes. He would see the slightest movement. If I released the blade he will be ready.

He held onto me as I placed one foot down onto the ledge, then the other. The lattice work of the bridge's side separated us now. That was good. It blocked his view. The river surged under my feet.

'You killed Mr. Chamberlain,' I shouted.

'What are you talking about?' He was right behind, speaking into my left ear: his blade gouging into my shoulder.

Keep it slow, keep it calm.

'The old man in the evening suit – murdered by a rabbit snare. Choked to death. That was you!'

'*I* didn't do it. He did that to himself. I told him not to move. I explained it to him. He didn't listen. I hope your girlfriend listened.'

I thought of her alone in that house, petrified, and next to that case, with its sickening photos. Was she sitting in blackness? I didn't know. It didn't matter: either way she will become increasingly uncomfortable and nervous of that house. She is scared of other's people's homes. She might not be able to control herself, keep still long enough for help to arrive. And the snare will tighten. If she's in the dark, she won't see the memories stored there but every creak, every groan will make her jump – a possible signal of The Tramp's return.

I needed to save her from any more torture.

'You have to jump now,' he said quietly.

My feet wavered on the slick surface. My bones rattled. The words burst from my mouth, 'His name is Don Gardiner. You have what you want – now leave us be!'

I saw the face of my Uncle James, head turned towards the camera, smiling. It was the wrong time. The image from that photograph wouldn't leave. It burned holes into my skull:

his smile as bright as summer sun through a magnifying glass. His hand was on the back of my mother's head – to caress it or to hold it in place.

'Jump!' he shouted.

'I won't. You have everything you wanted. You have the name. Now leave us – please. I have done enough. I have done what you asked.'

'It's not enough.'

'Then I am to blame. Get it over with and leave her alone.'

'I *will* leave her be – but *you* must jump. That's how you save her.'

'Why do you want to kill me? Can't you give me a reason, at least?'

'But *I'm* not killing you. When you jump you will be killing yourself.'

'How can you say that? It is *you* who are doing this to me. No-one will think it's a suicide. They *know* you are after me.'

'That's not the point.'

'What is?'

'I put the rope round your neck – that's all. That rope could stay there for the rest of your life and nothing would happen to you. I am not to blame for what happens next. It's only when you jump that it changes. *You* bring it on yourself. *You* are making the change – not me. It was the same with that fellow and the snare.'

'I'm not going to jump. If you force me off, you will be doing the killing.'

He yelled in my ear, 'Don't you get it? Do we have to go through it all again?' He was quiet for a moment and then he became composed once more. 'If you don't jump I will leave now and I will return to that house. I won't kill her either but I'll make sure she squirms and I'll watch and look on at the damage the snare does as it tightens and gouges and chokes.

Who is it to be then – you or her?'

Suddenly I am in a corridor, the corridor of my nightmares, I am young and I'm walking slowly towards the door at the end. I touch the handle – there is music coming from within.

I open it a crack and peer round. The music is louder. I see flesh – everywhere. In a corner there is a couple, one sitting on the other's lap. They are smiling. I don't recognise them. No-one looks up: they don't hear. I see the bright light in the corner and I see my father and my Uncle James. They are standing in the middle of the floor, tall, erect, and smiling at each other. My mother is between them – the three of them forming an H. She is the bar in the middle of the two uprights – my father is at the back.

I crouch down, my head level with my ankles, now below my ankles, as low as I can go, and I spring from the bridge like an Acapulco diver, jumping out, far and out, and away – except my hands are held behind my back.

Two ways to die – different and similar.

By gravity – a simple hanging. Or by water.

What is the length of the rope? Has he considered the rise in the Nith?

I will know soon enough.

The river is noisy as I fall to it. The rope has to be short enough. Too long and I hit the water. It will break my fall. It will cushion me, it will stop my neck from snapping: but the river will drag me under the bridge, it will haul on my body, pulling it downstream, yanking me against the noose – stretching me out on a watery rack. Throttling. The rope will hold my head above the river, saving me from drowning – but only to prolong death.

Or I go under completely. Strangled or drowned. I will know soon enough.

I'm flying through the air. It's a glorious feeling. And my

dearest Chiara will be safe. I was always going to do as he wanted: I could never take the risk. She didn't deserve that. I owed her. I told her I'd do anything for her – and this is better than moving to Gretna.

It places trust on The Tramp's word – but he came back to free my hands. I can never forget that. He didn't have to: he has shown some compassion. And I am honouring our contract.

Two ways to die. Two ways to live.

In the merest fraction of a second, the rope catches and a loud crack explodes in my neck. I'd barely got going: the rope is short. It could have been worse, much, much worse. Yet this sickening noise charges through my spine as the noose fights to rip each vertebra apart, battling to break my spine asunder. My full weight duelling with my frail neck. The rope clutches at my throat, ramming my jaw up and high.

I twist to face the bridge, my momentum swinging me under. I push on with my legs. Forward, propelling me forward, like on a swing. I'm swinging in the rain.

My legs shoot out, higher, and my feet reach and catch the underside of the bridge, one on either side of an I-shaped girder. My heels pinch in and catch on its narrow ledge – and I hold on.

He will think his work is done. He won't look over. He will go. I have jumped. I have done as instructed.

There was no sound from above. Has he gone?

I shuffled for a better grip, further under the bridge – if the train had hit, I wouldn't have heels to hold me here.

The rope was very tight but not choking. I could breathe – just. It ran up the back of my neck and supported my head. It held up my upper body. If I had missed my footing, if I had failed to grasp the beam, I would be hanging by my neck right now. But there would be another chance, another way to live: release the knife, slice away the bindings and the noose, plunge into the river, and take my chances.

I fumbled for the knife. If I dropped it now there would be little chance: I can't cling on for much longer. Cut through and free my hands.

The popper flipped away, the knife was in my grasp. The blade flicked out and I started to saw. My grip was firm: it was cutting.

There was a tug on the noose. He was still there. He hadn't gone. He was checking it. I needed to free my hands quickly. Suddenly the rope round my neck broke away: cut. At that instant, I heard his feet thump above me and felt the shake of the bridge as he ran.

No longer supported by the noose, my head and body fell away. I was hanging upside-down like a bat: my full weight held by my heels – my arms still uselessly behind.

One foot slipped. I lost my grip. I started falling through the air again towards the brown, raging, majestic River Nith.

I had broken my pact – in his eyes. What would he do to Chiara now?

I cut as I fell. It was short drop but a hard hit – headfirst, plunging into the surge. Underwater, sinking, turning, pumping legs for the surface. Briefly above. A gasp of air. The flow was fast. My legs hopeless in the current. I remembered the joke – the man who died in muesli – pulled under by a strong currant.

It rushed me under St Michael's Bridge. I hadn't dropped the knife. The river wanted it. I held on, rubbing, cutting, gasping for breath. Smothered in waves and waves of water, pushing down, tumbling me over, not wanting me here – the river wishing I would disappear.

The rope cut. I dropped the blade. I can swim better without it. My head broke the surface. I saw the bank and was heading towards it. The river curving. There was an overhanging bush. I grabbed it. The water was level with the path through the park. I dragged and crawled from the river like a croc coming onto land.

228

The rope, trailing like a leash, caught on a branch, and it released a huge burst of pain through my neck. I wrestled the noose over my head and threw it down.

The car had to be there. I needed to beat him back to the house. The water poured from my clothes in my frantic run over hard stones in bare feet. The throbbing in my neck was ugly and violent.

I could call the police from a phone box and raise the alarm – but I didn't have a clue where to find one. This was no time to search. I was puffing hard, my legs heavy, my head in agony.

I could go to someone's house. How long to raise them from their bed? Would they open up to someone in my state? If only I could get in touch with Asa – but it would be too dangerous for him to go round to that house. They could all go – safety in numbers. But I'd left my phone – I didn't know his number off by heart – and I didn't want anyone seeing that chest.

My car was there. The keys were still in the ignition. I bent inside and the movement was nauseating.

*

The car screeched to a halt outside Aunt May's house. It lashed through my neck. No time to consider it. I needed a weapon. My golf clubs were in the back. I grabbed the three iron, ran a couple of paces, returned, and swapped it for a seven iron – easier to hit.

I pushed the front door open. The yale lock had stuck, the catch hadn't flipped back out – not fully – that's why it hadn't shut properly. It needed oiling.

I burst into the hallway. Take time. I closed the door softly behind. The house was quiet – all the lights were on. I took the stairs one at a time, my clothes still squelching. And stopped – listening on the landing, club held high. There was no sound. The light was on in the bedroom; the door was ajar.

Was he here already?

Anger raged and I charged. He couldn't do this to us. Take him by surprise, smash him to the ground before he can set himself. I had the club in both hands – my latest golfing grip – the one to counter a slice. Chiara jumped in fright – she was alive, still attached to the chair, her eyes screaming. There was no-one else in the room.

I dropped my weapon and dashed across, working the ligature free from her neck. It was tight – there was a line where it bit in. I tugged off the tape at her mouth. It didn't hurt – she has no moustache.

I kissed her on the mouth, on her cheeks, her wet eyes. I kissed my way round the line on her beautiful neck. I collapsed in sobs, my head and neck aching and wet, supported by her lap. 'I'm sorry. I'm so sorry for everything you've been though.' I felt the blame – it was as heavy as a Gretna midfielder. 'Can you forgive me? You say it's not a good thing, but I'm sure I love you – more than anything. I couldn't take the risk. Do you see? I want you to marry me, Chiara. Will you marry me?'

'If I say yes, will you untie me?'

*

I ran downstairs. I had to take the risk: my seven iron wasn't enough. He could appear at any time. I'd snecked the front door shut – but it might not hold him. I grabbed two kitchen knives and raced back up the stairs. The house was large. He might have returned before me, inside, hiding, waiting. I didn't want to check each room, one at a time.

'Are you sure you didn't hear him?' I whispered. We stood side by side, crouched behind the open bedroom door, backs to the wall. I felt I was going to pass out.

'I don't know.'

We remained for five long minutes, expecting to hear his approach.

230

'You have to call the police, Jin. And you need to change your clothes – you're shivering.'

It was the signal for movement. I said, 'He's not coming – or else he's waiting for us – downstairs. I'll need to get rid of all this first.' I nodded in the direction of the box. It was a bad movement – it made me groan. My head was too heavy for my neck. The adrenaline, masking some of the pain, was ebbing away.

'It's disgusting, Chiara. No-one can see in that box.' With great difficulty, I managed to pick up my possessions from the floor, jammed into my shoes, replaced the photo in the box on top of the others, and locked it.

It was time to go. I held the box under one arm, the other hand holding the knife ahead. Chiara clung to me. We inched out of the room.

The stairs creaked with every step. We heard no other noises and left by the front door. The pavement outside was empty. We dropped our knives to our sides as we broke cover. We tried not to run – it lasted four strides. I had my key ready.

My front door closed. The relief was incredible. We crept through to my bedroom, not wanting to waken anyone upstairs, dumping the box on the ground. I found the painkillers and took a double dose.

Chiara slumped down on the bed. 'Call the police now.'

I grabbed some clothes, threw off the others, toweled, eased into them, and sat down beside her, rolling onto my side, gingerly, feeling the blissful relief of the support of my pillow, and then shuffled round to stare at the ceiling.

'Just give me time to gather my thoughts. I don't want to have to explain why we were in that house. We need to think of a good reason for going there at this time of night.' I tried breathing deeply. I felt exhausted but couldn't relax: the wild river was in me, flowing through my veins.

She shuffled and lay down beside me, both with weals

round our necks: the king and queen of Dumfries. She asked how I had escaped him. I told her I'd jumped from a bridge, that he had tied a rope round my neck and I'd escaped – keeping it simple, no need for more alarm.

'I gave him Don's name. I felt I had to,' I added.

'It's not your fault.'

'He'll track him down. Maybe we can set a trap for him – with Don's help.' I will have revenge.

'He might be on his way right now, Jin. You need to call the police. And, I think you need to see a doctor. Did you hurt your head in the fall?'

'There's no need to rush. Even if The Tramp could find out the address, Don's not staying in his own home. He's safe for now.' I paused. 'Something else happened on that bridge, Chiara.' I told her about my vision, relating each dreadful part.

'What do you think it all means?' I asked.

'A suppressed memory. Probably seeing that photo triggered it. You have the dream when you feel threatened or scared, isn't that right? It must be something like that.'

'I thought the nightmares were caused by you. And before you say anything, I know now it was only a coincidence – you just happen to be sleeping beside me when I've had them recently.'

'Let's not go over that again.'

'Sorry.'

'You were young when you witnessed it and it probably scared you. Perhaps the first time you felt genuine fright, and since then there has always been that link.'

'It was Aunt May's house, I'm sure of it – but I don't ever remember staying.'

'Well, for whatever reason, it seems you *were* sleeping there. You woke and decided to investigate. What age do you think you were?'

'I've no idea.'

232

'You might have been too young to fully understand what was happening but you must have known it wasn't quite – how shall I say – normal?'

'You think this is why I've been this way all my life?'

'How do you mean?'

'You're my first proper girlfriend – I've never had the urge, not really.'

'It's not something I've actually noticed,' she said coyly, before adding, 'You'd need to ask an expert that. But, I daresay, it might have shaped you in some way. It obviously had a big effect otherwise you wouldn't have submerged it.'

'There was music playing – it was loud. That might be what woke me. I'll always remember that tune.'

'What was it?'

'I don't know – I never listen to music...'

'Scared you might hear it again?'

I closed my eyes and breathed in deeply. The painkillers were starting to work. My headache was lessening: my neck dampening. 'What are we going to do with that box, Chiara?'

'Do whatever you think is best.'

'When I was ten, my father had the back gate bricked over – I remember it clearly. I thought it was odd at the time – that was my way in from the back lane. I was too wee to climb over the wall and had to go round to the front after that. It was a pest. He said it was to do with security – to make the house safer.'

'What about it?'

'Well, what if I *was* spotted keeking into that room? What if that put a stop to everything, all the goings on?'

'I don't follow.'

'If I peered into that room when I was ten then the two things could be connected. What if the guests to our house didn't just come from far away – what if there were others from town and they could slip in and out without the neighbours knowing? Along the back lane and in through the back door?'

'What does it matter now?'

'Some might still be alive.' I waited before carrying on, 'Onion Sanny used to come round on his big black bike – selling onions. He's old enough…'

'You think he was there? I would say that's a bit far-fetched. But, I suppose, you could ask your aunt.'

I thought of her: alone in the hospital ward.

'You need to forget about it for now, Jin. You need to start thinking about the police. Do you want me to call them?'

I turned my head, carefully, slowly, and stared at the two knives on the dressing table – the ones we'd taken from Aunt May's house. The handles were made of wood, part of a set, the only difference being the shape of the blades.

I said, 'I think we should destroy the box – right away. Burn it before the police arrive. I can build a fire in the front room – the fireplace still works.' I eased myself up into an upright position: it was bearable.

She did the same. 'You might want to look through them first, though – there could be other things in there you might want to keep. They might not all be like the top one. Maybe even photos of you as a boy – you never know.'

'That's just it – I never had my picture taken. And now there are all these. That seems to make it worse. And why would they want to keep them?'

She shrugged. 'For the same reason people have always taken and kept pictures: they wanted to keep a record of everyone who, eh, came on a visit. Why don't we have a look through it? Face your fears. Isn't that what people are supposed to do? It might help in the long run.'

'No, I can't – it will put me off for life. It's embarrassing enough to discuss that sort of thing with a parent, but it's much, much worse seeing them in the act.'

'I'll look through if you want?'

I gave a vague shrug. She carried the box over to the dressing table, sat down on the stool and studied each one, place them into different piles.

'When were you born?' she asked.

'1963.'

'So you reckon all this might have stopped in '73. It would have gone on right through the Sixties – the Swinging Sixties.' She muttered to herself, 'I never realised that was the reason for its name.'

I added, 'My mother was in her forties when she had me – and my father was older. Although he's probably not my father…'

She continued to size up each picture, sometimes turning it sideways, sometimes turning her head. 'So your parents were swingers. You know what I'm talking about?'

'Yes, I know. They were all at it – the whole family, my aunts and uncles, and the people who came to stay. By the end of the Fifties, they had managed to buy houses in this street, linked by the back lane and they were all at it.

But what I don't get is that my mother seemed to think Uncle James was my father – how could she possibly know? It could have happened at any time – by anyone. They appear to be doing it all the time. I thought the family came to our house for breakfast, but probably they never left the night before. I was always packed off early to bed – so they could get on with it. And every bedroom had a lock – again my father said it was for security – but it was more likely to keep me out, and one time they were careless.'

'So in '73, when the gate was bricked over, they would have been…'

'Fifty, or thereabouts. My uncles were older than my father. Getting too old for it, maybe. Do you think that'll happen to me? It's not so far away.'

She raised her eyebrows. 'I would hope not. I have plenty

more games.'

'As long as they don't involve other people.'

'Pity,' she said quietly, turning back to her task. 'Again, so much hair everywhere.' She added, 'Maybe it's not so bad, Jin, really – forgetting about your father for one minute. They were consenting adults – so where's the harm? People still do it nowadays and seem happy enough. I don't think it's something you should worry about. I'm sure I read about an actual hotel in France where you can book your holidays and go for that kind of thing.'

'They probably don't need to bother with room keys – that wouldn't suit Asa.' I hesitated. 'You've looked into this? Is this a suggestion for another holiday?'

She made a face. 'It might be better than in a tent.'

'Do you think they charged a fee, my parents – they all had large properties, plenty of room for guests, they had money?'

'Does it matter?'

I didn't intend to find out, and I had no questions for Aunt May. Was she still sleeping? 'Have you ever done that sort of thing, Chiara?'

'I've been to parties where they throw car keys into a pot.'

'And?'

'Well, I think you know I like to be in charge.'

'That's not much of an answer.'

'It will have to do for now – you will find out everything about me soon enough. What's the rush?'

'You know everything about me.'

She raised one eyebrow and patted the box. 'You surprise me every day. This here is one very good example.'

For the first time in an age I laughed. 'My mother must have felt something wasn't right, though. Remember my name – James and Sin. Do you think she was forced?'

'I doubt it. She seems happy enough. Even in the photo you saw.'

'She wasn't smiling.'

'She's concentrating. Her eyes don't say anything different. She's grinning in some of the other ones I've seen.'

'She used to tell me about the night elves.'

'What about them?'

'I thought the night elves were little creatures who tidied up and did the dusting while we slept but I think I misheard her. What if she meant the night evils? It was meant as a warning to me – she was really saying, 'watch out for the night evils.' I think she may have been forced into it.'

'It certainly doesn't look like it, Jin. She's happy in a lot of them. Do you want me to show you? Is this her with the three brothers?'

I turned away. How could it be right? Yet it was everywhere – and under my roof all the time. My families' houses didn't welcome guests with open arms but with open legs. Maybe that's what Chisel and High-Heid-Yin-Harris had been chuntering on about. Did Chisel's wife offer the same kind of service – favours in return for information? Harris is Chisel's informant: there would need to be a reason for that.

Chiara kept talking, 'It must have been strange for them to watch you grow up and without the usual urges – when they had all been so rampant.'

I was trying not to listen to her. I needed the debris to leave my mind.

'Does it seem dirty to you – all this?' She held up another photo.

'What? Yes.'

'And when *we're* together – how does that feel?'

'It feels the most natural thing in the world. It's always been that way with you.'

'What's the difference?'

I shook my head gently. I didn't want to think down those lines as other thoughts were forming. One idea and then the next. 'That's it. What you said about hair – a lot of hair around. I've got it – and the knives, the two knives.'

'What?'

'Put the pictures away just now, please. Lock the box and hide it. I need to go.'

'What are you talking about?'

'It's the two knives Jackie Gittes' killer had on him – one in his rucksack, one in his hand.'

'What about them?'

'The black handled knife in his hand didn't belong to him, and he didn't steal it from Jackie's bed-sit.' I stood up. 'I have to go. I gave Don Gardiner's name to The Tramp.'

'You're in no state to do anything. Anyway, you said he was safe: he's not at his home. You said he wouldn't be found at Jill's.'

'I was wrong. The Tramp will know where he is and he'll be on his way there right now. He has to be: he didn't come after us. *This* is more important to him. I need to ask you to let me go – on my own.'

'What about the police?'

'I'm quicker and they won't believe me. But, really, there is a better reason for not calling them: the people I'm dealing with won't want them there – and neither do I.'

'What if I say no? That it's too dangerous?'

'I won't be harmed – I'm sure of it. I need to see this finished – on my own. You have to stay here. What do you say? There are people who need my help. You told me I had to keep doing that.'

She hesitated – then gave the briefest of nods.

I stopped at the doorway. 'By the way, what's your father's name?'

'Why?'

'It would be one fact to hold. One fact about you for each day. We can do it like that – if you like?'

*

I took a knife from the kitchen – I didn't want Chiara to know I needed one. Now it sat on the passenger seat as I waited in my car, a little way down from Jill Gittes' flat. I didn't need the police and their interference – and I didn't want Don warned. I wanted to see how everything unfolded. Moreover, I needed revenge – but there was one worry.

No lights shone from Jill's window. I was in time: it hadn't started yet.

I waited for almost two hours – the windows open for the fresh air to hold the claws of sleep at bay – as the night began making way for the day. The vigil calmed me down, made me rational, cold. I wasn't sure how I would react to seeing The Tramp again, but only one thing mattered right now – Jill's safety.

I noticed the man in white trousers, white t-shirt, and black jacket walk to the door and ring the bell. He was clean-shaven, neat; his clothes were tight to his skin. He rang again and again – holding his hand on the buzzer far longer than was polite.

The door opened carefully, and then fully. Even from my position I could see the look of shock on a disheveled Jill Gittes' face. Some words were spoken – mostly by the man. It took her a while to move; then she went inside, leaving him on the pavement, waiting.

Don Gardiner stumbled out in slippers, with a coat slung over his shoulders, track suit bottoms hanging below, and stood beside Jill. She had her hands on her hips. There was a quick movement from the man in white trousers and Gardiner doubled up, staggering backwards to collide with the door frame, both hands to his eyes despite one arm held in a sling.

An envelope floated to the ground.

239

The man caught Gardiner's upper arm, stopping him sinking to his knees. Jill looked on, unmoving. I should have understood. Instead, I slipped from the car and stood motionless in the middle of the empty, gleaming road, the rain falling on my head, the knife obvious at my side – turning it in my hand to reflect the yellow streetlights off the blade. I shouted across, 'I don't want Jill harmed.'

Jill looked up, the man turned. He hesitated, then dragged Gardiner, still bent over, in front of him like a shield, and called back, 'This is not a good time for you to be here. Go away and leave us be.'

'I can't do that. I can't leave – not until I know she's safe.'

'Well, in that case, you might as well join us. Come over here and you can take her place – then she will be fine.'

'I don't think I'll bother,' I replied, taking a couple of deliberate paces forward. '*You* have to go. Now! And leave her.' My car door was opened, the keys in the ignition. I was twenty yards from him: he wouldn't catch me if he chased over – and Jill could escape inside. Or, I would fight him.

'Aren't you concerned about what happens to *him*?' He jabbed Don in the back, making him groan and stumble forward.

'Not really.'

'That's interesting. And you don't seem surprised to see me.'

'No, but it looks like you've scrubbed up well. What did you do with that stinking coat and the enormous hood?'

Jeremy Gittes whispered something, before bringing his hand out of the pocket of his jacket. Despite the distance and the filthy weather, I could tell it was a gun. It had a long barrel and it pointed in my direction. It was unexpected, shocking. It made me loathe him all the more.

I wondered how good a shot he was, if he could hit a

moving target, if my car was bulletproof, if I could run and leave without her.

Gittes shouted, 'What's it to be – you or her?' He gave a laugh. 'It always seems to be that way with you.'

I took a few steps towards him and his cologne was powerful, even from this range – but, then, it would have to be.

'Walk ahead of us so I can keep an eye on you. And leave the knife,' he demanded. 'And she can stay.'

*

We trailed on through the rain, along abandoned pavements – the three of us. I was in the lead, Don Gardiner behind. We wouldn't see the sun today – it would be a dark dawn and it wasn't far away.

Gittes told me to turn into a lane. I had dropped my knife down a drain, my father's switchblade lay at the bottom of the river – I had nothing up my sleeve. Jill had been allowed to return to her flat. She had stared unflinchingly at me – I couldn't judge what she'd wanted to convey. She wouldn't phone the police: Jeremy told her my life was in her hands.

We arrived at the new swimming pool complex. It wasn't far – not much more than round the corner. I hadn't walked down this way recently, only driven by on my way to find Chiara in room 43 – a lot of water had passed since then.

'You'll find a gap to squeeze through over there,' Gittes said.

We were in the muddy confines of the site: it looked like a normal chaotic construction site with bricks and rubble and machines. We moved inside the building. It had no roof yet – the walls were only half-way up. I gave a quick glance behind. Gardiner was still in difficulty. There was a gag over his mouth. Gittes held onto him, the gun fixed in his back.

At close quarters, it was obvious Gittes' nose had been broken, and his face was dappled with stubborn bruises: his jaw sitting at an odd angle. 'Careful,' he called. 'They've been

digging out the pool. You don't want to fall in. Not at the deep
end anyway: it's been concreted. The guard is about to come
round – as regular as a fig farmer, he is. We'll hide up there
until he finishes his rounds. He never takes long.'

At the end of the pool area a white column appeared
through the murk. The towering structure of the high diving
platform loomed over us like a giant conning tower of a
submarine.

'Climb up the rungs at the back, Mr. Johnstone – there's
no staircase yet. When you reach the top, go and sit at the far
end of the highest platform, legs crossed, your back to the
drop.'

I climbed up the metal, semi-circular rungs and a memory
returned of a similar but opposite time: descending into the
sewer. This was preferable: but no less dangerous. The
platform at the top was large. It had no railings. I shuffled
carefully to the end of the wet surface, sat down, and waited for
them. It took a while. Gardiner's head appeared finally. It must
have been a difficult climb up the slick hoops with stinging
eyes and fire through the head, yet without thoughts of
resistance. He had used both hands: the sling an apparently
unnecessary adornment. Gittes came into sight: pushing and
prodding his victim on.

Gardiner was guided half-way along, made to sit down,
cross-legged, to my right, at the edge, his back also to the drop.
Gittes pulled a roll of tape from a jacket pocket and wrapped it
round Gardiner's chest, pinning the arms in place: crossed over
like the dead. Then more tape bound his legs together. A
backward tumble would be the end of us both. It might be
difficult for Gardiner to keep his balance: soon the tremors
would begin through his body.

Jeremy Gittes sat down, cross-legged, matching me, back
straight, at the end with the rungs, the safer end; the one away
from the chasm of excavation, but still high enough from the

242

ground to provoke caution. The gun was in his hand: it pointed midway between his prisoners.

'Apparently it comes in one piece – this whole platform – and craned into position,' he said. 'They build the place round it.'

'Fascinating.'

He was relaxed. We might have been about to enjoy a picnic. I could almost imagine him spreading a rug out and offering pâté and crackers. Stealthily, the damp crept up into the seat of my trousers and another memory returned.

'What do you intend to do?' I asked him, estimating the distance. It was about four yards. Too far to leap – but what would be the point anyway? I didn't want to go over the side.

'What do I intend to do? I intend to shoot *him*.' The black, evil gun flicked at Gardiner, then back towards me. He went on, grinning, his mouth almost spread diagonally across his face, teeth missing. 'He doesn't deserve to live. I thought you'd have worked it all out by now.'

'I have – some – but not everything.'

Gittes slid the roll of tape across the damp surface like a curling stone on ice. It hit off my leg. 'Wrap that round your ankles – plenty of times, in a figure of eight, and make it tight. Please.' Another smile – either he was enjoying the power over us, or enjoying our company. I lifted the tape and wound it round.

He went on pleasantly, 'I would like to hear what you have to say. It will be interesting – you might know more than me, in fact.'

He was cajoling me into his amiable game. I thought of the moment he'd touched Chiara's skin with his foul hands, the snare he had fixed there, and the venom I'd felt then. It was still within me – it needed to stay at the surface.

'I know you killed Lewis Chamberlain,' I said: my voice flat.

243

'You mentioned that before – on the bridge. I've smartened up a bit since then, of course – which wouldn't be too difficult. I borrowed these from an acquaintance – if you're interested – and he kindly gave me the use of his bathroom – not that he had any say in the matter. I don't intend going down into the sewers again.'

'Who beat you up? Your face must have been a mess.' I enjoyed the notion.

'It was: jaw broken, nose broken, a mass of blood. But I thought you had it all figured out: I thought you knew who did it to me.' He gave a sharp laugh.

'I know you put a snare round Lewis Chamberlain's throat and watched him choke to death. He saw you up at the old hotel – it's mentioned in his diary.'

Jeremy Gittes dismissed my words with a series of shakes to the head. 'He was an old man. The next winter would have got him anyway.'

'How can you say that? How can you be so glib with someone's life? You have no rights to it.'

He nodded seriously. 'I understand that. I *did* explain to him…'

I couldn't wait to hear his ludicrous excuse again. 'And the fact that he hadn't gone to the police – did that not mean anything? Whatever he saw, whatever frightened him that night, he had decided to keep quiet. He *wanted* his life – and you took it away. Why couldn't you have let him be? He wasn't going to tell anyone. Perhaps he didn't see enough, or wouldn't be able to identify you – did you ever think of that? What right do you have!?' I was shouting – yet he hadn't told me to quieten down.

In return, he spoke softly, 'I'm afraid you are not quite correct there. It *was* necessary.'

'How could it be necessary? Why did you have to hunt him down? But it took you a while, didn't it? More than a month – because you're not very good at it. Just like with Gardiner, here?' I wanted to goad the man in front of me – turn him back to the person I hated.

He gave another nod and moved his hand. 'You are very brave for someone who has a gun fixed at the centre of their body. I admire that.'

'And I'm scared of heights.'

'Wait,' he whispered, and held up a finger. There was a noise in the distance. 'Not a sound or this goes off. It's the guard. Come closer to the middle of the platform. Shuffle forward so he can't see you.'

I moved from the edge. Gittes crouched, moved across, and pulled Gardiner a couple of feet in. The gun flicked between us. Gittes held the same finger to his crooked lips, and we waited as the rain fell. I saw the signs of the drug taking hold: Gardiner was beginning to shake, his eyes shifting back and forth, taking in demons, seeing the full danger for the first time.

After five minutes, I heard a motor start up, I hadn't heard it arrive. It drove away. He shooed us back to our original positions.

'Now what were we talking about?' It could have been a cordial conversation in the pub. He added, 'In case you're wondering, we have another hour before the guard's next visit.'

I couldn't hold back. 'You had to find Lewis Chamberlain. You needed him dead – but he was a sort of non-descript man. I didn't recognise him either without his evening suit. So it wasn't until you saw him all dressed up – perhaps by accident – on his way back from his dance night that you knew it was him. Or did you see him go there and hide, and lurk, and kill him when he set off back for home? Is that what happened?'

'Yes.'

For a moment his head bowed and the grip on his gun

loosened, the barrel dipping. I thought it might fall from his grasp. I placed both palms on the platform beside me. If it fell, I was ready to leap at him like a kangaroo, three bounds, if the binding allowed. My legs were crossed – that would make it harder, more awkward, but he had left my hands free.

Gardiner sensed it. He looked at me intently, nodded vigorously, urging me into action: shock, fear, terror filling his eyes.

'If he hadn't worn that suit to his dance, Mr. Chamberlain would still be alive,' I said, strongly. The thought rekindled my rage and the sound of my voice brought Jeremy Gittes back to life. His head came up, his hold of the gun returned. He wore no gloves.

'You could be right,' he said. 'But I want to hear about *him*!' The barrel whipped round to point at Gardiner. 'Tell me what you know about him. If we try, together, we should be able to build up the whole picture.'

I didn't mind going on – there was no rush. He wasn't going to hurt me – I'd told Chiara that. I started, 'Gardiner was involved in Jackie's death – I know that now. You must have found out as well and wanted revenge for your brother. But you couldn't find him, so, in some mad, roundabout way, you asked me – and now you have him at your mercy.'

Gittes said nothing in return, so I went on, 'When I gave you Gardiner's name on the bridge, you didn't ask me where to find him – you already knew. You didn't return to my aunt's house: you had to be after him instead. I imagine your brother told you about him.'

'Why did *you* turn up? You didn't need to.'

'I had to make sure Jill would be safe.'

Jeremy Gittes gave a nod. 'Jackie told me about the set-up with this new boyfriend. I remembered his name – but we'd never met, of course. I didn't know what he looked like.'

'It took you long enough to show up tonight – brushing

the skin, were we?'

He gave his angled grin. 'A lot of grime to be washed away – and by now it will have returned from whence it came. Down the plughole – and good riddance.'

He coughed: it seemed to hurt. 'My brother thought Gardiner was an okay guy – someone to be trusted, a good enough man for Jill. He thought she would be safe with him. He would protect her. That's what he told me – but then Jackie was never the sharpest...'

Gardiner was shivering, his nostrils flapping hard.

Jeremy Gittes continued, 'So you say our friend here was involved in Jackie's death? In what way? I thought they had the killer locked up last month.'

I hit back at him, 'Isn't that why *he's* here?!'

He shook his head. 'I'm afraid you're wrong about that, Mr. Johnstone. I didn't know for certain he had anything to do with Jackie's death – although it did seem likely he was behind it all in some way. But then the killer was caught...' He shrugged.

'Then why all this? Why bring him here?' I hesitated. 'So if this isn't about avenging your brother's murder, what is it? Ah, I see...'

He cut me off, 'How can you be so sure Gardiner was involved in the death?'

'It was all about the two knives. Once I figured that out, the rest came together. When we captured Jackie's killer he had two knives on him: one in his hand, a black-handled one, and another, brown-handled one, in his rucksack. But he didn't start out the night with two: he didn't have the black-handled, not to begin with. He didn't take it from Jackie's bed-sit because he didn't ransack it.' I pointed to Gardiner. 'That was him! *He* was the one who turned Jackie's flat upside down looking for drugs – and stealing the knife. *He* was the one carrying it that night.'

'Go on.'

A lot of what I was about to say was still guesswork – but I gave it a shot. 'Jackie received a shipment by mistake – maybe more than one shipment – and it made him scared, scared enough to move from his home and pretend to cut all ties with his wife. He needed to shelter Jill: he didn't want anyone coming after her.

But, of course, the dealers wanted their drugs back and this is where Gardiner comes in. He turns up in the area and starts poking about. He has a steady job, he seems respectable, so nobody is going to think twice about him – but really he's working for them. It wasn't by coincidence that he hooked up with Jill.

These are not the usual type of drugs: they are incapacitating compounds primarily for military use, probably stolen from an army base, and no doubt worth a lot of money in the right hands. It was Gardiner's role to find them and pass them on.' I turned on the man. 'Isn't that right?'

Gardiner shook his head. He wouldn't know where he was, but he would know I was right: he would remember his task.

I went on, 'I think Gardiner wanted bigger things for himself though – he wanted to take over this area, be the man in charge. He decided to get rid of anyone in his way. Your brother was killed as a warning to others. Gardiner didn't do it himself but he ordered someone else to – perhaps as a test to show their loyalty, or, maybe, it was under threat.'

Jeremy Gittes nodded.

'When Gardiner found out I was trying to catch Jackie's murderer, he volunteered to help. He wanted to cut his link to the killer – literally. He had that black-handled knife on him that night and, in a fight, it would have been put down as self-defence. He would say the killer came at *him* with the knife – so he wouldn't be blamed for the death. All nice and neat – and he becomes a hero, and fits in all the more.

But the attack went wrong: somehow he misjudged the situation and got the worst of it. Jackie's killer ran off, taking the weapon with him' I looked at Gardiner. 'That's right, isn't it?'

He stared back, blinking furiously in front of dazed eyes.

'Gardiner didn't find the drugs at Jackie's bed-sit, so then he turned his attention to you.'

Jeremy Gittes said, with a nod, 'That's good. Some of it tallies.' He tapped his middle finger on his lip. 'Now we have to consider some things. What do you *think* is going to happen here?

'I think I will return home in one piece and I think you will leave me and my friends alone from now on. I have done everything you've asked.' My voice stayed level – hiding the loathing I held for this man.

'Do you think *he* deserves to be left alone? Shall I tell you what he did to me?'

'Let me guess – he was the one who beat you up, made a mess of your face – and this is not about revenge for your brother, but merely to get even for what he did to you.'

'Merely? You haven't a clue.'

I said, 'Gardiner thought the drugs had been passed onto you – and he was correct.'

Gittes took it on, 'Jackie didn't want anything to do with them – but he held onto them for a while. Then he told me to take them. They weren't the normal kind – I could see that straight off. So I didn't know the market value or where to place them. I stashed them in a lock-up. Then this man caught me...' He flicked the barrel of the gun at Gardiner. 'Him and a couple of his thugs. See, he's not nearly so brave on his own!'

Gittes stopped to take in a deep breath. 'Someone, who I thought was a friend, pretended to tip me off in the pub. He told me people were looking for me and I should be careful. I went out the back way, over the courtyard wall – that's where they were waiting, on the other side.' He added, his voice low and gritty, 'I have no friends now – I've seen to that.'

He shrugged to dispel a memory, before going on, 'At first I tried to bargain with these men – but they wouldn't have it. Gardiner was the one giving the orders. They tortured me. I saw the pleasure in *his* face. I was held for over a day. They got the drugs, I told them where they were, but they wouldn't stop: they kept going and going.'

'They had no need to search your room.'

'Right. But it wasn't enough for *him*.' Gittes spat in the direction of his captive. 'They dumped me in that ruined hotel.'

'*You* were in the cellar!?'

He nodded. 'I was bloody all over. I had burns across my body. They wired me up and took turns to throw the switch. You've no idea what it was like, what they did. And then they put me in that hotel. They knew it was going to be demolished and they left me there, tied up, but still alive. It must have given them a thrill. I wished I was dead. Really I did.'

He hung his head for a moment, raising it to look me fully in the eye. 'I had time to think about a lot of things, Mr. Johnstone. I hoped I would die before the bulldozers showed up but I made plans as well – what I would do if I escaped. The mind works like that. There's seems to be a strand of hope at the core. That's something I've been trying to make you understand: optimism can exist in the darkest of places.' He sighed. 'I understood the need to change, to improve myself – but only after I had revenge on *him*.'

My mind was in a whirl now. 'You were there tied up? Mr. Chamberlain saw you *in* the hotel?'

He nodded again. 'I tried with all the strength I had to break free but it was hopeless…' His mouth tightened. 'Can't you see now why *this* man has to die? It's to make up for all he did to me.'

I looked over at Gardiner. I had been distraught when

he'd been stabbed. I blamed myself for his injury. I'd been fooled completely. How many other tortures and deaths were on his hands?

Jeremy went on, 'There is one thing, though, I have him to thank for.'

'What's that?'

'When he kindly reconstructed the bones of my face, I lost my lisp. It sounds like I have a new voice. I quite like it.'

'And you intend to shoot him?'

'I do.'

'What happened to all that stuff you spouted on about before – that you don't kill now?'

Are you really bargaining for Gardiner's life?

Jeremy shrugged. 'It's the bullet – not me.'

I snorted out a laugh. 'That's just plain nonsense – even you couldn't possibly believe that.'

He shrugged. 'Okay then, this is still the old me. The new one starts the moment this is over: when I finish what I planned. Once I have vengeance, I will change.' He twitched his shoulders. 'I'll let you into a secret, Mr. Johnstone – this is an old gun and it only has one bullet in it. That's right. It's all I have. I can't shoot you both.' He gave a weak smile. 'I intend to use it only on him. But, just in case I miss, we are up here as a back-up. If the bullet doesn't get him, if the gun doesn't work, he's going over the side. It's a fair drop down: a hard landing. I don't think anyone could survive it, do you?'

'And what do you intend to do with me? I know you won't harm me.'

Say it often enough and even he might believe it.

Jeremy shrugged. 'I hadn't budgeted for you to be here, obviously. I've wanted this moment with this man for such a long time. Sometimes, I imagined I wouldn't be able to control myself. I thought seeing him would send me into a fury. I thought I would kill him the moment he appeared in front of my eyes. It didn't happen. I was able to keep myself under control. But don't think for one moment he's not going to die this day. He will. I made a promise to myself...'

He shook his head. 'You see, I didn't want all that mess on Jill's door. It wouldn't have been proper. There you are, with all that time alone to contemplate, I can emphasise with people now.'

I decided against telling this gunman that he had the wrong word.

'A caring side has emerged in me.' Jeremy went on, 'I explained to Jill, told her what Gardiner had done to me but she couldn't have cared less: it meant nothing to her. She doesn't like me. Then I told her *he* was involved in Jackie's death, behind the whole thing. I didn't really know for sure but it was enough for her – maybe she suspected too. She was shocked to see me on her doorstep, of course, but that was swept away by her immediate hatred of this man. I've never seen anyone turn so quickly.'

I said, 'She was never coming along here, was she? I wasn't taking her place: she was never in danger, a hostage?'

'No, she wasn't. She wants this man dead as much as me. She would pull the trigger given the chance. I told her Jackie wouldn't want that, wouldn't want her in trouble. I promised her I would finish it for everyone's sake.'

'But what about *me*? Didn't she care I was trying to save her – and putting myself in danger?' I had helped Jill more than once in the past and had taken no payment – yet she had returned it by allowing me to leave in the company of a madman with a gun. I would never have thought it.

'What can I say?' he said, 'She wants me to go through with it. She won't rest until it happens. If we had allowed you to leave you might have called the police. We didn't want that to happen.'

He went on with a shake of the head. 'They seemed to

have had an intense love – her and Jackie. They'd go to any lengths for each other. I don't know what that feels like.' He stared at me for a while. 'Maybe you *do* – you jumped off the bridge.'

I could have played my 'love card', telling him about my feelings for Chiara, hoping it would bring leniency – but I didn't. To explain my emotions to this man – the man who had violated her skin – would be to dishonor them. I said, instead, 'I jumped to escape you and save myself – I knew I could.'

When do the builders show up for work – seven, eight o'clock? It can't be close to that yet. Too long to wait. How much rain has fallen in the last few days? One inch? Two? The excavated pool below will be filling up with water – but even three inches of rain wouldn't be nearly enough to take my fall.

'Cheer up,' he said, suddenly – and broke into another laugh.

'It's not easy. What are *you* so happy about anyway – I thought you despised this man?'

'I have the power over him. The thought of this moment has kept me going. The desire for vengeance has made each day possible – and justified everything. I've had to endure so much. You see the pleasure in the journey is in the moment of arrival – after that there's always the anticlimax.'

That certainly wasn't the case for visitors to my parent's home.

He may not waste the bullet on me but he could push me over. It's a long way down. My legs are tied – I'd be no match for him in a struggle. There had to be a way out. Chiara might have decided to call the police – I've been away for hours. How would they know where to find us?

I said, 'I don't think you will harm me. How's that – I'm trying out your optimism for size?'

He gave a deliberate nod, pleased with my statement. His smile was wearing me down – knocking me off guard. I needed to check myself: my hatred was evaporating as quickly as his cologne.

I went on, 'You saved my hands, you don't really want to harm me – not deep down.'

He shrugged. 'I've tried to be reasonable. It's difficult – there's always this struggle going on inside.'

'It's the drug, the anticholi-something compound. It's called Buzz. I had it in me as well. It makes you paranoid, persecuted – you see dangers everywhere, people turn into monsters. That's what's been happening to you. The chemical keeps well in damp conditions, it saturated the air of the sewer – there's a leak in the container. You must have known that. Didn't you realise you were being altered by it? You trusted no-one. Even your hanky, the one you stuffed into my mouth, was steeped in the stuff – enough to change *me* for a while. It's been affecting you all the time – until you are out in the fresh air and then it wears off. That's when you save me – do you see? You come to your senses.'

He nodded. 'I cut the noose to help you, let you go free.'

I didn't want to stop to consider that. 'Now you are rid of those clothes, away from any effects, out in the open, you can think rationally again. You can let me leave. Show compassion. What about it? I thought you would.'

He shook his head. 'Good try. The problem is – I don't like being stabbed all that much.'

'You're still on about that? I didn't want to mention it.'

If I let myself fall back I could land in the water – it just might be deep enough.

'You seem fine, though,' I tried. 'And you made me leap off that bridge – we must be even by now.'

Swimming pools slope to the deep end. The water will have gathered there. It'll be deeper – all collected below. Three inches of rain over the whole of the pool – it must be possible to calculate the true depth. But I'd stared out of the window during Maths lessons.

'I didn't make you jump – you *chose* to jump. I wanted the name and I wanted to punish you. You gave me the name: I was going to leave you on the ledge. I had what I wanted and I would have left you standing – but *you* chose to jump. I might even have done you a favour.'

'What are you talking about?'

'It showed how far you are willing to go.'

'It was only a couple of feet or so: shortish piece of rope.'

He went on, 'I bet it concentrated the mind, brought you in touch with your emotions, let you understand the important things. It works that way – am I right? When you are really up against it, things become clear.' His eyes roamed the space above my head. 'That's what happened to me as I waited in that cellar for the first fall of the masonry on my head. It sharpened my thoughts and brought meaning to it all.'

'Don't tell me – you found God,' I sneered.

'Why does everyone around here think that having one God is best? I have many. Surely that's better – the more the merrier.'

'So you've never had dealings with a committee?' Tread would have had a better repost, no doubt.

'Do you want to know how I'm fine?' he asked. 'How I escaped your knife?'

Topple backwards, close your eyes: it might be deep enough.

I played for time. 'A good wool vest?' Now I sounded exactly like Tread.

'The blade wasn't out.'

I shook my head. 'You're mistaken. I slid it out – all the way, its full length.'

'I picked up that Stanley knife – there was no blade showing. You never meant to do it – not really. I don't think you clicked it into position. It wasn't locked in place.'

'No, that's not right. I saw blood.' What was I doing? I should be agreeing with him: he'll look favourably on me and allow me to leave.

'There was no blood. It barely made it through my thick coat, certainly not to my skin.'

'I saw it,' I shouted. It made no sense to antagonise him.

He kept his voice level, 'You *expected* to see it. There was no blood. I hit my head as you pushed me back, that's all. Maybe there was water or a stain from before...'

'So no harm done?' It sounded friendly but I couldn't form a smile for this man.

'It's time,' Jeremy said, slowly, ominously, pushing himself to his feet – his shoes were kingfisher blue – taking one step closer to his prisoner, levelling the pistol at his head. Gardiner shrank within his shoulders and shuddered in anticipation. He wouldn't know how he had reached this place but he would know what happens with a gun and its bullet.

I shouted, 'You said you don't murder people!' I had no desire to help Gardiner. I detested him – but I didn't want to witness, or have any part in this reprisal.

Jeremy remained motionless. There was a slight stoop to his back – I hadn't noticed that before.

Does it just fire, or does the hammer need to be cocked first – like in cowboy films? 'You said you handed over the drugs,' I started. 'So how did you have them in the sewer then?'

I waited and prepared for the noise. It would be loud – even in this open area. Then the gun would be empty – if I believed him – and it would be the time to attack, or flee. Leap – but which way? Which was safer, which gives the better chance?

He kept still – as in a trance. I didn't dare speak again: scared it would startle him and the gun would go off. He hadn't fastened my hands. There had to be a reason. He could have given me no chance to fight back. When this is over, when the gun fires, he will let me go free.

It was taking too long. There was a brutal cruelty to the wait. Gardiner had collapsed slowly forward, sucked of life, his forehead resting on the platform, a tight knot of expectation. He started to make sounds – stifled sobs, then a high-pitched whimper. He was aware. And the gun had tracked his head.

The sound of Jeremy's voice jerked within me. 'You are right,' he said, and took a pace back, head still down. 'I am better than this now. In the tunnels I took the drug to make me forget for a while; forget why I was there and what every day in that stinking hole was doing to me. I took it so I wouldn't remember what it felt like to wake up and know there was another foul day to come in that cesspit. I had the pure stuff: the stuff he got had been cut. He thought he had it all: he got only half-strength.'

I said, 'You told me it wasn't too bad down there – no need to search for a toilet.'

He looked up and stared – as if woken from a dream and unable to place himself. 'I lied. I will never rid myself of its stench. *He* did that to me.'

'Why go there then – why not to a friend's?'

'I had to hide – I had no-one to trust. I'd been beaten and didn't want to be found. I was scared. It would be the last place anyone would look. I needed time to heal – so that I could go after *him*. I like things to be clean…'

'So I saw. Why would you even think of it?'

Jeremy held the gun in the flat of his palm – weighing it. 'At the time, it seemed the obvious thing to do: we go to any lengths when we are cornered and desperate. It is the nature of man: his success and his ruin.' He sighed. 'I had been there before – a long time ago. We were taken there as part of a school trip. Our primary teacher must have really hated us – but, at that time, I liked it. It was interesting.'

I agreed, mentioning my library book.

He shrugged. 'I was young. And I was silly enough to say to my classmates. Do you know what they started calling me?'

I shook my head, glad Tread wasn't here to guess.

'Germy. And it stuck – like a lot of things stick down there. It was funny for five minutes – but I was ridiculed for years on end. It affected me. They regret it now – every last one of them. I made sure of that, don't you worry.

I've disliked dirt from that time on. You would have seen that at my flat. I'm very particular: everything has to be dry-cleaned after it's worn. But you shouldn't have poked your nose in there – that's what cost you. Your snooping. I know what you're like and there are a lot of us who don't like busybodies prying into our town. There are some who want rid of you. I was doing them a favour – and I certainly didn't want you in my way, poking your nose in. You worried me.'

He gave a sad shake of the head. 'I was forced to hide like an animal in the humming bowels of the town, swilling around in everyone's muck, scrounging through litter bins in the middle of the night, searching for food. The smell will never leave me now, no matter how many times I shower, no matter how much perfume I use. I can taste it. I'll never forget; it'll never leave me. I'm not sure how I will cope. And it is all down to *him*. He forced me in there – he deserves to die.'

His hand clenched the weapon. He held it at arm's length, directly at Gardiner's bowed head.

I tried one last time. 'You said you don't kill – it has to start now.'

He kept still, his face blank. 'I have never delayed before – always acted. I never thought it would be this difficult. What's happening to me? Am I becoming good – is that it?'

There was a quick movement. 'Here.' He slid the gun across the platform. It bumped into my legs. I sat staring at it.

'Pick it up.'

258

I shook my head.

'Pick it up,' he yelled.

He pulled on Gardiner, raising him. 'This man doesn't deserve to live. Think about what he does with his life, what he's involved in, and the misery he injects. He deserves to die.'

'If you couldn't do it, how can I?'

'Because it *has* to be done – he tortures people. He enjoyed watching his men pulverise me into a bleeding mess. He destroys lives, he murders. *Pick up the gun!*'

'You couldn't kill him – you saw it wasn't right.'

'It *is* right – but not for me, not now. I have moved on – it has arrived.'

'And you think I'll do your dirty work for you?'

'Yes.'

'You can't force me.' If I had the gun in my hand, he couldn't stop me leaving.

He said, calmly, 'Pick it up, please. You wanted my knife in the sewer – well, here you are, one better. Pick it up and shoot him or you won't leave here alive.'

He took a step closer, Gardiner shuffling on with him.

'You won't do it,' I rasped back. 'If *you* can't do it to him then you're not going to harm *me* either. Think on it, Jeremy.'

I touched the weapon. I'd never held a gun before. It was heavier than I imagined. 'You won't do anything to me. You said you've changed. You're making no sense.'

'*He* will do it to you. *He* will do anything to escape. If I cut him loose, he will come after us both. He is cornered. Kill him now – to save yourself – or I free him.'

'I could shoot you and that would be an end.'

'But I'm the victim, Mr. Johnstone. He did it to me – and Jackie. What about Jackie? What about his wife – doesn't she get something for their years together? It's what *she* wants.'

He was right. I stammered, 'The body… who is the body… in the hotel? Tell me about the body, Jeremy. Who is it?'

'What does that matter now? Do this – and I will walk away. You will be safe.'

'Tell me about him,' I shouted back. 'You put the body there to take your place – to make people think you were dead.' I was shaking; I clung onto the gun with both hands – the way I'd seen in films.

'He was no-one. A Romanian. I'd had my eye on him for a while. He could have been a younger version of me. I arrange work for these people. He was an itinerary worker.'

'You mean itinerant!' The bravery of a gun.

'One phone call and he met me at the hotel. I was desperate. There was no other way: it had to be done, it was part of the plan. I was in agony but it had to be done. I hit him with the brick before he knew it. I had to force myself. He had beautiful hands – that's what attracted him to me first of all.'

'You cut them off to stop identification, fingerprinting, and then left a strand of *his* hair on the one brush in your room – so the DNA would match with the body. They thought the hair must be yours on that brush – but it was his.'

'No-one saw me. It was the middle of the night. It was my new start. I told you that.'

'Mr. Chamberlain saw you tie up the body.'

Jeremy shook his head. 'He didn't see me with the body. Nobody saw me. *He* was the one who untied *me*! I thought you knew that, I thought you understood. He was the one who set *me* free. I thought I was going to die in that cellar – and there, right in front of me, was an old man, in an evening suit, bending to untie the knots. I thought I was going mad.'

'He rescued you!?'

'He untied me and I stumbled away. I don't know how or why he was there – it was dark and it was a ruin. It didn't make any sense. Why would he be there?'

I felt sick. 'And then you killed him – as a reward for

saving your life?'

'I told you already. I didn't kill him. I don't kill anymore. I've changed. *You* have the gun – can't you see.' There was a pause. 'You must understand, *he* struggled, he shouldn't have struggled. It was meant as a warning to him. I told him he mustn't tell anyone about me. It was a threat only. So he wouldn't go to the police – ever.'

'I don't believe you – not for one moment.'

'It's true.'

'You killed him. You could have helped him free himself from the snare but you stood back and watched: just as you killed that boy. So much for your ludicrous improvements: you can never change. You are a murderer.'

'You have the gun – I've shown you. I saved *your* hands to make up for cutting off his – don't you see?'

I raised the weapon. He took a step closer, thrusting Gardiner ahead of him. Jeremy cried, '*He's* the one. *He's* the real killer. He did it all to me. I had no choice!'

'You're all monsters,' I yelled, the gun pointing at them, wavering.

Jeremy was shouting, 'Kill him! He will return for you if you don't. I am leaving. You will be safe from me. I promise. I'll be far away. You'll never be safe from *him* – nor will anyone you love. If you allow him go, he will come after you – and *them* – the people you know and care about. Do you want to live under that threat?'

No!

I closed my eyes and pulled the trigger.

The recoil rocked me back.

I sat in my blue, toy car, pushed the pedals, and raced round the front garden. I had a goldfish in a bowl: it didn't survive the first change of water. We played with plasticine on our first day at school and played tig in the playground afterwards. I won an egg and spoon race: I was the champion

for a year. The school trip was a cruise to Norway and I was
sick on the crossing. My first job was as a brickie's labourer,
working in a new estate in town. I bought my first gin when I
was eighteen. I returned home to stay the day after my father's
funeral. Chisel's son died in a car crash along with two other
boys – the driver survived. I have a girlfriend with beautiful
deep-black skin. And I love her.

The sound of the gun was loud.

When I opened my eyes I was alone.

I sat in the rain, motionless.

Sometime later I dialed Asa's number.

*

Asa's head appeared above the level of the platform. 'It's
me Jinky.'

'I have a gun.' I hadn't moved. The painkillers had worn
off. My head was pounding. It was a bowling ball balanced on
a paper straw. My whole body was aching.

'I know. You shouted it down. The police know. They
want you to put the gun down. Can you put it down, Jinky –
and move away from the edge?'

'I shot him, Asa.'

'Who did you shoot, Jinky?'

I stayed silent.

'Let it drop – for me,' he said. 'You have to – it's the only
reason they allowed me up here.' He hesitated. 'They're both
dead, Jinky. Do you hear me? They're both dead. Do you think
you can put the gun down now? I volunteered to come up here
– I didn't think you'd want to shoot me.'

'There was only one bullet.'

'One bullet? Are you sure? Did you check?'

'I don't know how to.'

'Put the gun down, Jinky. Slide it over.'

'But I shot him, Asa.'

'I know, you told everyone – but the medical examiner is

here and he's had a good look at the bodies. He can't find a bullet hole in either of them. There isn't one.'

'They fell?'

He shook his head. 'No, they didn't just fall.'

'What then?'

'They ended up a distance away. There was force. One way or another, they leapt.'

Monday 12th March 2007

We stood outside. The sun shone but the air was cold. We were resplendent in evening suits. I couldn't wait to see what my Chiara would be wearing.

Asa bent close to my ear. He held up the wedding ring. 'Don't worry – still got it. But I can't believe this is really happening.'

'What, me getting married?'

'Not that.'

'What then? Is it because I didn't allow you to wear a kilt?'

'No, it's not that.'

'Is it the colour of her skin?'

'Haud yer wheesht man, and don't be so silly.'

'What is it then?'

'Jinky, why on earth would you want to hold the ceremony at Gretna Green?'

THE END

Thanks for reading the trilogy.

Also available, <u>The Wrath Inside:</u> a thrilling, gut-wrenching, murder/mystery page-turner. Set in a fictional town in the Roman-controlled Middle East in 15AD, it highlights events of the period, giving it a sense of the time.

<u>A Different Place to Die</u>: is set in Glasgow, featuring a slightly different police duo.

RR Gall

Printed in Germany
by Amazon Distribution
GmbH, Leipzig